# THE CITY BLOCK

## BY

## GREGORY BRAZZIL

LIFE TO LEGACY

Cover Design and interior layout by
Legacy Designs Inc.
Legacydesigninc@gmail.com

Published by:
Life To Legacy, LLC
P.O. Box 1239
Matteson, IL 60443
www.Life2Legacy.com
877-267-7477

*In loving memory of*

*Vivian C. Page*

# SPECIAL THANKS

To my siblings during my research period of Chicago.

To Author Thome Selby for encouraging me to travel this road.

To a host of talented friends who inspired me to reach high.

# PRESENTED TO:

Reach out to the author at:
gregorybrazzil@gmail.com

# TABLE OF CONTENTS

# TABLE OF CONTENTS CONT.

# PROLOGUE:

Located in the Hyde Park area of Chicago near 51st and Harper, there's a neighborhood watering hole where you can relax to the smooth sounds of jazz legends. A melting pot of clients including people from the nearby university, the South side, Chinatown, and even some jazz lovers from up north that reside at some of the luxury condos on Lake Shore Drive.

It's a bar that has changed hands more than once, but has been in the community for decades. It's an old brick building both inside and out. The ceiling beams and rafters are exposed with leaf shaped fan blades hanging by chain above the beams. The bar is a classic antique handmade wooden "L" shaped pattern about twenty feet long. This is the kind of bar that you only see in the oldest of old taverns around Chicago. It's from a period when men drank bourbon instead of lite beer, before the corporates got into the market with their plastic and neon lights.

Around the room sits 10 to 12 tables that seats four people with candles flickering inside decorative canisters. At the far end of the room there's a stage that can hold a 4 to 5 piece band. Along the walls are autographed black and white photos of local musicians that made it big. Yes indeed, the City Block is the kind of bar where you can have a cold one, groove to mellow sounds, and unwind at the end of your day.

Our main character in this story is Private Investigator Sherman Brothers. He's not your typical brother. In fact he's only half brother! He's the product of a Black mom and a White dad. As a baby he was given up for adoption. At the age of eight years he was taken in by a wealthy and powerful White family.

Sherman is supported by a major cast of characters. His family is a roofless team of corporate lawyers, and his best friends own and operate the City Block. Like most gumshoes he has a local cop that hates the air he breaths! This cop's favorite past time is slapping Sherman around. In the mists of his investigations he's constantly interfered with by a lovely television reporter that will do anything to get him in bed.

# THE CITY BLOCK: 1

On a cold winter night you could see the crowd on the front snow covered lawn of a frat house. People could be seen through the windows and the music could be heard a block away. Midterms are over and the tomorrow is the first day of Christmas break. Tonight the roof will be blown off because this is the biggest and wildest frat party given each year on this night. It's not your normal party given by typical frat idiots. No sir, these frat brothers consist of spoiled well to do rich boys! Their parents earn over seven figures a year and have off shore accounts. There will be no kegs of Bud, instead Heineken will be served. Oh yeah, campus security, don't worry about them. They've been taken care of!

Upstairs in a private room the frat brothers toast with champagne. They tell stories of female conquests like little boys on the playground. The truth is that the only women that any of them ever had were either misguided, or someone who's affection was paid for with lavish gifts. Tonight will be different. There will be lots of girls that have heard about the parties that they throw. Like most young girls, they dream of marriage to a successful wealthy man, and tonight will be their chance to mingle.

As the party roars strong the frat boys separate and work the crowd. Several of them even manage to corral a drunken girl into an upstairs bedroom without being noticed.

It's nearly 3:00am. The band has packed it up and the crowd is thinning out. Finally the frat house is empty and quiet. The only remains are that of a huge mess. Most of the frat brothers have taken off for the holiday, but seven remain to clean up the mess. Their intentions are to leave the following day.

Stumbling in from the patio is the sexiest woman they've ever seen. No one knows who she is. They're helping her stand as she asks is the party over. One of the brothers says no as he starts leading her upstairs. Another one of them says no, we can't do this! The response is sure we can! The brother leading the girl pulls a small bag of white pills from his pocket. With a shit eating grin on his face he says that she want remember a thing.

They all start laughing as they led her up the stairs. Once they were all upstairs the games began. They each had their way with her and left her lying on a sofa passed out.

Morning came and they all began packing up to leave for winter break. The question of what to do with her came up. It was decided to leave her in the first floor bathroom. When found she'd just look like she passed out, and was overlooked. Before leaving they took an oath to never speak of this night again. A line of high end sports cars sped away from the campus grounds.

# THE CITY BLOCK: 2

## FOURTEEN YEARS LATER

After meeting a new client with an old problem up north in Lincoln Park, I decided to show myself a good time. What the hell, after the last few months chasing down leads and sleeping in my car, I had earned a little R and R. I only took this case as a favor to my brother the attorney. Normally these cases are cut and dry. A wealthy old lady believes that her husband is seeing a hot little cookie half his age. My job was to get the goods on the old man. That included photos, video, phone records, hotel records, etc. I'd have to cash in on a few favors owed to me, but it was doable. The old lady gave me everything I needed to get started. I had her husband's daily routine, business hours and places of social interest.

I had met Mrs. Lucille McCoy in a little coffee shop late in the evening, and it was now going on 8:00pm as I drove south toward the Magnificent Mile area. I figured that I'd try to find a room and do some bar hopping. Normally there are a few piano bars in walking distance of most of the hotels. It's a change of pace, plus they tend to attract the tourist crowd which is nice to be around for a change. You never know who you might meet. After having a couple gin and tonics I was getting into the rhythm of the crowd. The piano player was banging away at the keys as people at various levels of drunkenness were singing.

I found myself singing along with them. Thoughout the night I kept catching the eye of a good looking Latin woman, or was it just the gin and tonic making me think so? I've made a fool of myself before and decided to just cool my heels and enjoy the entertainment. After a couple of hours I stepped outside to have a smoke and decide on which bar to go to next. While looking at tall buildings and crazy taxi drivers, I heard a soft female voice ask me for a light. When I turned around it was my Latin friend from across the room.

I had left my lighter in my room and was using a book of matches advertising the City Block. When handing them to her I heard a horn blow and a car break hard. I turned around quickly because it sounded close.

When I turned back to the young lady, she had disappeared, just like that! I went back inside the bar, but nothing, she was gone!

While strolling down the sidewalk looking at designer wear, jewelry, and 500 dollar an ounce perfume, my stomach started talking to me. I'm thinking steak, medium rare, and a glass of Shiraz. I first needed to make a stop back at my room. While I was there I turned on the TV to catch up with a little of the local news. The next thing that I knew it was 9:00am and I was lying on the bed fully clothed. I smiled at myself and headed for the shower. As I got dressed, I finally got to see a little of the news. The typical reports like the weather, sports and entertainment were being aired. Next up was a young Asian female reporter.

"On a sorrowful note, we regret to report the body of wealthy Investment Broker Kevin Crocket was found slain in the wee hours of the morning. Police say that there were some unique circumstances involved. He leaves behind a wife and three children. Tune in tonight for full coverage with Candee Harris."

Oh well, in these times investment brokers aren't exactly saints! In the hotel lobby I ran right smack dab into a group of British tourist. As I made my way toward the door, a couple of them spoke to me, and I swear I didn't know what the hell they said! I gave them a warm smile and kept right on out the door.

I worked my way to a nice little outdoor café and finally had that steak with a couple of over easies. With a full stomach and a beautiful day ahead of me, I headed for the hotel parking structure. While I was walking I decided to give my brother Carlton a call. I needed to give him a update on the case I was working for him.

"I met with the client and you were right, she's pissed and money's no object!"

"Thanks man, I owe you one. Hey look Sherm, what are you doing today?"

"Why do you ask?"

"Abbigale is having another fundraiser this afternoon. You should come!"

"Man you know that I love Abby, but that's not my cup of tea!"

"Sherm, there's going to be lots of lovely, wealthy, single women there."

"You and I both know that these women ain't cheap, plus I like my freedom. I'll talk to you later."

CLICK.

Entering the parking lot I can see my baby parked a couple of rows over. I love my ride to death! It's a 1961 Corvette, silver with red interior, and a black rag top. Over the last six years I've put my life savings into it. It's the reason why I don't have a real baby. It's a real head turner, and I must admit it is an ego rush for me. Traffic was stop and go in the down town area. I was surrounded by a sea of delivery trucks, cabs and tourist driving rental cars. I don't care because it's a beautiful day!

I finally made it over to Lake Shore Drive and headed south. Passing the Field Museum, I could see that the lake front was bursting with life. Bicyclers, roller skaters, soccer games, you name it. With the top down I could feel the sun and the breeze at once. In my rear view mirror I could see a bright red sports car about two blocks behind me, and closing in fast. When it got within a block of me it quickly changed lanes and bleu pass me like I was standing still!

Now my car's no bucket, after all I've invested in a small block that's kicking 525 horses to the rear end. After weaving around a couple of cars I stepped on it! When I caught up to the red sports car the driver slowed down and fell in right beside me. It was a woman wearing a white halter top, with a White Sox baseball cap on turned backwards, and a pair of cat eye shaped shades. She gave me a wicket smile and stepped on it again. Racing or playing cat and mouse isn't my thing, so I let her go. I continued south on LSD, and when I reached my neighborhood I realized how good it felt to be back. After being away for a couple of days, I thought that I'd check my mailbox in the lobby of my building. Inside my place now, my first priority is to check on the girls, Thelma and Louise. The girls are my two Oscars that I keep in a 150 gallon aquarium. Everything looked good. Out of the dozen goldfish feeders that I left for them, one was left.

# THE CITY BLOCK: 3

Meanwhile back at the Remington residence Abbigale's fundraiser was in full swing. The who's who of the society world was in the garden, on the Patio, and in the pool area. All of which were looking to lend a hand to a local children's hospital, as well as a nice big tax write off! The host and hostess were well liked and appeared to have the perfect marriage as they made their way around the grounds. Waiters and waitresses carried trays of champagne flutes as they worked the crowd. Near the pool area Carlton spots his buddy Rex at the bar trying to work one of the social butterflies. The couple makes their way over to Rex to greet him. Abbigale gives Rex a nasty look as Carlton shakes his hand and says thank you for coming buddy.

"Carlton buddy I wouldn't miss this for the world!"

Abbigale is no big fan of Rex and gives him a nasty look.

"Hi Rex, you been out trolling the grounds for chum?"

"Ahhh come on Abby, I've come here in good faith. Let's play nice!"

"Yeah right!"

"Do you mind if I steal Carlton for a moment?"

"Why not, he doesn't wear a skirt!"

The guys walk away and Abbigale continues surveying for perspective donors.

"That's quite a woman you have Carlton!"

"What do you mean?"

"Look at the spread walking around this place."

"Come on Rex, what did you really want to talk about?"

"I've got bad news my friend."

"What's up?"

"I take it that you didn't catch the local news last night?"

"No I didn't. I spent most of the night preparing a brief for Monday, and then I hung out with the Silver Fox. He's out on his boat this weekend."

"So the old man still has some fire left! Good for him."

"So anyway, what's the bad news?"

"It's Kevin. He was found dead in his car late Friday night."

Carlton grabbed a flute from the tray of a passing waiter.

"What the hell happened to him?"

"I don't know, but the police say that there are some strange circumstances."

"What kind of strange circumstances?"

"They're not saying until they get a report from the coroner's office."

"Hell that could take forever! Do you think the other brothers have heard?"

"Well if I saw it it's possible."

"Where in the hell did this happen?"

"He was found over on Stoney Island."

"Stoney Island!"

"You know Kevin was one of our brothers and I loved him, but from what I recall, he always did have a flare for women of color."

"Dude you've got to be kidding me!"

"Well the cops did say that there were strange circumstances. All we can do is wait to see what comes up."

"Maybe we should contact his wife and arrange to have the brothers be pall bearers. We should help her out in any way that we can. Tomorrow is Sunday. Maybe if we divide up the numbers, we can catch the brothers at home."

The two of them part, and Carlton wonders off. Abbigale calls out to him but he keeps on walking. She catches up to him and grabs his arm turning him around.

"What's going on honey?"

"Nothing is going on. Now isn't the time!"

"This is the time! Look, we've got to start communicating. I know that something is bugging you! What the hell did you and Rex talk about?"

"I'm telling you that this is not the time!"

"Well you need to make it the time, because you're scaring me!"

"Rex told me that last night he saw a news report about a man that was found dead in his car."

"Well what about him? Was he one of your clients?"

"Even worse, he was one of our frat brothers from college!"

Abbigale takes him in her arms.

"Honey I'm so sorry! Is there anything that I can do for you?"

"No not really."

"I know that you're here today trying to support me, and I love you for that, but why don't you take off. As much as I hate to say it, maybe you and Rex should be together right now."

"Are you sure honey?"

"Yes I'm sure. You take off!"

# THE CITY BLOCK: 4

It's a little after 10:00am Monday morning and the City Block hasn't opened yet. The owners, Louie, Angie, and Carman are preparing for a new business day. In the storage room Carman is checking out the inventory and filling out a purchase order. In the bar area Angie is vacuuming and taking chairs off the tops of tables. She notices the strobe light flashing at the bar and yells out.

"Will somebody get the phone?"

Louie pops up from behind the end of the bar.

"I'll get it! City Block, can I help you? Sure thing buddy, give me a moment."

He hung up and headed for the front door. He opened the door for a delivery man and said good morning. He walked in rolling a dolly with five cases of bottled beer on it.

"Sorry man, but I knocked and didn't get an answer."

"Head on back, you know the way."

Carman comes in from the back.

"What is this, a funeral or something, somebody turn on the TV, radio or something!"

Making his second trip, the deliveryman comes in again, this time with a keg on the dolly. Carman sees him and calls out to Angie.

"Did you check out the deliveryman?"

"Carman girl, is your mind always in the gutter?"

"What? He's got a great butt!"

"You need to stop!"

"A girl's got to go out on a limb sometime. Stop acting like a nun!"

Angie just shakes her head and laughs. She then asks if anyone's hungry and suggests ordering a deep dish. Louie says pizza again! The girls know that he's secretly in the closet and Carman decides to tease him.

"Yeah I'd bet that you'd really love a nice polish sausage!"

Both of the girls began to laugh.

"That's real funny Carman!"

# THE CITY BLOCK: 5

The annoying sound of my alarm clock radio filled the air. I quickly reached over to the nightstand and shut it off. I sat up on the side of the bed and said to myself it's time to get to work. After taking a three day weekend it was now Tuesday and even being the boss has its limitations.

After showering and getting dressed, I grabbed the notes from my meeting with Mrs. McCoy. Well I guess that I'll start with the old man's office. My plan is to get a rental car just in case someone catches on to what I'm doing. Part of being successful sometimes means realizing that the best made plans can fail. I like to be prepared. If someone decides to run the plates, they'll only find out that the car's a rental. That could buy me a little time, and by time I'm discovered, I'll be long gone.

According to Mrs. McCoy, one of three offices that her husband manages is over in the City of Berwyn, on Harlem Ave. near 22$^{nd}$ Street. Having picked up the rental, I headed east on 55th Street passing through the so-called hood. The route I took is another reason for getting a rental car. No offense intended, but this is the real world, and if I'm going to be in it, I have to be real as well.

As I passed through an intersection crossing Western Ave., I see traveling in the opposite direction a plain black sedan with a bald guy driving it. It's a unmarked squad car no doubt. In my side view mirror I see the sedan make a u-turn about a block back. I keep going west as I see blue flashing lights and strobes mounted inside the grill of the sedan. The squad was rapidly approaching.

I signal and pull over to the curb to allow the car to pass me. To my surprise it pulls over and parks right behind me. It was a good thing that I had left my pistol at home. I keep my hands on the steering wheel and remain froze as the cop gets out of his squad. Shit! I see in the mirror that it's Lt. Lopez. What the hell does he want?

Stepping up to my window he says well, well, well with a strong Mexican accent.

"If it's not Sherman Brothers!"

"Lt. Lopez, what can I do for you?"

"Shut up, I ask the questions!"

With a shit eating grin on his face he asks me who's business was I sticking my nose in today? Before I could answer he tells me to step out of the vehicle.

"You know the drill!"

Stepping out of the car he pushes me toward the rear bumper.

"Put your hands on the trunk and assume the position!"

Lt. Lopez then began to pad me down.

"Where is your piece?"

"I don't carry a piece. I'm just taking a nice drive."

"Bullshit by friend! What's with the rental car? Where's that Corvette that you love so much?"

"It's in the repair shop."

"What did you do, get jacked in the hood? You should be more careful when you drive!"

"You're telling me!"

"What was that? Watch your fucking mouth boy! You wouldn't have anything under the seat, or in that glove box would you my friend? Wait here and don't move your hands!"

He went through the entire car before coming back to me.

"I guess I won't be seeing you around here again?"

"No Lt. you won't."

"Get the hell out of here!"

While I was putting on my seat belt, I whispered, you asshole son of a bitch! Signaling I pulled away from the curb and continued heading west. In my rear view mirror I saw this cock sucker following me. At Harlem Ave. I hung a right and headed north. Checking my mirror again I see that Lt. Asshole kept straight through the intersection. After passing under the Stevenson Expressway I stepped on it, trying to make up some lost time.

I try to focus and get my groove back. Finally reaching 22$^{nd}$ Street, I see the address. Pulling into the parking lot I take note of the time. It's a typical office building with a well manicured lawn. In the middle of the lawn is a rectangular shaped stainless steel sign with black plastic letters spelling out the words "Corporate Accountants Ltd.".

The lobby was furnished with attractive leather furniture and a sculpture of some kind. I didn't know what it was, but it looked expensive. What really got my attention was the 100 gallon salt water fish aquarium. While I was looking at the variety of different colored fish, a voice behind me asked can I help you sir?

It was a young lady, and before I could answer her, the phone on her desk rang.

"Please excuse me sir?"

As she writes on a note pad I notice her desk. It was very neat, and I like that. It says something about the person. She pressed the button on her headset and ended the call.

"I'm sorry, may I help you?"

"Yes, I'm here to see Leonard McCoy."

"Oh I'm sorry, but Mr. McCoy will be out of the office today."

"Is there any chance that he may be at one of the other offices?"

"I'm afraid not. He's taken a personal day off."

"Oh I see. Well thank you."

"May I say who called?"

"Umm, tell him that it was Lt. Lopez."

I smiled as I began to walk through the lobby. I couldn't help but notice a photo of Mr. McCoy standing on what looked like a 20 to 40 foot boat. On the rear was painted "The Good Ship Lucy". It was named after his wife. Ain't that a bitch! I stopped to make a comment.

"Wow, that's quite a boat!"

"Yes it is. That's Mr. McCoy's baby!"

"You wouldn't happen to know where he docks it would you?"

"He keeps it at the Burnham Park Yacht Harbor."

"Wow, sounds expensive. It must be nice! Oh well have a nice day."

Sitting in the rental I looked at my watch. It'll take forever and a day to make it over to that yacht harbor. I'll never make it in this traffic. My little run-in with Lt. Asshole didn't help! I may as well call it a day.

After having a good meal and a nice long nap, I decided to step out for a little bit. I put on some jeans, a sweat shirt, and my out of style Kango hat. Taking a stroll I found myself headed toward Harper Street. I decided to have a cold one at my favorite watering hole, the City Block. The crowd was light, which was typical for a Tuesday evening. Right away I saw Carman.

"Hey handsome!"

She gives me a hug.

"Hey honey, how are you doing?"

Taking a seat at the bar the ceiling fans felt great after my walk to the bar. At the end of the bar I saw Angie. This woman has taken my breath away from the first time that I met her. I know that there's nothing in the cards for the two of us, but every now and then I get drawn into her eyes! She sees me and approaches.

"Sherman it's good to see you!"

"It's good to see you too!"

"What can I get for you?"

"The usual."

"Coming right up."

The music is mellow, my beer is cold, my stomach is full, and I have a beautiful female bartender to serve me. Life is good! Sitting here I recap my day, and the thought of Lt. Lopez pissed me off all over again. My thoughts were interrupted by the flat screen mounted on the wall. The set was adjusted to closed caption mode and a news cast was on. It appeared to be a follow up on the story I saw in my hotel room. This time it was pre-recorded footage from the actual scene. The area had yellow police tape blocking off spectators.

In the background there were several squad cars with the lights going, and one unmarked black sedan that looked familiar. I was surprised to see that the crime scene was over on Stoney Island, not far from here. No wonder the cops said that there were unique circumstances. The next scene showed a young pretty reporter doing an interview with none other than Lt. Lopez. Angie was standing just to side of my view mixing a drink and I asked her who the reporter was. She turned around and took a look.

"Oh that woman, she calls herself Candee Harris. Why do you ask?"

"She looks familiar to me. Does she ever come in here?"

"No, not that I know of."

It wasn't long before Louie showed up and Angie took off.

"Looks like I'm going to be closing tonight."

"That's cool!"

I guess that maybe 20 to 25 minutes had passed when Louie appeared in front of me again. To my surprise he served me a gin and tonic and handed me a book of matches advertising the City Block.

"What is this all about?"

He points across the room at a table. I turned to take a look and couldn't believe my eyes. My Latin friend from the piano bar was sitting at the table. Of course I was up and on my feet in seconds!

"Hi, do you mind if I join you?"

She answered with her soft lovely accent.

"I'd be disappointed if you didn't!"

With a warm smile I say that my name is … She interrupted me.

"Mr. Sherman Brothers."

"Wow, I'm impressed! How did you know?"

She pointed toward the front door. I turned to see Carman smiling and waving at me. I had to drop my head and laugh.

"Well thanks for the drink, what's your name?"

Sticking out her hand, she says Maria.

"The drink is the least that I can do!"

"What do you mean?"

"Well I kinda disappeared on you the other night."

"Yeah about that, well, never mind!"

"So you're a jazz fan?"

"I like a little bit of everything."

"Is this your normal hangout?"

"You can say that. I live here in Hyde Park and it's convenient. I like it!"

Having a eye for detail, I see a thin red line of liquid and a couple of ice cubes in her glass. Taking advantage of the situation, I excuse myself from the table. Getting up I grabbed my lower back, and then stopped.

"You are going to be here, aren't you?"

She just smiled and laughed. Moments later I returned to the table with a Vodka cranberry for her.

"How did you know?"

Before I could answer her, she interrupted me again.

"You should let me fix that for you."

"Fix what for me?"

"I saw you grab your back silly!"

"What did you have in mind? Are you a surgeon?"

That got a real laugh out of her.

"No silly, I'm a massage therapist!"

I remembered how soft her hands were, and all the wrong pictures started running through my mind.

"I'm not sure that I can afford you."

"I wouldn't worry about that if I were you"

"Wow, so you have an office that I can come to"

"No, actually I do house calls. Over the years I've managed to build up a steady clientele of prominent business men and women that I see weekly."

"A self made woman, I'm impressed!"

The conversation continued for a couple of hours and I looked at my watch. It was past 10:00pm.

"It's been a real blast, but it's starting to get …."

"Ah came on Grandpa, how about a bite to eat?"

"The truth is that I cooked and ate before I came here."

"Wow, a man with culinary skills! Now I'm impressed. So what's on the menu? Show me what you're made of!"

I began to laugh.

"Not much, just some Shrimp Alfredo."

"Really, I love it! Let's go!"

I've heard of aggressive women before, but this takes the cake! I have to admit that it is nice to have the woman carry the ball for a change. When we got up I couldn't help but scan her body as she led me to the door. Once outside I remembered that I walked over.

"I'm sorry but I walked here from my place."

"That's ok, my car is right across the street!"

Climbing into her little 350Z I grabbed my back again.

"Grandpa!"

The ride didn't take long.

"I'm right here by the mailbox."

She gets out and goes straight to the car's trunk, and pulls out a duffle bag. I was thinking that this chick don't mess around! She noted the strange look on my face.

"Calm down, I'm not moving in Grandpa!"

"This Grandpa thing is starting to bug me!"

"Ah honey I'm going to fix that, don't you worry!"

In my place now, she's immediately attracted to Thelma and Louise.

"What kind of fish are these?"

"They're Oscars."

"They're very nice."

"Why don't you have a seat while I get you a glass of wine?"

"What I'd really like to do is take a shower."

"Well umm, ok."

"No silly, I meant by myself!"

"Sure I have towels in the hall closet."

She takes off for the bathroom and I'm thinking that this chick is on a serious mission, or either she's a serial killer! I turned on the stereo with the volume down low and go to my bedroom. I slipped on a pair of shorts and headed for the kitchen. Not wearing a shirt I put on an apron. I poured two glasses of wine and put some heat under the leftovers. With the music setting the mood I stood in front of the stove with visions of sugar plums dancing in my head!

As I was fantasizing, I felt two warm hands slip inside my apron, and slowly rub up and down my abs. Then to my surprise I felt soft moist lips kiss my back.

"Is this where it hurts?"

"Not anymore it doesn't!"

"Ok cowboy, let's sit down and eat!"

"I guess that was a step up."

"What do you mean?"

"No more Grandpa."

"We'll see!"

Man this chick has balls, but I like it! I can't wait to see what's next! I drank my wine and watched her as she ate.

"Well?"

"Well I'm not finished yet!"

As I watched her she slowly sucked in one large shrimp.

"Now you see, that's just not fair!"

"What?"

She wipes off her mouth, comes to my side of the table and takes my hand and leads me to my own bedroom.

"Take off that apron and lay down."

"You do know this is my place!"

"Yes sir I do! Is that what you wanted to hear?"

Maria was trying to keep her desires in check. She had seen a lot of bodies, but I could tell that she thought that mind was special. In her mind she had been craving a real man for a long time, and didn't know how long she could remain strong. I took off my apron and got in bed like she told me to.

"You know honey, if you want me to fix your back you're going to have to take off those shorts!"

"Are you sure?"

"Yes cowboy, I'm a professional remember?"

"Ok!"

I eased up off the bed and started taking them off. This time she had nothing to say. I imagined a big lump in her throat. Keeping her composure she squirts oil on my back and begins rubbing it in. My body slowly relaxed and the tension was going away. She kept one hand moving on my back while she was removing her clothes with the other without me realizing. My thoughts about her feelings were correct, and she proved that she could no longer fight her desires. Climbing into bed she straddled my body pressing her breast into my back.

I let out a low moan. She began putting soft moist kisses on my neck and worked her way up to my ear where she started nibbling on it. She began to moan, and through her moans she says that she's been longing for a cowboy.

"Come and get me!"

I turned over and it was on! The night got hotter and hotter until the passion subsided, and we fell to sleep together.

# THE CITY BLOCK: 6

My brother Carlton had asked me to be one of the pallbearers at Kev-in's service. Being one of the two people supporting the front of the casket meant that I was sure to be one of the first to have media camera flashes blinding me. It had been over three weeks since Kevin had been found slain. The coroner finally released his report. According to the media, the unique circumstances the cops spoke of included the fact that he had been given enough rat poison to kill a whole colony of rats! In addition to that he was found with his pants pulled down around his ankles. If that wasn't enough, there was a red lipstick kiss on his cheek.

Between the cops not having any leads and his body being found in his car in an area known for prostitution, the media was having a field day! In fact they're calling the case "The Lipstick Murder".

Stepping through the oversized cathedral doors, I see a mob scene of people. Every TV and radio station in the city was there.

On the corner of the church lawn I see my dad and Abbigale. There were so many media people, that if we didn't have the police presence, we never would have made it to the hearse without dropping the casket. At the cemetery the media showed a bit more restraint. Off in the distance I saw a red sports car coming up the narrow twisting road. A woman got out of the car but she was so far away that I couldn't tell who she was. While the priest was speaking I was focusing on the woman getting closer to the burial plot. Then it hit me! It was that woman reporter, Candee Harris.

Following the service, my family and I gave our condolences to Kevin's family. As we began to walk away I saw Miss Harris remove a small tape recorder from her purse. I spoke out loud. "Oh no you don't Bitch!"

Dad grabbed me by my arm.

"I got it son!"

He made a beeline in her direction and attempted to hand her one of his cards.

"Excuse me Miss Harris. I'm Carlton Remington of Remington, Remington and Jacobs at Law."

"I know who you are!"

"Well I represent Kevin's family, and this wouldn't be a good time to interview them. I'd hate to see your network in court for invasion of privacy during a funeral service."

Dad then got a shit eating grin on his face.

"What would your fans think about that?"

The Silver Fox returned and padded me on my back.

"It's taken care of son!"

After hugs we all separated and went to our own cars. I saw that reporter get back in her car and slip on a pair of cat eye shaped shades. I began to think. Shades, red sports car, well I'll be damn! She knew who I was all the time! I've been played! My first thought was to jump into my car and catch up to her. Not knowing what I'd say or do, I just let her go. As I was driving home I got the feeling that this wouldn't be the last time that I see Miss Harris.

Back at his home my brother Carlton was sitting in his study when Abbigale comes in. She tries to console her husband, but he's not feeling it. She pushes and pushes until he goes off. She then retreats with hurt feelings. He want's to communicate and let her in, but he can't for some reason. Sitting alone again, he knows that she didn't deserve that, but he wasn't in the mood for the supporting wife routine. Picking up the phone he speed dials Rex, the only person that knows how he feels.

"Hey buddy, what ya doing?"

"I'm doing the same thing that you're doing."

Rex continues talking as Carlton looks out the window into the garden. He see's Abbigale with a tissue in one hand, and a martini glass in the other.

"Great!"

"What was that?"

"Ah nothing man, you were saying."

"Are you sure that you're handling this alright?"

"Yeah I'm alright."

"Well what's bugging you?"

"It's me and Abbigale. We kinda got into it, and the timing isn't good."

"It never is my friend! You know that I'm always here for you. Do you want to get together and talk?"

"Yeah that'll be great! Abbigale would love that! I turn to you instead of her. What the hell, why not? Why don't you meet me at Grant Park, near the fountain?"

"Ok my friend. Let's say in about an hour."

"See ya there!"

CLICK.

While driving down Lake Shore Drive all kinds of things were crossing Carlton's mind. Among them was an old incident that happened 14 years ago. It was one that he swore never to talk about again. Actually he had forgotten about it until now. As he drove, every detail of that night came to mind, like it happened yesterday. He's a changed man now and it's eating him up!

After parking his BMW, he made his way across the park to the fountain. Rex was sitting on a bench holding two cups of coffee.

"Here you go buddy!"

"Thanks Rex. How are you doing?"

"I'm hanging in there buddy, have a seat. What do you think really happen?"

"Man I've been racking my brain! What's throwing me off is the whole Stoney Island thing! Why there?"

"Yeah I know what you mean. I'd like to believe that the murder took place somewhere else, and his body was taken there."

"That is possible, but it won't help. Why Kevin?"

"He was a successful married man. Sometimes when you're successful and have a family too, pressure can build up. That's when you have to be strong. I hate to say it, but maybe Kevin was weak."

"Do you really mean what you're saying about being strong in marriage?"

"Of course I do Carl! Look man, I'm not the scum of the earth that Abbigale thinks that I am. I've busted my ass to get to where I am. I'm a single man not committed to anyone. Why shouldn't I enjoy life? Do you think for one minute that she looks down her nose at those social butterflies? I know she doesn't. Well I'm no different than them!"

"In her head you are."

"Look Carl, are you going to get through this?"

"I've just been doing a lot of thinking."

"About what Carl?"

"Just stuff."

"What kind of stuff Carl?"

"Like the past."

Rex jumped up and threw his coffee cup in a nearby trash can.

"Damn it Carl, I don't know what you're talking about!"

"Fourteen years ago."

"Shit man, I swear that I will walk away and leave your ass sitting here! I'm going to tell you one more time. I don't know what the fuck you're talking about! Don't go digging Shit up! You got it?"

"Yeah I got it."

"You need to tighten up, and get your head straight! We'll figure this thing out!"

"You know Rex, I'd really like to tie up that Candee Harris and find out what she knows."

"Now don't go shutting at her! When she shuts back, she's shutting with cameras and microphones, and she has a million viewers that hate lawyers! All we need is that Bitch digging into the past! Go home to Abby Carl, she's waiting for you!"

# THE CITY BLOCK: 7

It's been weeks now since I closed the McCoy case. As in most cases, there are never any winners. I never got a chance to interview Mr. McCoy, so I did what comes natural. I followed him. With a sandwich and a couple of bottles of water in my back pack, I threw my bike in the trunk of the rental and headed for the harbor. It was another beautiful day in Chicago. I rode along the lake front enjoying the view and getting some exercise at the same time.

Just before reaching the yacht harbor I got off of my bike, had my sandwich and washed it down with a bottle of water. Riding along the harbor I knew that all I had to do was look for a boat named the "Good Ship Lucy". It was like fishing in a barrel! With my digital camera strung around my neck, I slowly paddled. Low and behold, there she was, "The Good Ship Lucy". Sitting on the deck was a young red head, about 26 years old, wearing a bright yellow string bikini. Riding by I snapped off about 3 or 4 good shots.

This was great, but not good enough. Her presence on the boat could be easily explained. I needed more. Later that evening I returned to Mr. McCoy's office and followed him at closing. About 15 minutes from his office he pulled into a Mexican Grill and Cantina. As he was getting out of his car I was pulling into the parking lot. Right behind me was a little white convertible with the top down. Driving it was the red head from the harbor. I decided to wait and see what happens.

Just as I suspected, McCoy stopped at the entrance. The red head greeted him with an embrace and a quick kiss on the lips, which I caught with my digital camera. From my rental I could see the host lead them to a table. I got comfortable and gave the couple about 30 minutes to enjoy their meal. Inside now I slipped the host a Ben Franklin. It turns out it they have the same table about twice a week. I then went back to the rental and waited.

After a while the couple came out and got in to McCoy's car. They took off and not ten minutes away they pulled into a small "U" shaped motel with parking in the rear, hidden from the main street. I was thinking man this is classic, straight out of a Hollywood movie! The red head gets out and goes into the lobby while McCoy waits. No paper trail. When she returns they join hands and head upstairs. On the way up he couldn't keep his hands off of her! The whole time I was clicking off shots.

I went inside the lobby and gave the night guy one of my brother's cards.

"I'm with Remington, Remington and Jacobs at Law."

The guy immediately gives me a nasty look.

"What the hell do you want?"

"I want to know who that red head is."

"I'm sick and tired of you people nosing around my place!"

"Oh really, why don't I get the Health Department over here in the morning, and you can really see what nosing around is! I've got half a dozen people that'll say that they got rashes from bed bug bites here at your establishment, with a doctor's letter to back it up!"

With a pissed off look on his face he grabs the registry and gives me what I want.

"The red head is a Miss Dorothy Latimore."

With her name, address, and credit card number I head home. It was a done deal!

After loading all of the details of this case into my laptop, I laid down in bed. After having my eyes closed for about an hour I heard my cell chime. It was a text from Maria. I hadn't heard from her in over a week. I sent a text right back.

"Where are you?"

"I'm right outside."

What the hell! I jumped up and looked out the window. She was running toward my building with her phone in her hand. At first I wondered why she didn't just ring the bell, but at this point it didn't matter. I ran down stairs to meet her in the lobby. She was crying and holding on to me like her life depended on it! Inside my apartment she was shaking like a leaf!

"Calm down, calm down, what the hell's going on?"

Still crying she turns and steps back.

"I was followed tonight by a man in a black car! He scared me so I sped up, and then suddenly these flashing lights came on!"

The anger was building up on my face.

"Then what happen?"

"I pulled over and this guy got out of his car and came up to my window."

"What did he look like?"

"He was bald!"

"God damn it, that son of a Bitch!"

"What baby? What?"

"What the hell happened next?"

"Seeing his face I realized that I had seen him before."

"Where? Why? You should've told me!"

"For what, I didn't know he was?"

"Go on, what happen next?"

"He asked for my driver's license. While I was going through my purse he yanked it out of my hands. He found a business card I had taken off your nightstand. Honey I'm so sorry!"

Maria tried to embrace me, but I pushed her away.

"Then what?"

"He pulled me out of the car and throws me against it. He then began to frisk me."

My anger got the best of me and I picked up a glass from the cocktail table and threw against the wall. Never seeing me like this before, Maria began to tremble and back away.

"Then what happen?"

"He threw my purse back at me and said that he wanted me to give you a message. He turned away like he was leaving, but spent around and slapped me!"

My anger then sent me back into my childhood. I was fantasizing about being slapped around by my so called fathers. I hear a voice calling, Sherman, Sherman, Sherman! Finally I came out of it. Back into reality now, I take Maria into my arms. With her face on my chest, she repeatedly says baby I'm sorry.

"Baby I'm sorry."

"No, it's not your fault! You haven't done anything wrong! Look, go take a shower and wash his filth off of you, and we'll figure something out."

As Maria showers, I sip scotch and pace back and forth. This shit has got to stop!

"YOU SON OF A BITCH, YOU WANT TO SEND ME A MESSAGE. NOW I'M GOING TO SEND YOU ONE MOTHER FUCKER!"

After calming myself down some, I lie in bed and wait for Maria. She finally came and climbed into my arms.

"In the morning I want you to go home and pack a bag. You're going to be staying here for a while. Cancel any appointments that you may have."

"I can't stay here! We hardly know each other!"

"What the hell are you talking about? You had no problem with knowing me the other night when you were screwing my brains out!"

She jumped out of the bed.

"You go to hell!"

I immediately grabbed her hand.

"Wait, wait please! I'm sorry! You didn't deserve that. Please don't go!"

While she was getting back in bed, a little smile crossed her face.

"What's so damn funny?"

"Did I really screw your brains out?"

I grabbed a pillow and threw it at her.

During the night I was restless. All I did was watch Maria while she slept. I finally got up and stared out the window at the streets the rest of the night. I managed to figure out a way to get back at Lopez. I knew that I couldn't hurt him physically, but I could hurt his reputation, at least for a little while.

By time morning came I had a plan. I gave Maria a spare key and the code to the lobby entrance.

"Make sure that you lock up when you get back, and don't answer the door. I'll be back."

"Sherman what are you going to do?"

"Don't worry, I got this!"

"Baby please be careful!"

"Don't worry, I will. He's the one that has to be careful!"

My first stop was the local drug store. Walking down the cold remedy isle I saw just what I was looking for, a plastic syringe. It was the type you use to give medicine to a toddler. I then strolled over to cosmetic counter. On a rotating stand I picked out a tube of bright red lipstick. Yeah I drew a little attention, but what the hell, it was worth it!

Now for step number two of my plan. The hardware store is a small Ma and Pa business. I like to support the independents. Once I got there I was greeted by a little old lady.

"Good morning son, may I help you?"

"Good morning Ma'am. I was looking for some rat poison."

"Ah, you have a mouse problem."

"Yes Ma'am I do. Well actually I haven't seen any, but I'm finding droppings that they've left behind."

I followed her and she ended up reaching for a small yellow box and handed it to me.

"May I help you with anything else?"

"No Ma'am, this should do the trick."

Walking back to my car I realized how I would look if I got stopped by the cops with this stuff in my possession. I opened my trunk, lifted up the spare and the floor panel beneath it. I threw everything in there and took off. Now all I had to do was find a way to plant the stuff on him.

On my way home I stopped off at a deli and picked up some things for Maria and me. When I pulled into the parking garage I noticed that she hadn't got back yet. That gave me time to put together my little revenge kit. I grabbed an old jelly jar from the kitchen and headed for the bathroom. While I was in the bathroom I heard Maria's key slip into the lock, and I quickly closed the door.

"Sherman I'm back."

I gathered up everything and put it under the sink in the vanity. I washed my hands and joined her in the kitchen. I grabbed some plates, glasses, and a bottle of Pinot. After we finished eating I noticed a huge suitcase in the living room.

"What the hell!"

"Come on, give me a hand."

"Damn baby, that thing's big enough to sleep two!"

"Ha ha ha, come on!"

"Really baby, you could've left the kitchen sink at home!"

She dragged it into the bedroom and I helped her put it into the chair. She then started taking things out and handing them to me. I placed them in drawers and on hangers in the closet.

"I'm almost done now."

She then starts giving me her underwear, things like bras, panties, etc. I had my back to her.

"Wow, these look great!"

"If you like those, you're going to love these!"

I turn around to see her standing there naked, and holding a pair of panties in her hand. We spent the afternoon doing what comes natural. Finally she drifted off to sleep, and that gave me the time to finish what I had started in the bathroom. I retrieved the kit from under the sink and turned the water on so that it could get hot. I opened the yellow box and poured it into the jelly jar. I then filled the jar about half way and put the top back on.

I shuck it until everything had mixed well. After removing the syringe from the packaging, I stuck into the jar, and filled it completely. Using a paper towel, I speared some of the lip stick on it to make it look used. Using an old rag, I removed my finger prints from each of the items. Using the same rag, I wrapped the lip stick tube and syringe in it. Now all I had to do was wait.

I figured that if Lopez is hassling Maria, then he must be watching me too. I'm sure that we'll be crossing paths soon. I still have the problem of planting these items on him.

Maria and I had been lying around watching TV when I suggested that we go over to the Block for happy hour.

"I'd love to honey, but I really need to do some thinking. This thing with that cop, and being here with you is more than I'm used to. I'm sorry honey, but I could really use some alone time."

"Yeah I guess that things have been moving pretty fast. Doing the work that I do, I forget that it's not a normal life style."

"Why don't you walk on over and have a good time. I promise that I'll be here when you get back."

I put on my jacket and a baseball cap and headed for the bathroom. I took the kit from inside the vanity and stuck into my jacket pocket. On my way out I stopped and gave Maria a goodbye kiss.

"Have fun honey!"

I was walking down the side walk wondering how this was all going to come together. Approaching the Block I crossed the parking area headed for the entrance. With so much on my mind, I wasn't paying attention to my surroundings. Without any warning I was grabbed from behind and thrown up against a car. Shit! How did I miss this fucker?

"What the hell do you want Lopez?"

With a sucker punch he nails me right in the kidneys. I folded over holding on to my side. He then spun me around facing him.

"Did that little whore you've been screwing give you my message?"

"Fuck you Lopez!"

He pulled a leather black jack from his rear pocket, and was raising it into the air when suddenly a black Corvette came screaming into the parking lot. The driver jumped out and yelled, hey! It turned out to be Rex wearing a twelve hundred dollar suit.

"I wouldn't do that if I were you!"

"Mind your own damn business!"

"You want to beat up my client? How about a nice big harassment suit just for starters?"

Lopez lowered the black jack and turned his attention to Rex. It gave me just the opportunity that I was looking for. With his back to me I reached into my pocket, pulled out the kit and leaned inside the window of his car and dropped it on the floor of the back seat. Lopez turned back around and gave me another nasty look.

"This ain't over punk!"

He then got into his squad and took off. Rex held me up by my shoulders.

"Are you alright man? Do you want to press charges against that asshole?"

"That won't be necessary. I already took care of his ass!"

"What do mean?"

"You'll see! Hey man thanks, let me buy you a drink?"

Inside we took a seat at the bar, but I had to ask him.

"Man Rex! Where did you come from?"

"I had a late lunch with a couple of Asian businessmen over in China Town. Leaving there I thought that I'd nose around over on Stoney because of this whole Kevin thing. I was working my way over to LSD when I came across you my friend."

"Yeah well, I'm sure glad that you came along when you did! Cheers."

"Wow dude! Who's that behind the bar?"

I had to smile.

"That my man is Miss Carman! She's part owner and a real fireball! Would you like to meet her?"

"Sure, I'm always up for a new adventure!"

I motioned to Carman to join us. When she arrived I couldn't get a word in!

"Where have you been keeping this gorgeous man?"

"Carman this is my buddy Rex."

"Well it should be Mr. GQ, because you're wearing that suit like you were born in it!"

I excused myself and headed for the John. Reaching into my pocket I took out three quarters and inserted them into a public phone mounted on the wall in the hallway. Searching through the phone book I find the W.L.O.K. Studios. I put the receiver to my ear and dialed the number.

"Hello, PLEASE hold. W.L.O.K., how may I help you?"

"May I speak with Candee Harris please?"

"I'm sorry sir, but I'm afraid that I can't put you through. May I take a message?"

"I'd rather talk to her personally."

"Who are you and what is this about?"

"Tell her that it's about the Lip Stick Murder."

I was put on hold.

"Hello, this is Candee Harris. Who am I speaking with?"

"Don't worry about that. The officer working this case is involved up to his dirty little neck! If you don't believe me, check the back seat of his squad the next time you come across him."

"Who is this?"

CLICK.

Well that should do it!

When I returned to the bar, it appeared that Rex and Carman had hit it off, and Carman was sticking one of his business cards into her bra.

"Sherman buddy, I've got to take off. You be safe out there!"

Carman then gave him a big smile.

"I hope that I get to see you again!"

"Trust me, you will!"

I decided to stay and have one more cocktail.

"Hey Carman, where is Angie today?"

"She hasn't been feeling well lately. She's taken the last couple of days off. What's it to you anyway? From what I saw a week ago, you should have your hands full!"

Laughing she walks away and I leave a ten spot under my glass before taking off myself.

# THE CITY BLOCK: 8

Maria was sitting on the bed polishing her toenails and I lay in bed watching the Cubs play the Reds. During a commercial there was a news break. A man's face was shown on the screen. Maria saw him and sprung up.

"Hey, turn that up! Turn it up! Oh my God, I know him!"

The scene changes and there's Candee Harris standing in front of an animal hospital.

"Hi, I'm Candee Harris with the W.L.O.K. news crew. It appears that the Lip Stick murderer has struck again. I'm reporting live from Oak Park where the body of Dr. Marc Kenner was found here in his office by the night cleaning staff. Tune in at ten for more details."

"Oh my God Sherman, I can't believe it! He was one of the appointments that I cancelled. I just talked to him two days ago."

Just as I sit up to take Maria in my arms, the phone rings. I pressed the talk button on my cell, but before I could speak I heard Carlton's voice. He was a basket case!

"Slow down, slow down! What the hell's going on? Is Dad alright?"

"Yeah, yeah, Yeah, he's fine! Did you see the news?"

"I'm watching the game, but I saw a news break about the doctor that was killed."

"Yeah well, that wasn't just any old doctor! That was another one of my frat brothers!"

"Holy shit Carlton! What the hell's going on?"

"Damn man, I don't know what the fuck's going on! Shit Sherman, I'm starting to get scared!"

"Calm down man, calm down!"

"Calm down, I'm losing my freaking mind!"

"Look, have you talked to Rex?"

"No, I was going to call him next."

"Look, first thing in the morning I want to see you and Rex here. Try and get some rest, everything's going to be alright."

I hung up the phone and turned to Maria.

"Honey you're not going to believe this!"

"Believe what?"

"That doctor friend of yours was another one of Carlton's frat brothers."

"You've got to be kidding me! Don't you think that's kind of creepy? Do you think something ..."

"Don't even say it! Carl's freaking out, and I don't blame him!"

"Sherman you know that something's up."

"Yeah I'm afraid that you're right. I just don't believe it."

"So now what baby?'

"I don't know where to start. I'm having Carl and Rex over in the morning."

"What are you going to say to em'?"

"I don't know. I mean, I don't want to piss them off with a lot of strange questions, but if there's something ugly in their past, I've got to know, or else I can't help them."

"What kind of stuff did the frat do in school?"

"They were normal college kids, you know. Silly pranks, parties, girls, football games, you know. They stood out because they came from wealthy families, but that's not a big deal, is it?"

"Well baby, maybe it's about money."

"The cops haven't said anything about money, besides it's been 14 to 15 years since they were in school. It does look like some kind of weird revenge, but I don't think that money is the issue. Did you know this doctor's wife and family?"

"No honey, I didn't. We always met at the hospital, but I feel sorry for them."

# THE CITY BLOCK: 9

Morning came and I found myself in bed alone. Sitting up on the side of the bed, I could smell coffee brewing. After brushing my teeth I made my way to the kitchen. I wrapped my arms around Maria.

"Good morning, man I can get used to this!"

"Yeah, you've got it pretty good cowboy!"

"What's that supposed to mean?"

"Just said down and drink your coffee."

"Yes Ma'am!"

"What time are the guys coming by?"

"I guess around ten. Carl's not really a morning person."

"Well I thought I'd make you guys some breakfast. That is if you don't mind!"

"Oh no, please, go right ahead! You owe me!"

"I owe you what?"

"I don't know, but I'll think of something!"

I could tell that Maria sees life differently because of the way that I make her feel. She was actually humming to herself when I walked into the kitchen. She's fulfilled, but I'm worried. While I was getting dressed, she came in and sat on the bed.

"You know it's a little different watching you actually putting clothes on!"

"Ha ha ha!"

"You know we've been doing this a while now."

"Yesss!"

"I've been waiting to tell you something."

"What, you used to be a man?"

For that comment I got punched on my arm.

"Don't make fun of me I'm trying to be serious!"

I continued laughing.

"Just forget it!"

She storms out of the bedroom, goes into the bathroom and locks the door behind herself.

"Open the door honey! Look, I, I, I love you too!"

There was a long pause, and then the door slowly opened. There were tears running down her face when she stepped out. For a moment we stood just looking at each other. Suddenly she sucker punched me in the stomach. She then ran and dived on the bed.

"Maria, what is it that you want?"

She rolled over and looked at me.

"I want you!"

"Maria you're crazy, you know that!"

"I'm not crazy! I'm emotional, get used to it!"

That's when I decided to leave well enough alone.

DING DONG

"That's the guys, baby."

I pressed to the intercom button and buzzed the guys up.

"Maria, this may get ugly honey, and you may not want to be here."

After I stepped out she closed the door.

"Come on in guys. There's a fresh pot of coffee in the kitchen. I'll be right with you."

I leave them alone and join Maria in the bedroom.

"So now you're kicking me out?"

I started laughing and shaking my head.

"There is one more thing."

"What is it?"

"About a block down there's a pet store. Can you pick up a dozen gold-fish feeders?"

"Hell no, I want do it!"

"Look honey, the girls have to eat too!"

"Ok then fine! I'll do it, but there's no way in hell that I'm going to put them in that tank!"

I gave her a kiss on the forehead.

"Thank you honey."

"Hey cowboy, are you going to be pissed off when I get back?"

"I am if you keep calling me cowboy! Why do you ask?"

"Because, I like it when you make love to me while you're mad!"

"See, I told you were crazy!"

When I walked back into the kitchen, Carl and Rex were going at each other.

"Ok guys, we've got to put our personal feelings aside. Just like you, I've been doing what I do for a while now, and from my perspective, you guys know something that I don't."

Maria walked in and the kitchen and there was sudden silence. Rex got a smile on his face after she left back out.

"Who the hell was that?"

That made Carl a bit pissed off, and I didn't blame him. Now wasn't the time.

"Jesus Rex, can't you focus for one freaking minute?"

That's when I interrupted them again.

"Carlton, your mom and dad welcomed me into their lives and gave me a life. You know that, and Rex, you're just as good as family. I'm going to ask you something that you don't want me to. What the hell did you guys do back in school?"

"Shit Sherman! That was years ago!"

"Look Carl, are we going to fix this shit or what?"

Rex was giving Carl the eye while I was talking.

"There had to be someone that didn't like you guys! You drove around in Beemers and Jags, give me a damn break! I know how I grew up, and rich boys weren't my favorite!"

Carlton begins to speak and Rex gives him the eye again.

"Look guys, there's a bitch out there that doesn't like you, so why don't we start there?"

Rex looked at me.

"Why do you think that it's a woman?"

"Good point Rex. You guys also had power as well as money."

"Sherman we were kids, what the hell do you want?"

"Maybe you guys don't get it! Someone out there is making a serious fucking point! You can bullshit me if you want to, but this ain't about money, it's got to be personal!"

Again Rex gives Carlton the eye. I love these guys, but I'm starting to think that it's their ass, not mind, but I can't let it go!

"Ok guys, this is what we're going to do. For the time being, I want to know your every move. Keep me on speed dial and call me twice a day. If you do anything out of the ordinary, I want to know. In the meantime I'm going to do some stooping around. Remember to watch your back, and spend a little more time at home. We don't want to make it easy for this bastard!"

The guys took off and I stretched out on the sofa. I've been stumped before in a case, but this time it's family. Maria came back with the goldfish and a news paper, which she dropped on my chest.

"What's this?"

"Check it out and see!"

I sat up on the sofa and unfolded the paper, and bang! There it was right on the front page, a picture of Lt. Lopez. The caption read "Decorated police officer Lt. Ricardo Lopez questioned in the Lip Stick murders". Detail in section A-7.

I jumped up in the air.

"I got that son of a bitch!"

"Got him how? What the hell did you do?"

"Honey, it's better if you don't know the details. Read the article, it should be self explanatory."

She turned to Section A, Page 7, and read it out loud.

"While covering the scene of the current Lip Stick murder, the W.L.O.K. camera just happened to pan past the squad car driven by Lt. Lopez only to see items inside that may have been used in these murders. The police department says Lt. Lopez will be on paid leave while an internal investigation takes place. Maria then gets a smile on her face.

"Ain't karma a bitch!"

# THE CITY BLOCK: 10

Sitting in my car, I finish off a cup of coffee. Not knowing where to start, I thought I'd go straight to the horse's mouth. I'm parked on Jackson Blvd., right outside the W.L.O.K. studios. I'm trying to come up with a way to get Miss Harris outside so that I can talk to her. Waiting for her to come out is not an option. It could take all day. I dialed up the studio switchboard.

"Hi, my name is Lt. Lopez. Tell Miss Harris that if she wants my side of the story, she should come outside and meet me near the guard's booth."

Without waiting for an answer, I hung up. Moments later, wearing her signature cat eye shades, she approached the guard's booth. She noticed right away that I wasn't Lopez.

"Who are you, and why are you wasting my time?"

I took off my shades and pointed across the street at my car.

"Remember me now?"

Removing her own shades now, she drops her head.

"Ah, the 61 Vette from Lake Shore Drive. Don't tell me that you're upset about my little stunt. I was just having a little fun!"

She extended her hand.

"Hi, I'm Candee Harris."

"I'm Sherman Brothers. I'm a private investigator."

She quickly drew her hand back.

"What is this all about?"

"Let's just say that I'm representing a future Lip Stick murder victim."

"Ok, I'm listening."

"I think that we can work together."

"How so?"

"There's a chance that I can save a life, and you can blow this story open. Here's my card. Think about it."

As I was walking away she yelled out.

"Hey, nice car!"

Back in my car now I get a text from Rex.

"At home now."

I hadn't talked to Maria all day, so I gave her a jingle.

"Yes Mr. Brothers, are you checking up on me?"

"Well you do have a history of disappearing!"

"That's real funny. When will you be home? We need to talk."

"About what, what's wrong?"

"It's nothing bad, relax."

"Ok, see ya soon."

While driving home I wondered if I had made a mistake by going to Candee Harris. After all, reporters aren't the most trusted people in the world. A lot of good investigative work has been screwed up because of reporters jumping the gun. My problem is going to be getting her to keep her leads between the two of us. There's always the chance that she'll just use me to get the story.

Pulling into my parking garage I wonder what it is that Maria wants to talk about. I like having her here, but I'm not ready for anything permanent. When I got to my door I froze.

"Oh my God!"

There was a note taped to my door with a red lip stick kiss on it! My heart started beating rapidly as I removed it. I rushed inside and yelled out.

"Maria, are you alright?"

She came running from the bedroom.

"I'm fine, I'm fine! What's wrong?"

I took her in my arms and held so tight that she almost lost her breath.

"Has anyone been here today?"

"No, no one!"

"Are you sure?"

"Of course I'm sure!"

I let her go and read the note.

TWO DOWN, FIVE TO GO!

"Damn it!"

I gave the note to Maria and said that it was taped to the door.

"There's one thing for sure, this person doesn't want to harm either of us."

"How do you know that?"

"Because they've already proved that they can get in and out of this building without being noticed, not only that, but they're challenging me!"

"Why you?"

"Carlton and Rex must've been followed here. This person has made the connection between us."

For a while the two of us sat down trying to remain calm.

"What did you want to talk about Maria?"

"I've been thinking about my place."

"What do you mean by your place?"

"My apartment, it's been a few weeks since I've been there. I'm thinking that we should check it out. I'm sure that my neighbors are worrying about me. I'd at least like to check my mail."

"Honey, don't do this to me again!"

"What are you talking about?"

"You scared the hell out of me with this, we need to talk stuff!"

"Whatever!"

"I'm not driving, we'll take your little rice burner!"

"It's not a rice burner!"

"Whatever!"

# THE CITY BLOCK: 11

In her sister's backyard, Lilly sits at a picnic table nursing a black eye and sore ribs. Trying to talk through tears, she tells her sister Dana that she doesn't know how much longer she can take it.

"I told you years ago about that bum! You're the one that decided to stay and let him use you for a punching bag!"

"But this time I really mean it!"

"Girl you've said that before. Are you really ready to end this shit?"

"I'll do anything!"

"If you mean it, I'll help you. Have you seen the papers lately?"

"No, Johnny doesn't let me, he keeps them."

"Does Johnny like spaghetti?"

"Sure, he'll eat anything!"

"Good, this is what we're going to do. Tomorrow morning after he leaves for work, I want you to pack a bag."

"Pack a bag?"

"Yes, pack a bag. Do you want to do this or not? "Look honey, you've GOT to trust me!"

The next morning Lilly did things according to Dana's plan. After he went to work she began preparing a spaghetti dinner for him. That afternoon Dana showed up with a small zip lock bag with a white powdery substance in it.

"Put this in the spaghetti sauce and be careful. It shouldn't take long to work."

"But what is it?"

"Look girl don't go getting weak on me now! I've got to go. I'll be back later. At 5:30pm I'll be parked at the corner. There's one more thing."

"Yeah."

"When that son of a bitch grabs his gut and folds over, I want you to pull the phone cord out of the wall."

"Then what should I do?"

"Damn girl! Grab your bag and come outside!"

If anything, Johnny was a reliable man. He was home within 15 minutes of his usual time. Being the asshole that he is, he demanded his dinner right away. He took a seat at the kitchen table and Lilly placed a plate of food in front of him. He had only eaten half, and just as Dana had said, he stood up and grabbed his stomach. Knowing what was happening to him, he tried to punch Lilly. Just as he raised his fist, he doubled over in pain and fell to his knees.

Holding his throat, he fell out on the floor. For a few moments Lilly just stood there looking at him taking his last breath of life. Taking a tube of red lip stick from her pocket, she put some on and then kissed him on his cheek. She suddenly realized that it was over and ran to get her bag, but stopped to pull the phone cord out of the wall. With that she was out the door.

From the corner Dana saw her come out and she hit the gas! She stopped in front of the house and threw the car door open.

"Come on girl, get in!"

Lilly ran around the side of the car and got in. Just like that the dirty deed was done and they were off! Lilly began asking questions.

"Where are we going?"

"We aren't going anywhere! You are!"

Dana reached into her purse and took out a envelope.

"This is a train ticket and one thousand dollars."

"A train ticket?"

"Yes girl, you can't stay around here anymore! There's also a phone number in that envelope. It's for a woman in Little Rock, Arkansas that has a vacation home in the woods. She helps battered women without asking any questions. Also, don't try to contact me, I'll contact you!"

With the typical Chicago summertime muggy days, it only took a few days before the neighbors noticed the pungent odor coming from Lilly's house. That combined with the lack of normal activity drove them to con-tact the police. Not getting an answer at the door, they kicked it in. They were greeted by thousands of flies. Due to the lip stick traces on Johnny's decomposing face, the police immediately assumed that he had fell victim to the Lip Stick murderer. The ladies had gotten away with it.

# THE CITY BLOCK: 12

It had been three days since I met with Candee. In the meantime Carlton and Rex had been keeping in touch with me like they agreed. The note that had been left on my door was still eating at me. What did they mean? Two down, five to go. Were five more of Carl's frat brothers going to be murdered, or even worse, did that five include Carl and Rex? As much as I hate to, I think that it's time to have a little chat with the remaining brothers.

What the hell did they do to earn a death sentence? I reached for my cell phone and it rang in my hand.

"Hi, it's Candee, we've got another one!"

"Damn it!"

"Look Sherman, I can't talk right now, but I want to take you up on your offer."

"Great, but can you tell me anything right now?"

"My sources tell that this one is a little different. His pants were on, but he did have the signature kiss on his cheek."

CLICK.

I immediately got on the phone with Carlton.

"You and Rex should split up the numbers and get on the phone!"

"Why, what the hell is going on?"

"It looks like she struck again!"

CLICK.

It seemed like time stood still while I waited to hear back from Carlton and Rex. I had to remind myself to keep it real! Everyone was present and accounted for, which made me wonder.

Maria and I agreed that since Lopez would be out of the picture for a while, it was safe for her to go back to her place. She wanted to get back to work and live in her own home. All of the togetherness was starting to get to us, so all and all it was a good decision for both of us. Days later after she was gone, my place was really quiet, and I could hear myself think, even when I didn't want to. From the bedroom I could hear my cell phone chiming. It was a text from Maria.

"I miss you!"

"Where are you?"

"I'm at a place where the cocktails are great, and the women are off the chain!"

I took that as an invitation to the City Block. I figured that it couldn't hurt, and walked on over.

As soon as I stepped into the bar I saw Maria, but I also Angie, and as crazy as it sounds, she still takes my breath away! I think that it has something to do with the fact that it's never going to happen between us. As I head for Maria I'm greeted by other friends along the way. Finally I get to put my arms around her, and what does she say?

"You know a lot of women here, don't you Mr. Brothers?"

She took the wind right out of my sail!

"How are you Miss Maria, it's good to see you!"

"Really?"

"Yes really!"

Louie came over and placed a gin and tonic on the table in front of me.

"So what have you been up to today?"

"Just spinning my wheels! By the way, there's been another victim."

"A third victim! God, when is it going to stop?"

"This time it wasn't one of Carlton's frat brothers."

"Maybe it's not about them after all."

"Maria, can we forget about this case for right now?"

"What else would you rather be doing?"

"Is that all that women think about?"

She laughed and tried to get Louie's attention, but she couldn't because he was making eyes with some guy at the end of the bar. That's when her eyes got real big.

"Whattt! Sherman, how long have you known Louie?"

"A few years, why do you ask?"

"He's gay!"

"You're crazy, he can't be!"

"Yeah, just watch!"

Angie walked up to the table to offer us another cocktail and Maria asked.

"What happen to Louie?"

She just pointed over to where he was standing.

"We'll have two more."

"Coming right up guys!"

"See, I told you!"

"He's just sitting there talking! That doesn't mean anything!"

Maria and I hadn't seen each other for a few days and was really having a good time. We decided to walk back to my place and leave her car at the Block. Of course she had something on her mind!

"Why were you so sure that I'd go home with you?"

"I don't know."

"I guess next you're going to try to get me in bed!"

I just laughed and we kept walking.

# THE CITY BLOCK: 13

It's 11:50 in the morning and I'm sitting in a coffee shop near the W.L.O.K. studios. I'm meeting here with Candee Harris. I tend to make it a point of arriving a little early when I'm meeting someone for the first time. Aside from giving myself time to collect my thoughts, it gives me the chance to observe a person's approach, and rather they're being followed or not.

In the studio's parking lot I see her red Porsche pull in. Good, she's right on time! Moments later she comes in and takes a seat at my table.

"Good morning."

"Good morning to you!"

She didn't beat around the bush!

"So why did you want my assistance in your investigation, why not the police?"

"You're a common ingredient in the case. You're always at the scene, and you hear and see things. How should I say, you have privileges that I don't. As for the police, we don't quite agree on things so to speak!"

"Well Mr. Brothers."

"Please call me Sherman."

"I like to know a little about who I'm working with. I hope you don't mind, but the name Sherman Brothers seems to have just appeared out of the blue."

"Wow, I'm impressed! I guess you do like to know who you're working with. The truth is I'm a foster child. I see no reason to make it public."

"I'm sorry I didn't mean to offend you."

"No offense taken, besides, some may say that I'm lucky!"

"How so?"

"At the age of seven I was adopted into a very loving family. What's your story?"

"I'm just a local girl who worked hard to climb up the ladder to get to where I am now."

"So what do you have on the latest victim?"

"For starters he wasn't a successful businessman like the others. He worked at a small plant, and lived in an average income neighborhood."

"That's interesting, all this time I've been thinking that it was money related."

"I think that we all did. What really throws me for a loop is Lt. Lopez. I don't care for him, but I don't think that he's our guy."

"I don't either, but let's try a different angle. What if it's not about the victims, but revenge against Lopez? Maybe that evidence was planted just to play with his head."

"I have to admit, it does sound possible. What do you know about Lt. Lopez?"

"He's been around for years, and the word on the street is that he's not exactly Officer Friendly!"

"I can do a background check on the other two victims. Maybe they've crossed paths in the past."

I wasn't ready to tell her that the other victims were frat brothers. It could lead her straight to Carlton and Rex.

"Are you convinced that the killer is a woman?"

"The truth is that anyone can buy a tube of lip stick."

"So Sherman, what's your next move?"

"I'd like to get a hold of Lopez's arrest records, but that's out of the question."

I was trying to throw her off of my brother's trail.

"Why don't I work on the backgrounds, and you work on Lopez."

"Well I guess that's a start."

"Ok, now that the business part is over, how about a little pleasure?"

I got a dumb look on my face.

"Pleasure?"

"Calm down Sherman, I just met you! I was talking about your car. What's in it?"

"It has a small block with a 10 bolt posi rear end."

"How many horses does it have?"

"It has 525 horses with a modified trans."

"Sounds great, did you do the work yourself?"

"No, I can't take credit for that."

"Do you want to sell it?"

"No Ma'am! Even if I did, you wouldn't want to pay for it!"

"Well can I at lease drive it one day?"

"I don't know, I've seen the way you drive! Tell you what, I'll think about it."

Our meeting ended and she walked out ahead of me. I was thinking man, this chick's got style! I mean Prada style, from head to toe!

# THE CITY BLOCK: 14

It's a new day and I don't know where to start. I haven't heard from Candee since we had our meeting. I wanted to call her, but thought it was best to wait to hear from her. Not hearing from Maria, I decided to give her a call. Her phone rang four times and then went to voice mail. Between Maria and this case, I haven't had time to spend with my old man. I dialed up the Silver Fox and waited for him to answer.

"Hi son, I'm walking into a briefing. Can I call you back? We'll have lunch."

"Ok Dad, bye."

CLICK.

It's time like this that I have to take a close look at my life. I have it all, but yet I'm in a rut. I decided to go for a ride and found myself headed for the lake front. I got lucky and found a parking space between the museum and the university dorms. After walking through the tunnel under Lake Shore Drive I came up in the park. I found myself a seat on the rocks near the shore. After putting on my head set I listened to music and watched the sail boats out on the lake. My mind was clear and my soul was fulfilled.

After 30 minutes of sitting on the rocks, I moved over to the grass and stretched out. I started out looking up at the activity in the sky, but soon I drifted off to sleep. Dreaming now I felt something wet on my face. In my dream I wipe it off, but my face keeps getting wet. I woke up realizing that I wasn't dreaming. With my eyes open I take off my head set and see a Jack Russell Terrier still licking my face.

In the distance I see a little old lady with a walker, and she's yelling.

"Barney, you stop that right now! Barney, get over here!"

I sat up and Barney jumped right in my lap.

"Hey little fella!"

Finally the little old lady makes it over to where I'm at.

"I'm so sorry! You're a bad boy Barney!"

"That's ok Ma'am, he's a great dog!"

"My name is Rebecca, and this is Barney."

"Hi, my name is Sherman."

Slowly she sits down beside me and catches her breath.

"What's a handsome man like you doing in the park alone?"

"How do you know that I'm by myself?"

"I was sitting right over there on the bench when you got here."

That's when I began to laugh. Rebecca was a breath of fresh air! After a little more conversation she ask me a crazy question, right out of the blue.

"What is her name son?"

"What is who's name?"

"Baby don't play with me, I'm too old! Anytime a good looking man like you would rather sit around talking to an old woman, he must have female problems. What's her name baby?"

"Her name is Maria."

"That's a pretty name. Is she a pretty girl?"

"Yes Ma'am."

"Is she Latin?"

"Why do you ask?"

"Is she?"

"Yes Ma'am."

"Now I see!"

"You see what?"

"She's exciting, head strong, and full of fire, right?"

"Yeah she's all of that. How did you know?"

"I didn't get this old my accident! So what's the problem?"

"Well lately she's been a little distant. I left her a message this morning, and haven't heard from her all day."

"Well baby, one of the things that this old woman has learned is that some relationships occur just for the experience. "The man upstairs gives them to us just for learning purposes." Mr. Sherman it's been a pleasure talking to you, but Barney and I must be going."

"Let me help you up Ma'am."

"Remember next time it's Rebecca, not Ma'am!"

"Ok Rebecca."

Back at home now I ordered a pizza and started watching a cowboy movie. Flopping down on the sofa I recall my encounter with Rebecca and Barney. I couldn't help but smile, however it didn't last long. The thought of Maria not answering my calls was starting to get to me.

# THE CITY BLOCK: 15

It's been three days since I chilled out over at the lake front. I'm still at a standstill on the case. The good thing is no one else has been killed. I've put three tasks on my plate for today. I really want to see my dad. It's not because I miss him so much, but he gives me the wisdom that I need sometimes when I'm working a case. He's an expert on people.

My second task may be a bit painful. I keep thinking about Rebecca telling me about the purpose of experiences. I will attempt to corner Maria again today, and maybe I'll find out what the hell is going on!

The last task of my day is going to be driving out to the south suburban town of Posen, Illinois. It's the scene of the last so-called Lip Stick murder. I believe that the suspect is a copycat killer that took advantage of the headlines. I need to prove that I'm right. If I am, I can eliminate the suspect from my case. What I'd like to do is arrive in the community during the daytime. I've learned that house wives and retired people tend to see and hear everything. In other words, they're a bit nosey. The seniors are especially nosey, because they generally are dying to talk to someone.

I think that I will start off with my third task. It's 9:00am now, and with most of the traffic going north, I should make good time going south. Using my GPS, I pulled into the neighborhood a little before 10:00am. Driving slowly I stopped and parked in front of the address of the murder scene.

Being a stranger in the community, I thought that I'd better prepare to show my Illinois State Private Investigator's License. It has my photo and registration number that can be traced back to the state.

Across the street I see an old lady wearing a straw hat with plastic fruit and vegetables all around it. With gardening gloves on, she was pruning roses. With my I.D. in my hand and the biggest smile I could put on, I approached her.

"Good morning Ma'am."

She turned around and looked at me.

"Good morning son, may I help you?"

She was trying to see my ID, so I moved it closer to her.

"My name is Sherman, I'm a Private Investigator."

"Are you sure you're not with the police son?"

"No Ma'am, I'm not."

"Do you like roses Sherman?"

"Yes Ma'am."

"Do you have a girl friend?"

I was thinking, what is it with these old ladies?

"Yes Ma'am."

"Here, take her these! Why don't you marry her? I see you're not wearing a ring!"

"Well Ma'am, can I talk to you about something else?"

"Do you mean the people next door?"

"Yes Ma'am, did you know them?"

"No son I didn't, no one did!"

"What do you mean by that?"

"Well son, he kept her under lock and key. If you ask me, she was a prisoner in her own house. I wanted to take her roses just to brighten up her day, but I was afraid to."

I thanked the old lady and headed for the house on the other side of the suspects. I saw a young mom loading a baby and a diaper bag into a minivan and I approached right away.

"Hi!"

Surprised, she took a couple steps back and held on to her baby tightly.

"Oh I'm sorry!"

I quickly showed her my ID.

"My name is Sherman. I'm a Private Investigator."

"Are you here about that bastard next door?"

"I take it that you weren't very fond of him."

She strapped her baby in and looked at me with a serious attitude.

"He was a pig! The other day I went to the door to invite her to the park, and she came to the door with a black eye!"

"Do you think that he was abusing her?"

"Abusing her, hell, he was kicking her ass!"

Well that was enough for me. I figured that I'd call Candee and tell her that our suspect is definitely a copycat killer, and we can take her off the list.

# THE CITY BLOCK: 16

After having lunch, I made my way back home. Now I'm trying to prepare myself mentally for my next task. I dialed up Maria and she answered on the third ring with a real drowsy voice. I had caught her off guard because she was sleep, and failed to read the screen on her phone.

"Hello."

"Hey honey, it's Sherman."

"Oh oh, umm, hold on a minute."

I was thinking what the hell? She returned to the phone with a depressed voice.

"Hi Sherman."

"Baby what the hell's going on? Why have you been avoiding me?"

"Please Sherman don't raise your voice at me!"

"Ok, but don't you think that you owe me some kind of explanation? I mean damn baby!"

There was a long pause, so I said hello again.

"Yes yes, I'm still here."

"What did I do to make you kick me to the curb?"

"Nothing honey, you're a wonderful man, and the best thing that ever happen to me!"

"So now you're going to give me that it's not me, it's you shit!"

"Look Sherman, I know that you don't understand."

"Yeah, you've got that right! I've got to go Maria!"

CLICK.

I was so pissed off that I began pacing the floor. I was mostly pissed off because I was too damn old to be falling for this school girl bullshit! I poured myself a double scotch and sat down on the sofa.

Thirty minutes had gone by when I heard the sound of a key being stuck in the door lock. She's got to be fucking kidding me! Before I could stand up, she had entered the living room. She tried to hug me but I pushed her away. That's when I started yelling again.

"You left me hanging for days! What the hell were you doing all that time?"

For a moment she just stood there crying.

"I'm so very sorry!"

"That's not good enough! What the hell were you doing?"

"I was trying to find a way to keep us happy."

"Well you've got a real funny ass way of showing it!"

She reached into her purse and took out a brochure featuring a resort in San Juan Puerto Rico.

"So what the hell does this have to do with us?"

With tears in her eyes she began to explain.

"Months ago I applied for a management position at this resort. There was no one special in my life at that time. I'd supervise an entire staff, and be with my mom in her final years!"

I couldn't believe that her logic told her to put our relationship in jeopardy instead of discussing it with me. I know how I feel about my career, and I couldn't stand in the way of hers. My anger was stuck and she sat down on the sofa. I sat in the easy chair and watched her as she slowly fell to sleep. An hour later she woke up with dry tear tracks on her face.

"Now what Sherman?"

"I don't know."

"Sherman I don't want to fight anymore! Do you mind if I take a shower?"

"Sure, go ahead, I'll be right here."

It had been a long day and I was emotionally drained, and had to go lay down. Maria finished her shower and joined me. Normally we'd be feasting on each other, but this time things were different.

Down town in the Gold Coast area at a steak house, a feast of another kind was about to take place. One hour before closing an unescorted woman appeared in the foyer. She was tall with long flowing wavy blonde hair. She wore a long black evening gown with black silky gloves over her hands, and a variety of what looked like high end jewelry. The host was so taken by her, that he could hardly escort her to a table. As she walked across the room to her table, every man in the steak house turned his head.

Forty-five minutes later she had finished her meal and two flutes of champagne. She left two hundred dollar bills on the table and went to the ladies room and stayed. An hour and a half later the place was completely silent. The staff had cleaned and left for the night. She could see the owner sitting at a stainless steel prep table doing some paperwork and sipping wine from a glass.

With her gloved hand she grabbed a small salt shaker and rolled it down the hall, where it hit a trash can. The owner immediately got up and left the kitchen to see what had fallen. Not seeing anything, he returned to his paperwork. He had made it far too easy for her. She stood in the shadows watching.

It wasn't long before the poison took effect. Holding his chest he fell face forward on his paperwork. She stepped out of the shadows and pushed him out of his chair. She quickly pulled his pants down. Still wearing her gloves, she removed the house keys from his pocket. Leaning over him she put a red lip stick kiss on his cheek, and just like that, she was gone! On the sidewalk now, she waved down a taxi and disappeared into the night.

# THE CITY BLOCK: 17

Awaken by the chime of my cell phone I realize that Maria isn't in bed with me. Her clothes are still on the chair, but my robe is gone. Reaching for the phone I see that it's a text from my dad.

"Hi son, I'm off for the next couple of days. Let's have lunch."

Just as I was putting the phone back on the nightstand, it rang again. This time it was Candee Harris and I answered it on the second ring.

"Sherman we need to talk! I'm sorry, good morning."

"That's ok, what's up?"

"Victim number four!"

"Damn it!"

"It happened last night. The body was found at a steak house down town in the Gold Coast area. All I know is the victim was an owner/ manager, and he was left with the usual calling card. Oh, there's one more thing, we've got surveillance video. I'm on my way to the scene now. Let's try to get together later. I've got to go."

CLICK.

The first thing that I did was call Carlton.

"Sherman thanks for waking me!"

"Hey man, get serious! You and Rex get on the phone again! Dial the brothers and watch WLOK this afternoon."

"What!"

"Yeah it happened again! Don't waste time, do it now!"

CLICK.

Maria came back into the bedroom wearing my robe.

"Can you come into the kitchen?"

She gave me a cup of coffee and we both sat down at the table.

"I'd like you to listen to me without any interruption. First I want to say that I love you dearly. This offer that I've been given rarely happens to people in my line of work. I don't feel very proud of myself right now. I wish that I could just disappear like I did at that piano bar. I have a window of time before I have to get back to these people. Rather you think so or not, this decision is both of ours. Now I'm going to go and get dressed."

I tried to hold on to my emotions but I couldn't. I threw my coffee mug against the wall and it shattered. Maria got up and walked over to my side and wrapped her arms around me, holding my head against her breast.

"Look at what I've done to us! Please forgive me!"

Maria took off after getting dressed, and I was left in silence making myself crazy. I sat around waiting for the noonday news report to air. I began to get nervous because I hadn't heard from Carlton or Rex. I got up and called Rex.

"Hey, it's me, why haven't I heard from you guys?"

"Sherman there's a problem. We were able to contact everyone but Donny. There's no answer at his home, or on his cell. I'm starting to get worried!"

"What's Donny's full name?"

"It's Donald Kelly."

"Have you gotten back to Carlton yet?"

"Yeah I have, and he's really freaking out!"

"Freaking out how?"

"He's incredibly calm. That's not Carlton!"

"Yeah I know what you mean! Rex you better sit down"

"Oh no!"

"Yes. We're going to have to get all of the remaining brothers together. I'll call and tell you when and where."

CLICK.

After talking to Rex I called my dad.

"Hi son."

"Hey Dad, lunch sounds great, but not now. Dad I have a problem. I'm doing an investigation and the client is someone dear to me. The problem is that all the negative roads keep leading back to him, and he's hiding information from me."

"Son I've had clients like that. You're going to have to cut him loose if he's not going to come clean."

"My case is related to the Lip Stick murders."

"You mean that woman that's running around killing guys?"

"Yeah Dad, and my client may be the next victim. I'm also kinda working with this W.L.O.K. news reporter."

It's not that damn Candee Harris is it?"

"Yeah Dad, it is."

"My God son, you really know how to pick em'! Son that Candee woman is a real hottie! Don't let her work you! I'm sure that you know what I mean!"

"Yes sir!"

"I'll talk to you later son, good luck!"

CLICK.

It was getting close to noon so I grabbed the remote and turned on the TV. While waiting for the broadcast to air, all kinds of things were going through my mind. Finally bold letters ran across the screen. LATE BREAKING NEWS! There she was.

"Hi, I'm Candee Harris with the W.L.O.K. news crew, and I'm coming to you live once again from yet another murder scene. The police believe that it's the work of the Lip Stick murderer. I'm here in the Gold Coast area of down town standing outside of a popular steak house, where the body of Donald Kelly, owner/manager has been found slain. The police say that the killer left behind his or hers calling card. They now firmly believe that they have a serial killer on their hands. They won't say rather or not the victims have anything in common. Like the other victims, Kelly leaves behind a wife and children. The chief of police says that these murders are now the department's priority. I'm Candee Harris with the W.L.O.K. news crew."

From the beginning this killer has held us at bay. He or she is in control. The only thing that I know for sure is that seven people may be killed. I'm beginning to get desperate, and I'm thinking about bringing someone into my investigation that I truly hate! He can be the very tool that Candee and I need to add to our toolbox. That person is the one and only Lt. Ricardo Lopez.

Yeah, that's right! I guess that this is the length that I'm willing to go to save lives. Due to the fact that my adoption records are sealed, neither he nor Candee can find out that Carlton is my brother. The only problem that I have is explaining how I knew about the frat brothers to begin with.

I can't believe that I'm considering this. I could very well be inviting him back to finish the beating that he started! To get the ball rolling I sent Candee a text, and she agreed to meet with me. Next I called the Block to see if they'd let me hold my meeting there before opening. I spoke to Carman and she was fine with it. Now for the hard part, I had to reach out to Lopez. I called the police department switchboard.

"Good afternoon, Chicago Police Department. Is this an emergency?"

"No. it's not."

"Please hold while I switch you over. Have a nice day."

"Chicago P.D., this is Sgt. McNally, how may I help you?"

"Lt. Lopez please?"

"Hold on."

In the background I hear, hey Lopez, line three!"

"Lt. Lopez here."

"Can we get together and talk Lt.?"

"Who is this?"

"Sherman Brothers."

"What the hell? Why would I want to waste my time on a punk ass gumshoe like you?"

"I think that you may want to hear what I have to say."

"I'd doubt it!"

"It's about the Lip Stick murders."

"Look Punk, don't be nosing around on my streets!"

"Ok Lopez, but I can do this with you or without you!"

"Let's get one thing straight punk, don't be yanking my chain! You'll regret it!"

In my mind I was already regretting it!

"Where do you want to meet punk?"

"The City Block, you know the place."

CLICK.

# THE CITY BLOCK: 18

I knocked on the front door of the Block and Carman let me in. In the back I could see Angie and Louie milling around doing their cleaning duties. She took my hand and led me to a table where we both took a seat.

"What's up?"

She first looked over her shoulder.

"Girlfriend is sick."

"Really, I'm sorry to hear that!"

"I'm not sure what's wrong, but it's not female. As close as we are, she can be real mysterious when she wants to be. Hey, I've got to go before they miss me."

A few minutes later Candee arrived at the door and I let her in.

"Hey, how are you doing? I'm glad that you got here before Lopez. It gives us a chance to line up our ducks! When he gets here I'm going to introduce some information that I've discovered. He and I are not friends by any means. In fact we hate each other! Keep in mind that he may just take over the whole case, and lock me up for interfering with a police investigation."

"Yeah, I can see your point, but do you mind letting me in on it first?"

"I've found a connection between our victims."

"Why didn't you tell me?"

"I was waiting to hear from you, but then things started happening."

"Ok, let's have it!"

"It appears that our victims all belonged to the same frat club back in college, and they all come from wealthy families."

"You mean a rich boy frat?"

"Yeah exactly!"

"Do you think that it would be safe to say that these are revenge killings related to something that happen back in school?"

"It's definitely a possibility."

"I found this note taped to my door. Here, read it."

Candee's eyes got big when she saw the kiss on the outside of the note.

"Two down, five to go! Why would they leave this with you?"

"I've got a better question! How did they get to my door?"

"What do you mean?"

"I live in a gated security building."

"Is there anything else that you've been holding back?"

"No that's it."

"So the big question is why these seven guys?"

"That part I haven't put together yet."

"So I guess that's why you wanted to bring Lopez into the game?"

"Bingo!"

"Well don't look now, but he's here!"

I looked over my shoulder and saw Carman letting Lopez in. Standing behind the bar I saw Angie and Louie whispering, and Angie was leading.

"Isn't that that reporter Candee Harris?"

"Yeah, and I saw that bald guy on camera the other day beating up on Sherman! I wonder what the hell is going on!"

Carman joined them and said be quiet, let's listen!

Lopez took a seat and asked…

"What the hell is she doing here?"

He said it like she wasn't even there.

"She's here for the same reason you are."

"How the hell do you figure that punk?"

"Look, we all have a personal reason for catching this killer."

"I can't think of any good reason not to run your ass in right now!"

"Yeah you could do that, but we all know that you're here because you're not getting anywhere on this case."

"So what is it that you want from me?"

I handed him a list of names.

"What the hell am I suppose to do with this?"

"For starters you can see if they have rap sheets."

"Why would I do that?"

Candee and I both gave each other the eye, and I placed the note on the table. He picked it up and read it.

"Where the hell did you get this from punk?"

"It was taped to my apartment door a few days ago."

"Are you saying that your list includes these five?"

"Well now it's these four! By the way, the guys on that list all belonged to the same frat club back in college."

"You're kidding me!"

"Do I look like I'm kidding you?"

"Where did you get these names?"

"I can't say right now."

Lopez then looks at Candee.

"What's your part in this?"

"Let's just say that Sherman and I are partners."

Lopez got up from the table to take off, but stopped.

"You guys better not be yanking my chain!"

He then left the City Block. Candee looked at me with a smile.

"Thanks for having my back partner!"

"Hey, as long as we're here, how about a cocktail, they're going to be opening soon anyway?"

"Are you trying to hit on me?"

"Not at all."

"Well I guess that one can' hurt, besides, you're kind of cute!"

"What would you like?"

"How about an apple martini?"

"Coming right up!"

While we were sipping on our cocktails, Candee got a strange look on her face.

"What's up?"

"Sherman I've been holding back myself. After we met the other day, I went back to my sources and discovered something about your past that

I'm curious about."

"Well I told you that I'm a foster kid, what else could it be?"

"I'm just going to put it out there! Have you been in touch with your sister?"

I choked on my drink and backed up in my chair!

"Sister, what sister?"

Candee put her hands up to her face in complete shock.

"Oh my God Sherman, I'm so incredibly sorry! It was none of my business! Oh my God, what have I done?"

I just sat there, completely dumbfounded! Candee reached across the table and took my hands in hers trying to show some sympathy.

Just about then Maria walks in. With her hands wrapped around her face, she stopped walking just short of our table. With tears running down her face she turns and runs out! Candee sees what's happening and quickly stands up.

"I guess I'm just a one woman wrecking ball!"

I sat there alone at the table, and I guess that Angie and Carman had seen the whole thing. They both came over and wrapped their arms around me. Louie brought me another gin and tonic and then they all left me sitting alone.

# THE CITY BLOCK: 19

I've been lying on the sofa in darkness for hours now. After several attempts, Maria's not answering my calls. I guess that the decision has been made. I sat up on the sofa and was about to call it a night when strangely, I heard my doorbell ring. I looked at the clock and wondered who the hell it could be. I went to the intercom panel as asked who's there.

"It's me Candee."

I buzzed her up thinking you've got to be kidding me! A minute later there was a knock at my door. When I opened the door, there she stood with a bottle of Tequila in one hand, and two limes in the other.

"Do you have a couple of glasses?"

Shockingly I said come right in! Stepping in she kicked her shoes off, set the bottle and limes on the cocktail table and took a seat on the sofa. I went to the kitchen for glasses. I began slicing a lime and she opened the bottle. We clicked our glasses and she slammed back the first shot.

"Sherman, do you ever wonder why things happen?"

"Most of the time I just wonder why things happen to me!"

"Yeah, I know what you mean!"

"Oh you do? Well tell me how I feel Missy!"

"You're just like everyone else!

"What do you mean everyone else?"

"You think that I'm just a spoiled little thing with expensive clothes and a flashy car. Women hate me, and guys are afraid of me, and you fit right in with them!"

I couldn't help but laugh. She was mostly right.

"Should you be drinking?"

"Don't laugh at me, it's not funny!"

"Well how do you see yourself?"

"I'm just a hard working girl that's had some good luck."

"What about the toys?"

"What toys? You mean the car, it's in my dad's name."

"So why do you scare men away?"

Tears began to run down her cheeks.

"I don't know! What's that girl's name?"

"Her name is Maria."

"She's very pretty!"

"Yeah well!"

"I didn't mean to burn you today."

"Well it was falling apart anyway!"

"Do you know that for sure?"

"Yeah, I'm just waiting for the final notice!"

"I feel responsible!"

"It was in the making before you came along."

I excuse myself and went to the bathroom. When I returned Candee had stretched out on the sofa and was sleep. It was getting late so I just went to bed. During the night I woke to the feeling of weight on the other side of my bed.

"What the hell?"

I couldn't freaking believe it! I rolled back over to go sleep, but what I didn't know was that she had opened her eyes and was watching me with a smile on her face.

# THE CITY BLOCK: 20

It was late in the morning when I woke up. The first thing that I noticed was the light blinking on my cell phone. Remembering that I had an unexpected guest, I turned over to take a look, but she was gone.

Checking my messages I see that Candee had left one.

"Hi Sherman, it's me Candee. Sorry but I had to be at the studio at 4:00am. I'll call you later."

The next message was from Lt. Lopez.

"Hey punk, I've got something for you. You can reach me at this number."

I called Lopez back right away.

"This is Sherman. What do you have?"

"I got two hits off of that list. It looks like two of our boys were arrested for attempted sexual assault, but the charges were dropped before the case went to court."

"Paid off no doubt!"

"One of the guys was our victim number three. When he was arrested, the date rape drug was found in his possession."

"You said that there were two hits."

"Well my boy, for that one I want the pleasure of seeing your face when I tell you! Give me 20 minutes and meet me outside of your building."

CLICK.

While I was quickly getting dressed, I couldn't help but think that it was Carlton. I also wondered why Lopez would be so happy. In any case, I went down stairs and waited. Moments later a black sedan pulled over to the curb.

"Ok Lt. who is it?"

Instead of answering me, he handed me a business card. I couldn't believe my freaking eyes! The Lt. actually learned something. The card was from my dad's law firm, and it boldly had Rex's name on it. It was the same card that Rex gave him in the City Block parking lot. The Lt. took off with a shit eating grin on his face!

I was pissed off, because I now knew that this whole thing was about sex! It also explained the killer's calling card. It was time for me to get real damn ugly! I got Carlton's ass on the phone.

"Carl it's me! Get everybody together and meet down at the fountain at 6:30pm, and Carl, I mean everybody!"

CLICK.

I then left Candee a text message.

"Hey, it's Sherman. We've got something, give me a call."

I went back up to my apartment and prepared to take a shower. That's when my cell rang. I was surprised to see that it was Candee. Evidently I answered it the wrong way!

"This is about sex!"

"Ok, I'm game!"

"I mean the motive for the killings. Lopez came through for us. Can we get together later?"

"How much later?"

"Maybe around eight o'clock."

"Ok, but no liquor!"

CLICK.

The afternoon rolled on and still there was no word from Maria, which I expected. I'm sure now that the decision has been made. With nothing to do but sit around and worry, I sat my cell phone alarm for 5:00pm and put on my head set. I stretched out on the sofa but my mind kept racing. I guess the main thing that was killing me was the possibility that my brother may be a freaking scum bag! That thought led me to think about poor Abbigale. She's the one poor unsuspecting victim in this whole thing, and I really don't believe that she could handle the mental strain. As for my dad the Silver Fox, he's going to be torn between having has heart broke and killing Carlton. If the media makes a connection, this whole mess could shine an ugly light on the law firm. Carlton Jr. has always been his pride and joy, and he may end up looking like a piece of shit!

Finally I managed to drift off to sleep. At 5:00pm sharp I was startled by the sound of my cell phone alarm. I sat up and slowly got my act together. 15 minutes later I headed down to the parking garage. It wasn't long before I was north bound on Lake Shore Drive. I didn't know exactly what I was going to say, but at the same time I knew what I wanted to say. I wanted to say that you guys are a bunch of assholes and I'm walking away from this shit!

At the fountain in Grant Park, Rex was the first to show up. He stuck out his hand for a shake, and wanted to talk. I told him to wait for the others. They all came one by one.

"Carlton, is this everyone?"

"Yeah, but let me explain!"

"It's too late for that shit!"

For a moment they all stood looking at me, but then started looking at each other. I took a deep breath and started.

"Now I'm not fucking around here! Your college administrators were forced to shut down the frat house because of you guys! I believe that one evening seven of you guys got the bright idea to do a dirty deed. This is what I'm going to do. I'm going to take seat over on a bench, and while I'm gone I want the remaining four dead men to remain here. The rest of you fucking losers can take off and thank your lucky stars!"

After taking a seat I saw the group scatter like cock roaches caught under a light! There were four men remaining. Two of which were Carlton and Rex. I walked back over and took a deep breath.

"Ok guys, I'm going to lay it all out on the table. I'm not the only one that's on to your game! The biggest, nastiest son of a bitch carrying a badge would love nothing better than cleaning the streets with your ass, and locking you up for life! The only card that you hold is me, and that's because I don't carry a badge! As you all know, three of your brothers have been murdered. In addition to that, the killer has been in touch with me."

With shocked faces they began to pace and argue between each other.

"Hey, knock it off! You haven't heard shit yet! The killer informed me that seven of you guys will die. From my point of view, this person is on a fucking mission! Not only that, but they're damn good at what they do! The cops say that each of your dead brothers was found with his pants pulled down around his ankles, with a red lip stick kiss on his cheek. "With that said, does one of you guys want to step forward?"

No one moved an inch.

"Ok, let's try it this way! My nasty little friend with the badge did a background check on all of you."

Out of nowhere Rex said ah shit!

"Pay close attention to Rex guys, because he's already had the pleasure of meeting Officer Friendly! Does anyone want to know what he found out?"

This time Carlton says ah shit!

"If you're having trouble keeping up, let me tell you. Two of you guys have a record for attempted sexual assault. Well let me correct myself, only one of you now!"

Carlton stepped forward and no one tried to stop him.

"It was the night before Christmas Break, and we decided to throw a big party."

At that point Rex stepped up and interrupted him.

"It was me, I'm the other guy. We were both drunk and she acted like she wanted it. My parents paid her off before it went to court."

Carlton then continued.

"The party was wild, girls were passing out, and everything was crazy. When it was over this girl wondered in wasted. Donny took out some little white pills. Morning came and she was still out cold. We thought that she wouldn't remember a thing. You know the rest."

"Yeah well, obviously you assholes were wrong!"

After hearing their story I was lost for words. Not one of them would look me in the eye. They just stood there looking at the ground like little boys!

"I don't know about you other guys, but Carl and Rex, you guys can be disbarred, and also go to jail, and that's if you don't killed first! Do you guys even know the woman's name?"

They all stood around looking at each other.

"For crying out loud, you guys are pathetic! Go home, lock your doors, and wait to hear from me!"

I got in my car, jumped on Lake Shore Drive, and put the pedal to the medal!

# THE CITY BLOCK: 21

When I got home I took a shower and threw my robe on. I was due for another break from reality. The meeting down at the fountain not only drained me, but made me not want to think at all! I turned my stereo on to a jazz station and poured myself a double Jack on the rocks. I took a couple of good swallows and stretched out on the sofa. The music was mellow and the whiskey was starting to touch all of the right spots!

DING DONG!

Damn, I forgot about asking Candee to meet me. At this point I wasn't even in the mood for discussing the case. I knew that it couldn't be anyone else, so I buzzed her up. A few moments later I opened the door and there she stood.

"Please, come right on in!"

The first thing she did was kick off her shoes.

"I didn't know that this was a pajama party!"

"Please don't, I'm not in the mood!"

"Who put salt in your tank?"

"It's just been one hell of a day!"

"Why don't you lay down and tell mommy all about it!"

I know that she meant well, but I ignored her and stretched back out on the sofa. At that point she headed for my bathroom. I didn't know what she had in mind, but I was trying to get back to where I was. Things were going fine until I suddenly felt warm flesh on my back. I jumped up knocking my drink over and kneeing Candee in her thigh in the process.

She fell back on the sofa moaning in pain.

"Jesus Sherman, I was just trying to make you feel better!"

During the excitement I didn't realize that she was only wearing her bra and panties.

"Well you could have given me some warning!"

"Well don't look now, but your robe is open!"

I looked down to see my entire body exposed to her. She was somewhere between enjoying the view and rubbing the pain out of her thigh.

"Look Candee, you're incredibly sexy, and a man would be crazy not to want you, but I'm just not feeling it."

"Well that's just great! I swear I've never been more humiliated before in my life!"

"Why don't you just relax and have a drink?"

"I'm here now Sherman. Do you mind if I take a shower and a nap before going home? I promise I want stay pass midnight."

"Sure, why not!"

She went to do her thing, and I did mine. The place was now quiet again. A little past ten o'clock I got up off the sofa and went to bed. Candee was on the other side of my bed with her back to me. I assumed that she was sleep. I crawled in bed and was surprised when she reached over, grabbed my hand and wrapped my arm around her fully nude body.

Despite all that had happen, it wasn't the worst thing that could happen to me, besides, she felt incredibly good! We went to sleep in that position. At 11:00pm I felt her moving my arm away. It was time for her to get ready to go. While she was getting herself together, I went to the kitchen and made her some coffee. When I came back she was in the bathroom and I got back in bed. Moments later she was standing in front of the mirror wearing my robe and applying makeup.

"Candee, did the cops share the surveillance film from the steak house with you?"

"No they didn't, but they did say that sense the place was closed for business, the lights were dim, and the killer could have been any one of a dozen people."

"I'm thinking about providing surveillance for the remaining guys of that list."

"And just how to you plan on being at four places at one time?"

"I don't know, but I do know that most of murders have taken place at the victim's place of business."

Candee got dressed, gave me a kiss, and took off. Morning came and I wasted no time putting together a list of the items that I would need to get the ball rolling. Next I did the one thing that my brother Carlton hates, I woke him up. At this point I really didn't give a damn about how he felt!

"Sherman, why do you do this is to me?"

"You should be happy that you're not answering a prison phone! I need some information."

"Ok, what is it?"

"I need names and phone numbers, as well as home and business addresses of all the guys. I'm also going to need everyone's daily routines. There's one other thing Carlton. I need that information right away. Everyone's life is depending on it!"

CLICK.

While Carlton was gathering the information that I needed, I hopped in a taxi and went to pick up a rental car. A couple of hours later I was good to go. I started off with a Mr. Frank Mallory, a family man and owner/operator of a new car dealership. I'll park my car in front of his place and mount a dashboard camera in it and monitor it from my laptop.

Next up was Mr. Leo DeSanto, manager of several multiplex movie houses. I'll use the rental car to watch his place. I talked to Frank and Leo to let them know what my plan was. Leo told me that his wife packs up the kids and drops them off on her way to work. He normally sticks around until the mailman comes. He sorts the bills and leaves checks for his wife. I knew that my plan wasn't full proof, but it was better than waiting for these guys to get killed. Tomorrow morning I'll put my plan into action and hope for the best.

It was 6:00am and I was already sitting parked across the street from the DeSanto residence. I opened my laptop and activated the dashboard camera in my Vette which was parked in front of the Mallory home. Even though it's early in the morning, my mind is turning like it's the middle of the day. Stake outs are the part of this job that I hate. You never really blend in because the locals know that you're out of place. Killers try to blend in as well, but sometimes have tunnel vision because they're on a mission.

As the neighborhood began to wake up there was activity. Just as Frank had told me, I saw a couple of kids come running out of the house avoiding a bike, a skateboard, and some other toys on the sidewalk in front of the steps. They were followed by his wife carrying a back pack and a lunch box. Around 9:30am things began to quiet down.

Just before 10:00am the air was filled with the sound of a nearby lawn mower. It wasn't long before I saw the mailman making his way down the block. So far everything had gone just like Leo said it would.

# THE CITY BLOCK: 22

Every 2 or 3 minutes I take a look at my laptop. It appeared that the same basic activities were taking place over in the community where the Mallory's live as well. I guess you could say that this was a typical American morning.

It was close to 11:00am when I saw the garage door open on the Mallory home, and a Jaguar backed out with Frank behind the wheel. Once he left for work there was no point in me staying. I closed my laptop and headed for his place of business. I parked at the multiplex and gave him a call on my cell. He met with me and I gave him the key to my Vette, and requested that he put it in his garage tonight. Things were going well with him so I took off.

My morning was coming to an end and I was headed back home. There was a lot of things on my mind while I was driving, mostly the news that Candee gave me regarding me having a sister. As soon as I can, I'm going to get to the bottom of this thing.

As crazy as it sounds, I decided to pour salt into the wound by stopping by Maria's place. When I pulled on to her block I saw her car parked on the curb. Walking toward her place I did a double take when I saw a for sale sign on the windshield of her car. I rang her doorbell and it wasn't long before another tenant came to the door.

"May I help you?"

"I'm a friend of Maria's, my name is Sherman."

"Oh, so you're Sherman! I'm sorry but Maria's not here anymore. She moved back home."

"You mean Puerto Rico?"

"Yes, and I'm really going to miss her! She left the sale of car in my hands."

I said thank you and turned to leave. For the first time I truly knew that it was over. My darling Maria had disappeared for the last time!

# THE CITY BLOCK: 23

It was day two of my stake out. It's been close to a week since our murderer has struck, and again I lay in wake. As I sip on my coffee I turn my attention to my laptop. I see a woman carrying a briefcase and stepping up the sidewalk to the Mallory home. I immediately put my coffee down and call Frank on the phone.

"Crack the door a little and ask who it is."

I could hear the woman say that she was with a local church.

"Frank, tell her to go away. She'll have to come back another time. If I don't see her turn and leave, I'm sending the cops immediately!"

A moment later I saw her turn and walk away.

"Ok Frank, you did well. Now calm down and stick to your routine."

CLICK.

I turned my attention back to where I am. School buses had come and gone, and the neighborhood was getting quiet again. It was around 10:00am and the mail lady was making her way up the side walk. She had a stack of letters in one hand, and a small package in the other. Just about on time like yesterday. On my side of the street I watched an old elderly couple taking a walk.

Out of the side of my eye I saw the mail lady ringing the doorbell at the DeSanto home. The door began to open and that's when I said SHIT! It's supposed to be a mailman, not a mail lady! Jumping out of my car and running, I damn near got hit by a minivan. Inside the house just as Leo was signing for the package, she stuck him, injecting him with poison. Holding his head up, she kissed him on the cheek.

Running up the sidewalk, I jumped over a bike and a skateboard. She must've heard me, because as I reached the steps she came barreling out of the door. Pushing me I staggered back and as she ran by I grabbed her ankle and she fell forward breaking her fall with one hand. I stepped on the skateboard and it shot from under my foot causing me to fall back. My rib cage landed right on one of the pedals of the bike. Slowly getting up, I hold on to my ribs and start out after her, but she was at least 50 yards ahead me and approaching the corner. Just as I reached the corner and stepped off the curb, a car was hauling ass straight at me. I turned to get out of the way, but the bumper clipped my knee and sent me spinning. I lost my balance, fell and hit my head on the sidewalk.

Slowly waking up I could smell the strong scent of disinfectant, and feel the warm hand of someone holding my wrist. Fully awake now I could feel my head throbbing like a jack hammer in a steel mill! Attempting to sit up I felt severe pain in my mid section. Looking down I see that I've been wrapped in bandages. This time I feel two warm hands on my chest pushing me back down.

"Please Mr. Brothers I wouldn't do that if I were you."

Looking at the nurse I asked if I were in heaven.

"No sir, you're in the hospital."

"What happened?"

A much lower voice answered.

"You almost became victim number five."

I was pretty drugged up, and it took me a moment to put it all together.

"What do you mean number five?"

"Yeah punk, you screwed up!"

Lt. Lopez took a small note pad from his pocket.

"It seems that a Mr. Leo DeSanto became the latest victim this morning. Who the hell do you think that you are? If you weren't in this bed, I'd lock your ass up right now!"

"This morning?"

"Yeah hot shot! It's now going on 7:00pm."

"7:00pm!"

"Look, I'd love to stay here and ream your ass, but I've got to get back over to the crime scene!"

"Hey Lt., how did you know I was here?"

"The local police department found my number on your cell. I've got to get the hell outta here, but don't think that I'm finished with you!"

After the Lt. left, I asked the nurse to help me sit up so that I could go to the rest room.

"I don't think so Mr. Brothers."

"Why not?"

"Have you taken a look at your knee?"

"My knee?"

Looking down I see that my knee is swollen to the size of a cantaloupe. It was then that the pain set in.

"Maybe tomorrow if the swelling goes down."

"What do you mean tomorrow? I'm not staying here!"

"Oh yes you are! We're keeping you here for observation."

"But I can't stay here!"

"Mr. Brothers, I really don't think that you want to fight with me. I have a distinct advantage over you!

She then gave me a bed pan and took off. It didn't look like I'd be going over the wall anytime soon, so I did my best to relax and get some rest.

I wondered what had happened to that angel that I saw when I first woke up!

Thirty minutes later I woke up to another angel, but this one I recognized.

"Hey there tough guy, you made the news!"

"Candee, how did you know?"

"I picked it up on my scanner. Let me see now. A private investigator involved in the hottest murder case in the city, maybe this will earn you some business and you can buy yourself a Porsche!"

"Oh that's real funny! Kick a man while he's down!"

"Honey this is far too easy! I have other ways of kicking you while you're down!"

"So did you come here to harass me, or to take me home?"

"Have you ever heard the saying, you can catch more flies with honey?"

"Yeah, so what!"

"If you want to get out of here, you need to start being nice to that nurse."

Just about then the nurse walked in with my meds and a cup of water.

"Here you are Mr. Brothers."

After she left Candee gave me a kiss on my forehead.

"I've to go, see ya around!"

"That's it?"

"Hey, I did what I was supposed to do! I'll check on you."

A few minutes later my meds kicked in and I was out like a light.

# THE CITY BLOCK: 24

At 6:30am sharp, I was greeted by Nurse Friendly! In her hand she held a small cup with a red liquid in it.

"Here, take this."

Just as I was about to ask what it is, she seized the moment and poured it down my throat. Grabbing my wrist, she looked at her watch.

"Excuse me nurse."

"Yes Mr. Brothers."

"Can we start over? My name is Sherman."

With the biggest, sweetest smile I've ever seen, she said hi, I'm Linda.

"I'm sorry for the way that I behaved yesterday. I know that you're only here to help me."

She didn't comment, but she continued to smile. Lifting up the sheet, she looked at my knee.

"Well Sherman, it appears that the swelling is starting to go down."

"Good, does that mean that...?"

She turned and gave me a stern look.

"Never mind."

Lying in bed I went over the events of yesterday. The bottom line is that I blew it! I knew for a fact that Leo had a mailman, not a mail lady. Even if I thought that she was a sub, I should have been on my game. I couldn't help but feel responsible.

On my third day in the hospital Dr. Shammere paid me a visit. After introducing himself he asked how I was feeling.

"You look much better than you did when you arrived. Let's have a look at your knee. Ah, it looks good! The swelling is going down and it doesn't appear to have fluid in it. Have the headaches gone away?"

"I'm not normal, but I feel a lot better."

"That's good, the medication is working as well."

"So doctor, how soon do you think I'll be able to go home?"

"Well Mr. Brothers, for starters I want to get you on your feet. We're going to get you some therapy and teach you how to walk with the aid of crutches. You'll need them for about two to three weeks. Trying to walk without them could result in the need for surgery. "Let me make myself clear? The knee does need some exercise, but don't overdo it." Tomorrow morning I will meet with your nurse and the therapist, and we'll find out when you may go home."

"Thanks doctor."

Just as the doctor was leaving, Dad, Carl, and Rex walked in.

"Why didn't you call us son? How are you feeling?"

"Dad I've been so drugged up that all I could do is sleep. How did you guys find me?"

"We saw the news report on Leo that mentioned a private investigator. We contacted that Candee Harris woman at WLOK and she told us."

I looked at Carl and Rex.

"Hey guys, I'm really sorry about Leo! I screwed up!"

That's when dad spoke up.

"Who's Leo, and what is this all about?"

OPPS!

Before Carl and Rex could speak up, a nurse's aide came in and handed me a vase of flowers. I took the card from the flowers and sat them on the nightstand. I read the card and I swear, if I wasn't lying down, I would have fallen down! Dad immediately took the card from my hand.

"Once again I'm going to ask what the hell this is all about!"

The card read Sherman, please let it go! I didn't mean to hurt you! It was signed with a red lip stick kiss.

"Ok you two, get the hell out of here, I'll deal with you later! Close the damn door behind you! Alright son, why are you three yanking my chain? I want every damn detail, and I want it now!"

"Well Dad, you already know that I'm working on the Lip Stick murder case."

"So what does Carl and Rex have to do with that shit, and don't bullshit me son!"

"Dad, all of the guys that have been murdered was their frat brothers back in college."

"You mean to tell me that this shit is about a kid's club?"

"Yeah Dad, but it's bigger than that."

"How is it bigger son?"

"The killer has promised to kill seven of them, and now there are only three of them left."

"Let me guess son, two of them are Carl and Rex!"

"Yes sir."

"Son of a bitch, so what is it? Money, revenge, what?"

"It's not about money Dad."

"So it's revenge? Wait, you said that the killer is a woman. Sherman, don't lie to me! Is this shit about sex?"

I couldn't look at dad, I just dropped my head. That's when he kicked the nightstand causing the flowers to fall over.

"Damn it, I'm going to break their fucking necks! The firm doesn't need this shit, and I'm too damn old for it! I swear I'm going to kill em' myself!"

Linda and another nurse came crashing through the door.

"What's going on in here? Mr. Brothers are you alright?"

That's when Dad spoke up.

"I'm sorry nurse, I'm Sherman's dad, and I got a little emotional."

The nurses left and Dad started cleaning up the mess that he had made.

"So where are you at now son?"

"I'm stuck right now, but there's a guy name Frank Mallory that's one of the three remaining. He has my Vette parked in his garage. Every morning I have him park it in front of his house."

"So how does that help you?"

"I have a dashboard camera mounted in it, and I can monitor it from my laptop. I also have a rental car parked outside of the last victim's house. You'll find my laptop in it."

"Well son, it looks like I don't have much time to waste. I'd better get out of here! Get well, I'll be in touch."

As soon as dad left I gave Rex a call.

"Hey, it's me."

"How did it go?"

"Not good! You should know that he plans to rip you guys a new one!"

"Yeah, I expected that."

"Look. I need you to get away, and come back to see me. I need a special favor!"

"Anything you want Sherman!"

"Don't tell anyone about this conversation. Visiting hours are over at 8:00pm."

"Got it!"

CLICK.

After talking to Rex, it occurred to me that I hadn't heard from Candee, oh well!

# THE CITY BLOCK: 25

That same day there was another gathering of sorts over at the City Block. It seems that Angie has been off work the last couple of days, and has returned with a surprise. Carman greets her and immediately yells out.

"Louie, get in here!"

He came running in from the storage room and took one look at Angie.

"What the hell happen to you?"

The two stood starring at her with a cast on her arm and in a sling.

"Oh I feel so stupid!"

"What happened honey?"

"I fell down the stairs in the lobby of my apartment building."

"What were you doing?"

"I was rushing instead of paying attention. The doctor says that I'll have to wear this thing for six weeks!"

"Well sit down girl! How do you feel?"

"I'm fine, I'm fine!"

"What can we do for you?"

"Nothing girl, don't make a fuss! I feel so embarrassed!"

"Ah honey it could've happened to anyone!"

"Look guys, I still want to work."

"There's nothing you can do here."

"I can still mix drinks, and I'm sure there are other things I can do."

"Ok girl, it's up to you, but I'm going to be watching you!"

Meanwhile back at the hospital I had just finished my first therapy session. I was now lying in bed watching TV. The phone rang and it turned out to be Candee.

"I had just about given up on you!"

"I'm sorry but things have been a little crazy here at the studio. How are you feeling?"

"I feel a little better. So when will I see you again?"

"Gee Sherman, I don't know."

"Yeah, I'm sure that you're busy."

"I hope that you understand."

"I'm a big boy, don't worry about it!"

"I really have to go Sherman!"

CLICK.

I started thinking about Candee. This woman drove into my life and tried to force herself on me sexually, and now she's dropped me like a bad habit! Here again I'm thinking about what Rebecca told me. At least now I know what Candee is about.

As much as I hated to, I gave Lt. Lopez a call.

"Yeah punk, what do you want?"

"I was wondering if you found any witnesses?"

"There was a few. They all said that the car that hit you was green, and everything else happened too fast, but they all gave a perfect description of a strange man sitting in a parked car all morning!"

Laughing, the Lt. hung up on me.

CLICK.

# THE CITY BLOCK: 26

It's morning again, and all of the poking and prodding is right on schedule!

"Good morning Sherman."

"Good morning Linda."

"Sherman, can I ask you something?"

"Sure, what is it?"

"I've noticed that no woman has come to visit you."

"Yeah, I've noticed that too!"

"I just thought that I'd ask."

Nurse Linda left and I had breakfast. Shortly after that Rex walked in.

"Hey buddy, how are you feeling?"

"Pretty good Rex, close the door and have a seat. What I'm about to say must stay between us. I mean nobody can know, not Dad, not Carl, not anyone! This is extremely personal, and you're the only one that I can trust!"

"Jesus Sherman, you're scaring me! What is it?"

"I think that I have a sister."

"You've got to be freaking kidding me!"

Look, I don't care how much dirt you get under your nails, or what rocks you have to turn over. I want you to dig up everything you can find on my natural mother, my father, I want it all! I don't care how disgusting it may be!"

"Sherman I'm sure that those records are sealed and I'd need a court order."

"I know that Rex, but I also know that you know people! You have more power under your little pinky than the person that told me that I have a sister! I know that I'm asking a lot, but what would you do?"

"Ok Sherman, but I've got to tell you, this can get real ugly!"

"Yeah well, my life hasn't been a bed of roses lately!"

"Man buddy, this is a big pill!"

"Remember don't say a word to Dad or Carl."

"Speaking of the Silver Fox, I've got to go bend over and take it the hard way!"

"Thanks Rex, good luck!"

After Rex left I started fantasizing about having a sister. While fantasizing Nurse Linda came in to take my vitals.

"Excuse me Linda, but can I ask you a question this time?"

"Sure, what's up?"

"Do you have brothers and sisters?"

"Yeah, I have a younger brother and two sisters. Why do you ask?"

"How do you get along?"

"My brother is a first class jerk when it comes to women. I fight with one sister every time we talk, and my other sister gave up on men and took to pizza and cup cakes!"

"Wow, I'm sorry that I asked!"

"In all honesty Sherman, I wouldn't trade them for anything in the world! Are you having sibling problems?"

"No not really. In fact that's the only problem that I don't have!"

"Ah ha I see!"

"You see what?"

"What is her name?"

"That's all Nurse Linda!"

Mocking me with a low voice, Linda says, "That's all Nurse Linda!" as she leaves my room. A few minutes later Dad called me.

"Hey Dad, how is it going?"

"I don't want to say how it's going!"

OPPS!

"I picked up your car and dropped it off at that bum Carlton's house! I put my own people on the Mallory residence, so you can relax and get better."

"Thanks for everything Dad."

CLICK.

Man I've got to get out of here! I buzzed Nurse Linda and she came in right away.

"What's wrong?"

"Give me the scoop!"

"What scoop?"

"The doctor told me that you guys were meeting this morning."

"Oh, that!"

"Yeah, that!"

"The jury is still out on that, but you can take a walk if you like."

"You know, that's a damn good idea!"

"You're not going to try anything stupid are you?"

"I'm just going to take a walk, like you suggested."

Linda left and I started wondering who I could call that wouldn't ask any questions. I came up with the idea of contacting Abbigale. No one would ever thing that she was up to something. First I've to take a look at the grounds and see if my knee can take it.

I found myself sitting at a table on a large garden patio. Nurses sat around on coffee breaks, and patients soaked up the sun. The patio was bordered on three sides by the hospital. The one open side was bordered by hedges, three feet square with one foot spacing between them. On the other side of them was the parking lot. While sitting there I put together a plan.

Back in my room now I gave Abbigale a phone call. She wasn't crazy about my plan, but she agreed to help me. I gave her the details of the grounds and she said that she could be here in an hour or so. While waiting I tried to act as normal as possible. I remembered the doctor telling me not to overdo it. Between my walk to the patio and back, everything that I could feel was hurting, but I couldn't take this place another day!

An hour and ten minutes later the phone on my nightstand rang. It was Abbigale. She had made it and was sitting in the parking lot. Through all of the pain, I managed to get dressed and make it to the doorway. I looked in both directions and the hall was completely clear. I felt like I was being set up, but I figured what the hell, I went for it!

In the courtyard now, I could see freedom just a few yards away. When I stepped between the hedges I saw Abbigale. She pulled her car over to where I was standing and pushed the passenger door open. She got out and helped me into the car. Just as we were about to pull away, Nurse Linda came running up to the door.

"Here you are Sherman, you forgot these!"

She handed me my cell phone and a bottle of pain pills. She then turned to leave but stopped. She gave me a big smile and took off.

"Well I'll be damn!"

# THE CITY BLOCK: 27

Abbigale had proven to be heaven sent. At my place I had no choice but use the service elevator, which I hadn't used since moving in. Getting out of the car was a painful experience! Once inside Abbigale got me comfortable on the sofa and asked if she could do anything else.

"That should do it Abby, you've been absolutely wonderful!"

"I guess that I'm your partner in crime now?"

"Well I won't tell if you won't?"

"You've got a deal. Before I go let me get you your phone charger, the remote control, and a of glass water for those pills. I'll just put it all on the cocktail table in front of you."

"You're an absolute angle! Thank you so much!"

"Ok Sherman, I'm going to get out of here, but call me if you need anything."

"Thanks again."

After Abbigale left I took a much needed pain pill and went to sleep. Somehow during the day I managed to make it to my bed and slept through the night. I guess I must've needed it. I woke up the next day feeling better than I had in the last couple of days. I sat up on the side of my bed and began planning a little outing. The most important part of my outing will be plenty of rest stops!

I'll be seeking lots of bus stop benches. I was hoping that I wasn't biting off more than I can chew. The problem is, once I'm out there, I'm out there! Getting bathed and dressed was more than a notion! It took me forever to get down the stairs. Each step had its own method of torture! At the bottom I took a rest. After a few moments I adjusted the crutches and took off slowly.

I had taken over a dozen rest breaks, and it took me forever and a day, but finally I made it to the front door of the Block. For about ten minutes I just stood there, and finally I knocked on the door. A minute later Louie came to the door. He took one look at me and froze.

"Sherman, what the hell happened to you?"

Before I could answer he yelled out to Carman and Angie. Angie was the first to show up at the door, and I was shocked to see that she had a cast on her arm. That's when Carman walked up and folded her arms starring at the two of us. I turned my attention back to Angie.

"What on earth happened to you?"

"I feel down the stairs at my place. What happened to you?"

"I got hit by a car, among other things!"

Both Carman and Louie began laughing until Carman caught her breath.

"It's like you two guys came from the same egg or something!"

Everyone got a big laugh out of that, but it made me think about the task that I had given Rex.

"Tell me something Sherman and then I'll leave you guys alone. How is it that the both of you get hurt on the same day?"

"I don't know Carman. It beats the hell out of me!"

She began laughing again.

"What's so damn funny?"

"If you guys are going to get hurt like this, you should at least do it together and enjoy each other!"

That's when Angie spoke up.

"Carman girl, please get your mind out of the gutter!"

"If you guys don't mind, I'd like to park somewhere!"

"Why don't you take a seat right over there Superman!"

Louie and Carman joined me at my table, and Louie was curious.

"So what's the extent of your injuries?"

"Well I have fractured ribs from falling on a bicycle for starters. I also have a mild concussion and a busted knee from getting hit by a car, but that's all."

"You know something Sherman you're a lot dumber than I thought you were! I knew that you were an idiot when it comes to women, but this takes the cake! I should take you home right now and tie your dumb ass down to something!"

"Thanks for caring Carman, and by the way, I love you too!"

"Honey you ain't missing a damn thing here! Both you and Angie have lost your damn minds!"

"I'm sorry buddy, but she's got a point. You should be in bed with someone taking care of you."

"Well hell, he can't do that because he got caught by his new girl holding hands with that other dummy Candee Harris!"

"Now I know why I came here Carman. It was because I missed you so much!"

I hung around the City Block until they're late afternoon crowd started showing up and then I said by goodbyes. Offers of a ride were extended to me, but I had things on my mind and I needed the exercise. I made the same stops along the way, but I got home alright.

# THE CITY BLOCK: 28

The next day my phone was blowing up with offers of help, but I didn't want to become dependent on anyone. I was getting stronger and it gave me the courage that I needed. So much so, that I called for a taxi to take me over to the lake front. Of course it was challenging making my way through the park after the taxi dropped me off, but I managed to find a seat that was just right.

The lake front was just the way that I had left it. There was plenty of sunshine and activity. This was just the rehab that I needed. The only thing that I forgot was my head set, but there were no telephones, no Carmans, and no cars trying to run me down!

I sat there enjoying myself for about an hour. Even though my knee was getting stronger every day, my ribs still gave me a wakeup call every now and then. Right now they're telling me that it's time to go home. Along the way I took another break on a bench. Just as I was sitting down I heard the sound of a dog barking and claws clicking on the pavement. It was my little friend Barney jumping up and down in a frenzy.

"Hi ya boy, it's good to see you too!"

Following at her usual pace was Rebecca. She took a seat next to me to catch her breath.

"Sherman baby, what happened to you?"

"I had a little accident at work."

"At work, what kind of work do you do?"

"I'm a Private Investigator."

"Well what happened baby?"

"I was hit by a car."

"Hit by a car! Did they catch the guy?"

"No Ma am', it was a hit and run."

"So what does your lady friend think about it?"

"She doesn't know about it."

"Oh Sherman, is she gone?"

"Yeah, it's been a while now. How are you and Barney?"

"We've been fine baby! I've been working in my garden and playing a little Bingo, but mostly we come here."

"If you don't mind me asking, is there a Mr. Rebecca?"

"Yes baby, but he's been gone now for nine years."

"I'm sorry!"

"Don't be sorry baby. We had a wonderful life together, and now I have Barney. He's all I need, but you on the other hand are too young to be alone. Look at the mess you're in. Some pretty little thing should be taking care of you!"

"Someone is taking care of me."

"Who?"

I leaned over and gave her a kiss on the cheek.

"You are!"

"Sherman baby I know that you're just trying to make an old lady feel good, but you shouldn't live your life alone!"

We talked a little while longer and then went our separate ways. Over at the City Block they were getting ready for opening, and Angie was the last to arrive. She walked in with a very serious look on her face.

"We need to talk. Please sit down guys."

Louie and Carman asked what was wrong at the same time.

"You guys know that I've been taking some time off. Well I had some test done."

With that said tears started running down her face.

"The test showed that I have Sickle Cell Anemia."

Carman and Louie got up and wrapped their arms around her as she continued to cry.

"My bone marrow doesn't produce enough, or the right kind of cells."

Can't anything be done, asked Louie?

After taking a few moments to pull herself together she replied.

"A bone marrow transplant may help, but there are no guarantees. For starters I have to find a matching donor, and that's like a needle in a hay stack!"

That's when Carman started to cry.

"The procedure itself is very painful. I'd have to wear catheters. It's just a mess! It can take four to six weeks in the hospital, and that doesn't include recovery time at home."

Louie told her that she's not alone, we're family here! Silence fell across the room as they embraced. Finally Louie broke the silence.

"Look, the bar has been doing well lately, and we're going to remain closed for today."

"Honey you go home and get some rest while Louie and I put our heads together. We're going to beat this damn thing!"

Angie left to go home, and Louie gave Carman a strange look.

"You know what we have to do don't you?"

"Yeah, but where?"

"We can do it here! This bar sticks out like a sore thumb! I'm sure that we can get some of the other business owners in the neighborhood to support us. We can run the blood drive for three days. We can start on a Friday morning and end on a Sunday night."

"I don't know Louie. It's a lot of work, and we're going to need a lot of help."

"We can start by getting on the internet and do some research, and then get on the phone."

"I guess that that's a good place to start. Louie I'm scared!"

"I am too, but we have to be strong for Angie. If she sees one of us break down, she's going to give up! Let's get busy!"

# THE CITY BLOCK: 29

Just sitting around I decide to give Rex a call to follow up on my request. With a less than a cheery voice he answered.

"Hey Sherman."

"Is it that bad buddy?"

"I hadn't called because I didn't know quite how to tell you what I found."

"I love you for that, but let me have it."

"Ok, here goes! For starters you do have a sister, and not any old sister, but a twin."

"A twin!"

"Yeah."

"What did you find out about her?"

"That's where it gets a little hairy. In most cases the mother doesn't name the child. As the child goes through different foster homes, the parents take it on their own to create and change the kid's name. After a while the kid falls off the radar."

"What about DNA?"

"Back then DNA was a up and coming science, but not perfected yet. There was no reason for the hospital to keep samples."

"Ok, what about my parents?"

"Your father is listed as unknown and that's common in most cases. I can tell you that he was Caucasian, but I'm sure that you know that already."

"What about my mother?"

"Your mother is listed as African American."

"I always thought that she was either that or Latin. Go on."

"There is no record of drug or alcohol abuse which is usually the reason for giving up the child."

"Why do you think she did it?"

"Sherman she gave birth in a county hospital using a false name. I took that name and did some research. I found that she had several aliases. Through my contacts in the police department archives, at least one of these aliases had a rap sheet."

"For what?"

"Solicitation."

"She was a hooker?"

"Not just any hooker, a high class hooker!"

"High class!"

"Yeah Sherman. Bankers , politicians, clergy, etc."

"So what does that mean?"

"That means that she's been buried."

"Buried!"

"Not under dirt Sherman. She doesn't now, or ever did exist! You see, these are very powerful men. It's not about being exposed or having their personal lives destroyed. The power and connections that they have would start an avalanche and tie up the court system coast to coast for years."

"So they protected each other?"

"Yeah Sherman, it's a good ole boys club! She was just a pawn, but a pawn that someone couldn't take risk with. Her having babies could not be in the picture and someone went to great lengths to make the three of you disappear! I'm sorry buddy! What do you want me to do now?"

"Gee Rex, I don't know. I need a little time to absorb all of this."

"I understand."

"Hey thanks Rex, I owe you one!"

"Well I'll settle for you keeping my ass alive!"

"I'll try my best! Talk to you later."

CLICK.

For hours I sat around feeling sorry for myself. The only good thing was that none of the remaining brothers had been killed. Now I'm both physically and mentally helpless. I left one jail, which was the hospital, and went to another, which was home. Until I get back on my feet, there's nothing that I can do.

# THE CITY BLOCK: 30

Waking from a nice nap, I reach for my phone. There were no messages, and no missed calls. Just as I was placing it back down on the table it rang.

"Sherman here."

"Hi Sherman, it's Carman."

"Not now Carman, I have a headache!"

"Ha ha, that's real funny!"

"What can I do for you?"

"Sherman this is serious!"

"What's wrong honey?"

"It's Angie."

"Angie!"

"Yeah, her illness has gotten worse. A group of us are getting together tomorrow and we want you to be here."

"I'm already there, you can count on me!"

"Do you need help getting here?"

"No honey, I can make it on my own. Hey Carman, are you alright?"

"I'm fine, but it's sweet of you to ask, Dummy!"

"Dummy!"

"How the hell do you think I'm doing?"

CLICK.

I spent the rest of the evening thinking about Angie. Even though I had the possible murders of seven men on my lap, all I could think about was the possible devastation that could fall on the trio at the Block. This is the first time in a month that I wasn't focused on myself. I don't know the details of Angie's illness, but it must be serious if people are coming together for a meeting.

The following morning I got up moving slowly, which really I had no choice! I started brewing some coffee and headed for the shower. As I prepared for my adventurous walk to the Block, I wondered what was really wrong with Angie. Aside from being a beat up cripple, it was a pretty nice day.

As I approached the Block I could see that there were already several cars in the lot. When I stepped inside there were people scattered in small groups. The meeting hadn't started yet. Off in the corner I saw that Carman had Rex pinned down. That in itself was no surprise, but Rex being here at all surely was!

It appeared that Angie wasn't here, and maybe that was intentional. Tables and chairs were being pulled together. The meeting was starting and Louie took the floor.

"First of all I want to thank you all for coming. I know that over the years we've all come to love Angie. You all know that she's become ill, but some of you don't know the details. I'm going to get right to the point. Angie has Sickle Cell Anemia and she needs a bone marrow transplant. We have you all here because we intend to use this place as a donation center for a blood drive. By taking blood samples from people in the community, maybe our prayers will be answered, and we'll find a matching donor. It's going to take time and effort. We asked you all here because you're all prominent people in the community. We need your help and connections."

Wiping his eyes, Louie gave the floor to Carman. With a note pad in her hand she began speaking.

"As you all know, time is important here. I'm going to read off some items that Louie and I think would be helpful. As I read them off just raise your hand if you think you can be helpful in that area. I'll write your name down next to that item. For starters here at the City Block we're going to offer discount prices to anyone that will sign up for the drive. The first item is printing services for the flyers. The other items are as follows:

Experienced medical help

A receptionist

Ushers

Help with refreshments

Also keep in mind that this list may grow. Please, before you volunteer, think about the commitment. We're going to be here for a while, so think about it."

The crowd broke up into small groups and talked among themselves. Rex came over to where I was.

"Hey buddy."

"Man, this is incredible news!"

"Yeah it is, but Sherman, there are some legal notifications that should be printed on those flyers before they go out. I can write something up, but I'm going to have to talk to the lead person with the medical team."

"Excuse me Rex, but I need to make a surprise phone call."

I dialed 411 and got the number to my former place of residence. The call was automatically put through for me.

"Hi, my name is Sherman Brothers."

"Yes Mr. Brothers, how can I help you?"

"Can you put me through to the nurse's station please?"

"Just a moment please."

I heard the phone ringing.

"Nurse's station, may I help you?"

"Yes, my name is Sherman Brothers."

"Well, well, well!"

"May I speak to Nurse Linda?"

"Sure, hold on."

"Hello, this is Linda speaking."

"Hi Linda, this is Sherman."

"We used to have a Sherman here, but he escaped!"

"Alright, I guess I deserve that!"

"The funny part is that we were going to let you go!"

"What!"

"Yep! Anyway, how can I help you?"

"I have a major medical issue regarding a dear friend. It's a lot to talk about right now. When will you have more time to talk?"

"I'll have time after I get off work this evening."

"Will you call me back at this number?"

"Sure I will."

"Thanks Linda."

CLICK.

As the morning went on the crowds came and went. People were signing up for various duties. Some were offering to do anything that they could. It was obvious that Angie had touched a lot of lives during her years at the bar. Attempting to have the blood drive was definitely a step in the right direction. It was after 4:00pm when my cell vibrated. It was Nurse Linda.

"Hi Linda, can you hold on a minute please?"

"Sure."

I went to the back office and took a seat.

"Hello, thanks for holding on."

"So Sherman, tell me about this friend of yours."

"Well her name is Angie. She has Sickle Cell Anemia and she needs a bone marrow transplant."

"Sherman I have to tell you, this is a very slippery slope! Does she have any family?"

"That's the problem! We're her family!"

"So what's the plan so far?"

"A group of business owners in this community is putting together a blood drive to try to find a matching donor."

"That's a good start Sherman, but you can't do it if you're not a licensed medical professional. You should also know even a matching donor may not work."

"Yeah, that's what the doctor said, but we can't sit and watch her die!"

"Does your group include a lawyer?"

"Yes, a very good one!"

"I'm reluctant Sherman, but I'll help you."

"Thank you so much!"

"Don't thank me yet! There are some conditions!"

"What kind of conditions?"

"I'm going to have to put together a team, and those people will have to be compensated."

"Ok, what else?"

"It's going to cost you personally."

"Cost me what?"

"Dinner and I want it tonight!"

"Dinner! Tonight!"

"And that's not all!"

"That's not all?"

"I want an apology from you for making me look stupid!"

"Nurse Linda I'm truly sorry for behaving like a child and making you appear less than professional in front of your peers."

"Where are you right now?"

"I'm at a place called the City Block."

"I know where it is!"

"You've been here before?"

"No, but I saw one of their business cards in your wallet the day they brought you in here."

"Well I guess I'll see you when you get here."

CLICK.

Wow, this is going to be interesting!

When I turned around Carman was standing behind me with a look on her face that I've seen far too many times!

"I know what you're thinking Carman, but we need medical help."

"Tell me it's not a woman!"

"Damn Carman, I'm trying to help!"

Carman walked away shaking her head. I joined everyone else and gave them the good news. At this time the crowd was starting to thin out. I asked Louie how things were going.

"So far everyone has been very helpful, but I think that we're going to have to find a way to reach more people. I mean more than we can reach with flyers."

"What did you have in mind?"

"What would really be cool is radio, or something like that."

"Yeah, but we don't know anybody like that."

"What about your hot little friend with W.L.O.K?"

"Louie you seem to have forgotten that that hot little thing cost me the best girl I've ever had!"

I agree with Sherman Louie, said Carman.

"I know that Maria meant a lot to you, but that Candee chick has a million viewers tune in every night!"

"Well I'll give it some thought."

"I'm just saying that sometimes you have to take one for the team!"

"You know sometimes I hate you guys! Just for the record, she wouldn't even visit me in the hospital, and she's been avoiding me lately, so don't get your hopes up!"

I noticed that Rex's attention had turned toward the door. He then said wow! Louie and I both turned around at the same time. Standing just inside the door was a curly haired brunette wearing a red halter top, skinny jeans and red high heels.

"Who the hell is that, asked Rex?"

It was Nurse Linda like I've never seen her before, and Carman was directing her my way.

"Gentlemen, may I present our medical professional?"

I made the introductions and then Nurse Linda and I got the hell out of there! Once we were outside I had to tell Linda what I was thinking.

"You know Linda I've got to tell you, you really look different!"

"So do you."

"How do I look different?"

"You don't have your butt hanging out of your gown!"

"Well that's just great, a medical professional with a sense of humor!"

I followed her over to her car and she opened the trunk.

"I have something for you."

She reached in and took out a cane.

"You're going to need this if you intend on keeping up with me!"

She then took my crutches away.

"You know Linda you're just full of surprises!"

"Slow down slugger! Let's see what the evening brings!"

"You've got it!"

# THE CITY BLOCK: 31

Nurse Linda stored away my crutches in the trunk, and we climbed in her car, well at lease I climbed in.

"Ok Mr. Brothers, where are we going?"

"What did you have in mind?"

"I really don't have much time. Can we keep it simple?"

"Well in that case, will delivery be alright?"

"You're a very lucky man! Delivery will be fine."

"Will Chinese be alright?"

"Sure, but where are we having it delivered to?"

"My place if you don't mind?"

"I'm going to agree to that, but only because I know I can take that cane and kick your butt if I have to!"

All I could do was smile, because as a woman she was taking a risk that under normal circumstances she would not. I gave her directions and we took off. When reached my place I knew that she was waiting to see me do the stairs. Using the cane now instead of the crutches, I too was curious. I pulled it off, but there was a shift in my body weight that put unexpected pressure on my ribs, and that resulted in me moaning out loud in pain.

Linda responded right away.

"Are you ok Sherman, you'd better let me take a look at that when we get inside!"

Once we were settled I ordered the delivery food and she began unbuttoning my shirt. It was a strange feeling, because I no longer felt like a guy that had this incredible woman entering my home for the first time. It was more like she was once again a professional that had me under her care.

"Jesus Sherman, when was the last time you changed these bandages?"

"I try, but it's hard to do by myself."

"I'm going to go out on a limb here, do you have any supplies?"

"Yes, Nurse Linda! You can take a look in my hall closet."

She returned with the supplies and went right to work. She began by cutting and removing the old bandages. The fresh air touching my skin felt wonderful. Next I got a feeling that I remembered so very well, and that was Nurse Linda's warm soft hands.

"Sherman I want you to wear these new bandages for one week, and I'm going to you a support."

"Yes Nurse Linda, I'll do whatever you want!"

"Don't go getting kinky on me!"

"I'm not getting kinky!"

"Yeah, I know what you guys say about nurses!"

Before I could comment the doorbell rang. The food was here and I gave Linda money to pay the delivery guy. With the bag in one hand, she used her other hand to lead me to the kitchen. It was like she lived here or something! After we sat down to eat she stopped and looked at me.

"Can I ask you a question Sherman?"

"Sure, go ahead."

"Do you have time to waste?"

"Whoa, you don't mess around!"

"Well I guess that's my answer."

"The truth is recently I've been jerked around more than I care to say."

"So, do you like it?"

"Do I like what?"

"Man, that fall you took must've affected your brain! Do you mind if I get to the point?"

"Hell, don't stop now!"

"Sherman I take my career very serious, and I work a lot of double shifts, but I'm no different than any other human being. I don't make it a habit of hitting on my patients. Every blue moon I believe that I see a good thing, and when that happens I take the ball and run with it! It doesn't always work in my favor, but it is what it is."

"Linda before you go on I want to say something. I appreciate your directness. When you walked into the bar today I was on cloud nine. Even though I knew that you were there on business, you were there to see me."

"Sherman I think that we both know that we can't let our careers or our past stop us from living."

"For right now why don't we just enjoy dinner?"

We laughed and talked while eating. She also gave me instructions on how to take care of myself. We finished and headed for the door.

"Linda I really want to thank you for helping our group out."

At the door she gave me a warm moist kiss on the lips. It was quick, but tasty!

"There's one more thing Sherman."

"What's that?"

"Please get well soon!"

With that she was gone.

# THE CITY BLOCK: 32

Morning came and I was carefully putting my words together for when I call Candee. The last thing that I wanted to do was give her the impression that this was a mercy call. I want to be all business and not reflect one ounce of regret or anger. I wanted to keep it brief, direct, and to the point. If she says yes, that will be cool, if she doesn't, that will be cool too!

I dialed Candee's number and got her voicemail. I left her a message giving her the details of Angie's illness. I had done my job, now it was on her!

I decided to give my new cane a workout. Once I got out I was really starting to like the independence that it gave me. While I was walking along my cell phone vibrated. I was thinking wow, Candee's calling back already! I was wrong, it wasn't her. It was Nurse Linda instead.

"Good morning, this is Sherman."

"Hi, this is Nurse Linda. I hope I didn't wake you."

"No, I'm out giving the new cane a try."

"How are you feeling this morning?"

"It's funny that you should ask! I was just wondering why I feel so good this morning."

"Well Sherman I'm calling on business."

"What can I do for you?"

"I need your lawyer's phone number please."

After I gave her Rex's number she said thank you, good bye."

CLICK.

Wow, I guess that was her business side! Keeping my spirits high, I kept on trucking! I got about a half block down the street and my cell vi-

-137-

brated again. This time it was a text message from Nurse Linda.

"I feel especially good this morning too!"

Now that's what I'm talking about! Even though her text made me feel a bit light hearted, I had to take a seat on a nearby bench. I needed to remind myself that I'd been down this road before. Things were going fast, and as I had recently learned, that could be a bad thing. I recalled Linda using the phrase, slow down slugger! Right about now it was making sense.

She had shown me her professional side this morning, and it was now time for me to do the same. I had to get back into my murder investigation. At the risk of being humiliated, I dialed up Lt. Lopez.

"Hello, Lopez speaking."

"This is Sherman Brothers Lt."

"Hey hot shot, have any women kicked your ass lately?"

"Look, can I talk to you about the murders?"

"Go ahead, I'm listening."

"I'm trying to put together a profile on the killer."

"Let me ask you a question hot shot? How the hell did you know our killer would show up at the DeSanto place?"

"I really didn't, I just took a shot in the dark! I staked out their place and the Mallory home. I thought that the police would do the same thing."

"I'd bet that you did hot shot! The media would have a field day if they knew the P.D. was using their resources to protect a bunch of rich perverts!"

"Yeah I guess you're right. You got any ideas on why our murderer has been quiet lately?"

"Witnesses say you both took a fall, maybe she got injured too."

"What's your next move Lt.?"

"I'm going to try not to be a hero slick!"

CLICK.

I wanted to talk to Lt. Asshole some more, but oh well! I didn't get the chance to tell him about the flowers and the note that I received at the hospital. I really wanted to know what he thought about the killer regretting hurting me. I'm sure that he would have had something sarcastic to say, but even that may have helped. He made me wonder why the department wasn't putting more effort into the case. They've got to be getting close to having a public outcry. On the other hand I had to consider the possibility that the Lt. is just keeping me out of the loop.

What the frat brothers had done was unspeakable, and maybe the cops just don't give a damn what happens to them! If Carl and Rex wasn't involved I wouldn't give a damn either! I don't know what was discussed between my dad, Carl and Rex. All that I know is no one is talking. I can only hope that they've put together some kind of legal defense in case this mess comes to light.

The firm's reputation is truly on the line. You can steal other people's money, get factories excused for dumping waste, and even close down hospitals, but no one wants legal representation from a firm that has sexual assault attached to it! If the media ever gets a hold of what happened four-teen years ago at that frat house, all hell is going to break loose! I can see the headlines now.

MILLIONAIRE FRAT BOYS RESPONSIBLE FOR THE LIP STICK MURDERS!

If that happened, there wouldn't be enough spin in Washington to save the firm!

# THE CITY BLOCK: 33

After having lunch I felt pretty strong, and was craving a drive in my Vette. I needed a ride over to Carlton's place so I gave Rex a call. I know that I've been leaning on him a lot lately, but he doesn't have a family to look after, and I'm sure that he's trying to avoid my dad!

After making arrangements with him I gave Carl a call. Abbigale answered the phone.

"Good morning, Remington residence."

God, they're so formal over there!

"Hi this is Sherman is this my partner in crime speaking?"

"Good morning Sherman, are you regretting leaving the hospital yet?"

"I do kinda miss being pampered!"

"Did you want to speak with Carlton?"

"You can just let him know that I'm on my way over to pick up my baby."

"I guess by baby you mean that car of yours?"

"Why of course!"

"Ok Sherman, I'll let him know that you're coming to get your baby!"

"Thanks Abby!"

CLICK.

I was surprised that Abbigale didn't come on like Florence Nightingale! I know how much she cares, and right about now she needs someone to take care of.

While I was waiting for Rex to pick me up, I got a call from Louie. He informed me that the blood drive had been scheduled. It would take place on Friday, Saturday, and Sunday from 10:00am to 7:00pm. He said that there was more that he needed to discuss with me, but it could wait. Excited now, I went down stairs to wait for Rex. For some reason my phone was blowing up this morning. Once again it vibrated, and once again I thought that it may be Candee. Again I was wrong. It was Nurse Linda.

"Hi Sherman, I'm sorry to bother you again."

"That's ok, you're not a bother."

"Sherman I don't want to wait until you get better!"

I was shocked at what she said, and there was a long pause on my behalf.

"Hello, Sherman, are you still there?"

"Ah yeah, I'm still here. I was just getting up off of the ground!"

"Well at least you didn't say that you were going to run for it!"

"I am a little blown away! I mean, I'm mentally game, but physically, I'm not sure."

"Good, how about tomorrow?"

"Tomorrow!"

"Hey. I'm being paged. We're not finished talking yet. I'll call you back!"

CLICK.

Never in my life have I ever been afraid of having a lovely woman throw herself at me, but this was different. With Candee she came on too strong, too soon. She completely ignored the fact that she destroyed my relationship with Maria. As sexy as she is, it wasn't that hard to blow her off. I get the feeling that Linda has gone without for a long time due to her job and for some reason, she feels comfortable enough with me to let her feelings hang out.

When Rex and I arrived at Carlton's door, we were greeted by Abbi-gale. The look on her face showed that she was surprised to see me walking with a cane. She was also surprised to see Rex standing beside me. At this point I was hoping that they both would behave.

"Why don't you guys walk around to the garage? I'll have Carlton meet you around there."

"Thanks Abby!"

By time we walked around to the garage, Carl was already there wait-ing for us. He immediately stuck has hand out to Rex for a shake.

"Thanks man!"

"Thanks for what?"

"Thanks for not starting something with Abbigale."

Both Rex and I smiled."

"How is my baby Carl, you didn't scratch her did you?"

"No, but I did take her for a spin! She's no BMW, but she's got a lot of get up and go."

"You just remember that the next time you're paying for German re-pairs!"

"Here's the key buddy. Are you sure that you can get in?"

"Just watch me!"

It was a challenge getting into my baby, but once inside, I felt right at home! Just the feel of the rumble coming from the engine gave me goose bumps! I gave Carl and Rex a wave, and I took off like a kid on a new bike! I was ripping down the highway with my stereo cranked! I felt like the road was mine. Not having to use my cane gave me a new found freedom. Just as I was pulling up in front of my place, my phone rang.

"Hello, this is Sherman."

"Hi, it's me, how are you?"

"I'm in love!"

"That's real sweet, but talk about pushing it!"

"Oh, I'm sorry I just picked up my baby!"

"What the hell!"

"I'm talking about my car."

"That's just great! Now I have to compete with a damn car!"

"Relax you're far more special than this car is!"

"In that case can we talk about tomorrow?"

"When do you want to talk?"

"Right now, look across the street!"

I turned around and looked across the street to see Linda sitting in her parked car. I backed up my car and parked in the garage. By time I made it back up to the sidewalk, she was standing there. We smiled at each other and she followed me inside. It was time to let her know how I feel.

"Linda you told me some things about yourself and that's fine, but now I'm starting to worry."

"Sherman I'm just trying to keep the excitement going, but if you want me to stop I will."

"I love your aggressiveness, but like you, I like to be in control sometimes."

"I understand, but I'm afraid to act like an average woman. A man like you might get bored."

"Linda you're anything but boring to me. In fact you're driving me crazy!"

"So what are we going to do now?"

"Why don't we relax and watch some TV. You get comfortable, I'll be right back."

"That sounds fine to me."

"Are you sure that you're going to be alright?"

"Stop worrying, I'm not going to be naked when you get back!"

"No comment!"

When I returned she was stretched out on the sofa and looking at me.

"Is this how it's going to be?"

"I'm not sure that I understand."

"Can we at least watch TV in the bedroom?"

"Do you promise to behave?"

"Why don't we compromise?"

"And just how are we going to do that?"

She got up and took me by the hand.

"Come on, I'll show you!"

In the bedroom she picked up the remote off of my nightstand and gave it to me.

"Why don't you turn on the TV."

I turned around to turn on the set.

"I'm warning you, I'm going to be keeping an eye on you!"

"Sherman I think that you would be better off keeping both eyes on me!"

I quickly turned around to see her lying completely nude in bed.

"Don't panic Sherman, just take off your clothes and join me. Rather you know it or not, I've already seen your junk at the hospital. This is a compromise. All I want to do is snuggle."

I started taking off clothes, but I was mumbling to myself at the say time.

"What was that you said?"

"I said that it's not junk!"

With that she busted out in laughter!

Morning came. Seeing that I didn't sleep very well, I was first to wake up. As I watched her sleeping I began to feel guilty for being so hard on her yesterday. I know what it's like to overreact when you see something that seems real. At the risk of looking like a jerk, I rolled over absorbing the pain from my ribs and lightly wrapped my arm around her. I then kissed her on her neck.

"Good morning Nurse Linda."

She slowly opened her eyes.

"By the way, it's Mason, Linda Mason."

"I think that I'm ready."

"Well it's about damn time!"

"Remember that I'm not a well man!"

"Whatever!"

# THE CITY BLOCK: 34

Today is Thursday, and tomorrow the blood drive begins at the Block. So far I haven't got an answer from Candee and that's a drag! I know that she doesn't run the station, but I thought that I'd at least get an answer back from her. Maybe she called the Block.

I gave Carlton a call and had him check on all of the guys to make sure that they were still among the living. After talking to him I got a phone call from an unknown number. Normally I don't answer those because more than likely it's a telemarketer. Considering all that's been going on, I decided to answer.

"Hello, you've reached Sherman."

I waited a few moments but there was no reply. I said hello once more and got the same thing, so I hung up. I still hadn't planned a lunch date with my dad, but I really didn't think that he was in the mood. I had warm thoughts of Linda on my mind as I grabbed a cold beer from the kitchen. I headed out to my balcony to enjoy the evening air.

After a couple of swallows I heard the phone ring in my bedroom. I put the beer down and went to answer it.

"Hello this is Sherman."

Once again there was no reply.

"Ok, it's you again! I'll just sit here and listen to your breathing! You can hang up whenever you're ready!"

After 5 or 6 minutes I hung up. Now that it's happen twice, it dawned on me that it may be the killer trying to reach out to me in some strange way. Now I'm thinking that maybe I should let the Lt. in on this. Before I could go back out to my beer, the damn phone rang again.

"Who the hell is this?"

"Hey, calm down, it's Dad! What's going on over there?"

"Sorry Dad, some nut's been calling and not saying anything."

"Well son I just wanted to let you know that I've got a little time now. Why don't I swing by?"

"That sounds great Dad!"

"See ya in a bit!"

CLICK.

I took a couple of rib eyes out of the freezer and thawed them out in the microwave. Out on the balcony got some goals fired up. Back in the kitchen I got a salad going, and before long I had dinner for two on the way. All I had to do was wait for Dad and throw the steaks on the grill.

While waiting for Dad I gave the guys over at the Block a call. They hadn't heard from Candee either, but they had received some medical supplies. They had also talked to Linda who had given them instructions on how to arrange an in and out traffic pattern in the bar. I really felt good about bringing Linda into the picture.

It wasn't long before my doorbell rang and I buzzed Dad up. I opened the door and waited for him to make it up.

"Hey son, how are you doing?"

"I'm great Dad, how about you?"

"Kinda beat, but I guess I'm alright."

"Make yourself comfortable, I hope you're hungry!"

"I'm starving son!"

"Great, I'm going to throw a couple of steaks on the grill."

"You want a beer?"

"Sure, why not!"

We both took a seat on the balcony while the steaks slowly smoked to perfection. After some small talk, I threw a curve ball at Dad.

"I've been thinking about this case Dad."

"So what have you come up with?"

"Seeing that the killer has been so quiet lately, why not try to flush her out?"

"How would you do that?"

"Why not have Candee Harris interview Lt. Lopez on the air. Have him say that they have a suspect on the run, and that's why there haven't been any murders lately."

"I don't know son. That might piss the killer off!"

"Yeah I was thinking the same thing."

"You do have one thing in your favor."

"What's that Dad?"

"She screwed up by telling you that her targets are seven men."

"The truth is, if I had had the support of the police department the last time, we'd have her right now."

"I thought that you and that Lt. were working together."

"Yeah Kinda."

"What do you mean?"

"Let's just say that catching the killer isn't his priority."

"Why the hell not?"

"He believes that these guys are getting what they deserve. You know Dad, I don't think that this woman is a real killer."

"Why do you think that?"

"She's making too many mistakes. At the steak house she allowed herself to be recorded on camera, and then she damn near let me catch her. A professional never would have let that happen!"

"Hey son how are those steaks doing?"

"There's a salad in the refrigerator, do you mind grabbing it?"

"Sure son, coming right up! Do you want another beer?"

"That sound great Dad."

After eating we sat around talking a bit, and then Dad caught on to the wheels turning in my head.

"You look like you've got something to say son."

"Well, something other than this case has been eating at me."

"Before you start, am I going to need something stronger then a beer?"

"You just might Dad!"

"Well let me run to the kitchen first?"

I tried to put my words together carefully while Dad was gone.

"Ok son, let me have it!"

"When I first met Candee Harris she didn't trust me."

"And?"

"She had her sources run a check on me. Keep in mind that not all of her sources are legit. Well to make a long story short, she found out that I have a sister. She let it slip out by mistake. It turns out to be true. In fact, my sources found even more information."

Dad had no comment. Actually he was visibly shaken.

"Not only were we separated at birth, but my dad was White, and my mom was African American. Dad, my mom was a high class call girl that catered to wealthy men. Evidently one of these men got her pregnant. She was forced to give us up for adoption, and she was conveniently disposed of. Records show that her name was false to begin with, and none of us really exist."

Dad just sat quietly, white as a ghost! He had a look on his face that I've never seen before.

"Dad, are you alright?"

"I'm fine son. I just don't know what to say. When your mom and I were looking to adopt, we were just looking for a little boy. We had no idea that you had a sister."

Deep down inside all the Silver Fox could think about was the life-style he used to live thirty something years ago.

"I'm sorry son. You've been through a lot, and you deserve better."

"Well Dad, through it all, I came out alright. What bothers me most is knowing that I have a sister out there that may not know she has a brother."

"Well son, I'm not going to keep you any longer, and again I'm sorry about the news you received!"

We said our goodbyes and Dad took off. I think that he took off because the news was too much for him. I can't say that I blame him. After Dad left I began cleaning up behind our meal. That's when I received a text message from Linda.

"Tomorrow I'm going to be Nurse Linda, and I'd appreciate it you kept your hands off of me!"

Oh I had to text her right back!

"Ain't that the pot calling the kettle black!"

She replied, LOL.

She made me smile and I really needed it at the time. I called the Block one more time to check on things and Louie told me that a package had been delivered there for me. I assumed it was the back brace that Linda ordered. I told him that I'd be right over. Maybe being there will clear my mind for a bit.

When I got there I decided to stand at the bar instead of climbing up on a stool. About the time that I was ordering a beer from Louie, Carman showed up to give me my usual amount of hell!

"Hey Lover boy, I've got a package for you!"

"Yeah I know. It's a back brace."

"Yeah I'd bet it is! It's more likely to be some kind of sex toy!"

"Just go and get it Nosey Rosy!"

"Here's your beer buddy!"

"Thanks a lot Louie."

Carman came back carrying a box, and Louie handed me a pair of scissors, which I gave to her.

"Here you go Rosy, they a look for yourself!"

"I'm not touching that filthy thing!"

Louie started cracking up!

"You need to stop! I told you it's not a damn sex toy, and even if it were, you need to stop acting like you're Mother Theresa!"

"Whatever! Just open it up lover boy!"

I cut the seal on the box and opened it. With the flaps spread apart it was plain to see that it was indeed a back brace.

"Now what do you have to say Nosey Rosy?"

Carman just rolled her eyes at me and walked away.

"Sherman what would you two do without each other?"

"Just taking a wild guess Louie, I for one would be very happy!"

"You know that you love her!"

"Yeah, but don't tell her!"

Back at home I put on a pair of shorts and stretched out. Before going to sleep I sent Linda a text.

"Late night dinner, tomorrow, my place, don't me late!"

She texted me back right away.

"You must think that I'm yours now!"

"I'm just making a kind offer."

"I'll think about it! Good night."

# THE CITY BLOCK: 35

Friday morning came fast, but I was ready for it. Nurse Linda had instructed me to start putting in about twenty minutes or so each day without the aid of my cane. Standing up was a challenge, but once I was on my feet it wasn't too painful. One thing for sure, I had really gotten used to the cane, and Linda was right. If she wanted to kick my butt, she could. I spent the twenty minutes doing my regular routine. I did things like going to the kitchen to make coffee, shaving and getting dressed.

Just past 8:30am I grabbed my extra leg and headed down to the parking garage. With the aid of the new brace wrapped around my ribs, it was a lot easier getting into my car. On my way over to the City Block I stopped by the bakery and picked a couple of dozen donuts for the volunteers. I pulled up to the Block's parking area just in time to get the last parking space.

I walked around to the front of the bar and was shocked at what I saw. The drive was scheduled to start at 10:00am, and here it was only 9:00am, but there was a line of people half way down the block. It was visual proof that there is hope for our society. The drive was no longer just a kind gesture, it was real!

At the entrance sat a male nurse handing out wrist bands and forms to be filled out. Behind him was three more nurses sitting at tables with one extra chair in front of it. There was a table at the far end that was occupied by Nurse Linda. At the entrance I was given a form and a wrist band.

"Thanks for coming Mr. Brothers."

"Wait a minute, how did you know who I am?"

At first the nurse just smiled.

"Aren't you the patient that went over the wall a couple of weeks ago?"

"Jesus, does everyone know?"

"Pretty much sir!"

I took the donuts over to the other side of the room where a table was sat up for refreshments. At the side door, Louie thanked people for coming just as they were about to exit. He saw me and said good morning.

"Wow man, this place looks like a well oiled machine!"

"That Nurse Linda really knows her stuff!"

"If you only knew!"

"What's that?"

"Nothing, just thinking out loud. So what can I do to help?"

Before Louie could answer, a voice behind me spoke.

"Just keep your cripple behind out of the way!"

"Good morning Carman! What were you saying Louie?"

"Why don't you go behind the bar, handle questions and man the phone."

"Aye-aye Captain!"

Things were going well. The crowd would get small and then start growing again. At lunch time a couple of the nurses switched off, but I still didn't get a chance to talk to Nurse Linda. The action was non-stop, and Linda was a different person. It was strangely exciting to me. About an hour later I went to the men's room. When I returned, Linda and another nurse had left for lunch. I had missed my chance to talk to her.

I noticed that Louie was standing just outside the side entrance, and he motioned for me to join him.

"Hey Sherman, you're not going to believe this!"

He pointed across the street and there parked was a WLOK news van. The satellite dish on top of it was telescoping up into the air. At the rear of the van, a guy was taking out a shoulder mount camera. Louie and I went to the front of the bar just in time to see Candee stepping out of the passenger door. Wearing her usual designer attire, she looked like she had just finished a photo layout. By this time Carman had joined us.

"What's she doing here?"

"I know how you feel about her, but for now we need her."

She shook her head and walked away. Candee crossed the street and stood just in front of the bar and the cameraman gave her a five finger count down.

"Good afternoon, I'm Candee Harris with the WLOK news crew. We're coming to you live from outside of the City Block Cocktail Bar. They're in the middle of a desperate blood drive to find a matching donor for Angie Cruz, one of the owners here."

She then stepped over to Louie.`

"We're talking to Louie Malano, another one of the owners. Louie what can you tell our viewers about Angie?"

"Thank you Candee. Angie is in need of a bone marrow transplant, and you can see by the turnout that she's well loved in this community. I don't have to tell you that it's a needle in a haystack situation. Even if we find a close enough match, there's no guarantee that her body will accept it. Candee this is why we need the WLOK viewers to pitch in. For every person that can take a little time out of their life today, we might save Angie's life. We'll be here until 7:00pm today, Saturday and Sunday."

"Thank you Louie. There you have it folks. If you can find the kindness in your heart and the time in your day, please make your way down to the City Block. They're located here in Hyde Park. For directions and more information you can call the number on the bottom of your screen. I'm Candee Harris coming to you live from the City Block."

She gave the microphone to her cameraman and Louie walked up to her.

"Thank you Miss Harris. You have no idea of how much this means to us. I'm sorry that Angie can't be here to tell you herself."

"That's ok Louie, and you guys are very welcome. Is Sherman here my any chance?"

"Yeah, he's around on the side helping out."

Looking at her watch she quickly went around to the side of the building. At the side door she rushed up to me, put her arms around me, and gave me a kiss on both cheeks.

"Sherman I'm sorry for not returning your calls. Give me a call honey, and we'll hook up!"

With that she ran across the street, jumped in the van, and they took off. Louie then joined me at the side door.

"What the hell was that all about?"

"Louie this bitch has lost her damn mind!"

We both stood watching the van as it ripped down the street. With all that had just happened, I was a combination of shocked and pissed off. I was so caught up in it that I failed to see that Nurse Linda had returned from lunch and had witnessed the whole thing. I started to approach her, but she gave me the hand.

"God damn it!"

I was so pissed off that I hit the side of the bar with my cane and broke it in half! At the same time I folded over in pain from my ribs. To avoid creating a bigger scene, Louie and Carman quickly rushed me into the back office.

"Damn it Sherman!"

"Not now Carman!"

"I knew that that high class bitch was no good when she ran your Latin friend out of here! Just sit back here for a while and relax."

I sat for a while not believing what had just happened. I felt my cell phone vibrate on my belt. It was a text message from Linda.

"Your ass is grass! You can damn bet that I'll be at your place tonight!"

At this point I didn't want to hear from anyone else, so I turned my phone off. I got my act together and headed for the side door.

"Louie I'm sorry, but I think that I'm going to call it a day!"

"Sure buddy, I understand. Go home and have yourself a tall one."

"Yeah I just might do that!"

I got into my car and the first stop that I made was at the drug store. I needed a new cane. When I got home, I did indeed pour myself a double shot of scotch. After calming my nerves I began preparing a late night meal at the risk of looking like a fool. In any case I still had to eat. After getting things ready to go, I grabbed my bottle and went to the sofa.

I tried not to think about her, but I couldn't get Candee off of my mind. She had already proved to me what kind of woman she is, but yet I let her get to me. From the moment she arrived at the bar I should had prepared myself. My behavior was inexcusable, but damn, I couldn't lose another good woman because of this chick! Even Dad told me in the beginning that she was a piece of work!

I wish that Rebecca was here. I wonder what she'd have to say about this mess. After a couple of glasses of scotch I closed my eyes and the time drifted by. At around 7:30pm there was a loud pounding on my door that scared the hell out of me! If I didn't know better, I would've thought that it was the police. Through the peep hole I could see a white uniform pacing back and forth in the hallway. I was now wishing that was the police!

Just as she started pounding on the door again, I opened it. She wasn't expecting that and her next attempted pound on the door hit me right in the chest. I staggered back and Nurse Linda came barreling in shouting at me.

"What the hell was that shit all about?"

"Linda honey please calm down!"

She kicked off one shoe.

"Is that what you like, high class tramps?"

She then kicked off the other shoe.

"I come back from lunch to find you in the arms of some celebrity wannabe that doesn't even give a damn about you! Well I guess that I know you now!"

With that she stormed out the door, slamming it behind her. A moment later she was pounding on the door again. I opened it and she reached in grabbing her shoes and left again with another loud bang of the door.

# THE CITY BLOCK: 36

I sat back down on the sofa and did what any man would have done. I poured myself another shot of scotch. After a while I went to the kitchen to heat up my dinner. When I came back to the living room, I thought that I heard something out in the hallway. I opened the door and there was Nurse Linda sitting on the floor leaning against the wall, holding her shoes.

Without saying a word I took one of her hands and led her back inside. I sat her down on the sofa and I took a seat in the chair. Picking up my glass, she poured herself a shot and downed it. Still not talking I went to the kitchen to check on my meal. While making myself a plate I could hear the shower come on in the bathroom. At this point I lost my appetite. I went to my bedroom and got a tee shirt and hung it on the bathroom door knob. I then climbed into bed.

About fifteen minutes later she joined me in bed. I had my back to her still not talking, but waiting to hear what she had to say. With my back to her I could hear her softly crying, but did not respond. I could feel her tears dripping on my neck, but I remained silent.

"Sherman you hurt me."

"We'll talk in the morning."

"Why do we have to wait until morning?"

"That's the best thing for me."

I got out of bed and went to the kitchen to put the food away. I was trying really hard not to go off again, but I had to say something when I got back in bed.

"Linda do you really think that I'd do something like this to you in front of your peers when you're trying to save the life of a friend of mine?"

"Well why did she think it was alright to throw herself at you like that?"

"A few weeks before I came to the hospital we had a one night stand. Following that night she broke off communication, and I wrote it off and considered it over."

"Well how do you know her?"

"She and a Chicago cop have been working with me on the Lip Stick Murders. I almost caught the killer until she ran me over, and that's where you came in."

"I don't know what to think Sherman."

"Do you believe me?"

"Yeah, but I still don't like it or her. I don't want you to think that I'm spying on you, but it is alright if I stay here until the drive is over? It will be a lot easier than driving home every night."

"By the way, you never did say where home is."

"I live in Richton Park."

I didn't say yes or no. I just got out of bed and went back to the living room. In the morning we drove both our cars to the drive. I gave her a 30 minute head start so that we'd walk in at different times. At 11:30am things were completely blowing up! The line outside had reached the end of the block, and around the corner.

To save time, Louie and I took forms and wrist bands out on the sidewalk and began giving them out. About half way down the block I had to rest on a bench. While sitting there I heard a familiar voice calling out the name Barney. Just as I turned to take a look, Barney jumped up into my lap.

"Hey little buddy!"

Coming behind him was Rebecca with a young man. Nearly out of breath, she took a seat next to me.

"Rebecca, it's good to see you. How are you doing?"

I stuck my hand out to the young man.

"Hi, my name is Sherman."

"Sherman this is my grandson Tony."

"It's nice to meet you sir."

"So what brings you to this neck of the woods?"

"I saw that pretty little thing on TV talking about that poor young girl! It's such a shame! Now honey you know that I'm too old, but I had to do something. I brought my grandson, he's a good boy."

"Thanks for coming Tony."

After a little small talk, the three of us headed for the bar. Tony stopped just inside the door to register while Rebecca and I took a seat. As we sat Rebecca started looking around.

"That nurse over there is sweet on you!"

She was referring to Linda.

"Rebecca!"

"Well she is!"

"How do you know?"

"As soon as we walked in she perked up."

"Maybe it was Barney. You know how women love little dogs."

"Do you know her?"

"Yes, she was on the staff that took care of me at the hospital."

"So there is something that you're not telling me!"

Just about then Carman came over and started rubbing Barney's head.

"Who is this little guy?"

"See Rebecca, I told you!"

"Honey what's wrong with this boy?"

"He's a dummy! Hi, I'm Carman."

That's when I got up and walked away.

# THE CITY BLOCK: 37

It was Sunday morning and the blood drive had been a huge success. It was mostly due to Candee's on air coverage. Afternoon rolled around and to my surprise, Abbigale, Dad, Carlton, and Rex walked in. After greeting everyone they were all given wrist bands and forms to fill out. While Rex was waiting, Carman made a bee line for him. Abbigale took one look at Rex and started shaking her head.

When the day ended Carman closed and locked the door. Moments later Louie rolled out a cart with buckets of champagne on ice in them. Everybody started cheering and exchanging hugs. A couple of the team members took off their shoes and put their feet up on empty chairs. After flutes of champagne were passed out we toasted to a job well done. The house music was turned on and everyone let their hair down. For the first time, the crew of the bar got to know the medical staff a little. There was lots of laughter and talk about Angie's future. It must've been past 8:30pm when the medical staff began to pack things up. Linda was the last of them to remain at the bar. She then stood up and took the floor.

"Can I get everyone's attention for a minute?"

Carman turned off the music and we all gave her our attention.

"Look, I hate to rain on this festive occasion, but there's something that needs to be said. As you all know we took in over a thousand donors in the last three days. What you may not know is that it can take weeks for the lab to go through all of the blood samples. Even if we get lucky, and I do mean lucky, maybe we'll find two or three matches in the first three hundred samples. Even if we do, those matches will have to be tested for a variety of diseases before we can even think about any kind of medical procedure. When and if everything goes great, the donor will have to be screened and counseled so that he or she will know exactly what their getting into. With that said, does everyone here completely understand me?"

With sad looks on our faces, we all said yes. Just as we all started milling around again, Linda said wait!

"There's one more thing that I want to say. I'M IN LOVE WITH SHERMAN BROTHERS!"

I don't know what in the hell possessed her to say that! Maybe it was insecurity, but it freaked me out, and I'm sure that it freaked out everyone else as well! They had no choice but to start cheering again and welcome her to our family. They then left Linda and me alone.

"I know that everyone is shocked. I hope that I didn't screw up."

"Don't worry about it, it's all good."

# THE CITY BLOCK: 38

The sun shining in my face woke me up the next morning. The first thing that I wanted to do was to go down stairs and check my mailbox. Opening my door I saw the murderer had paid me another visit during the night. This time the lipstick smeared note read, IT'S NOT OVER YET. I MADE A MISTAKE THE LAST TIME, BUT IT WON'T HAPPEN AGAIN!

"Damn!"

I immediately called Lt. Lopez and left him a message saying that I had been contacted again. Thirty minutes later he returned my call.

"Hey hot shot, it sounds like your girlfriend wants to finish your ass off!"

"I don't think so!"

"Why not?"

"When I was in the hospital she sent me flowers along with an apology."

"You've got to be freaking kidding me! Ok hot shot! This bitch is right under your nose! Not only that, but I think that you know her! At the very least, she knows you and your habits."

We agreed to meet outside of my place at 11:00am. A little before eleven o'clock I went out on my balcony. Looking down on the street, there was Lt. Lopez. Checking him out from my balcony, you'd never believe that he was a cop! The only real thing that gave him away was the 40cal pistol on his belt. Leaning on his car he wore jeans, cowboy boots, a blue wife beater tee shirt, and a diamond ear ring. The model police officer!

I went down stairs and handed him the note with the lip stick kiss on it. Removing his mirrored shades he read it.

"This chick is a real piece of work!"

"Look hot shot, you may think that you don't know her, but sooner or later, we're all going to know who she is!"

"I have a plan if you're interested?"

"A plan, here you go playing cop again! Ok, let's hear it!"

"Why don't you go on the air and have Candee Harris interview you?"

"Are you crazy?"

"No I'm not, listen. Just make up a story saying that the police have a possible suspect. Show a hand sketch of any woman fitting her description. Say that the murders have stopped and you believe that she's on the lam. Indicate that an all points bulletin has been placed and she can't get away."

"This woman is on a mission hot shot! If we play her cheap, she's going to get pissed off! All we have to do is stake out the remaining possible victims. When she shows up, we'll grab her."

"If you guys were there the first time, we'd have her already!"

"You've been watching too many movies! First of all I don't like it! Second of all, the department's not real big on going on the air, especially to sell wolf tickets! What makes you think that this Candee Harris is going to go alone with this?"

"She'll do it because she's in love with herself. She's an egomaniac!"

"What if her station won't allow it?"

"Trust me they will. It's all about ratings. They'll jump all over it!"

"Have you spoken to this Harris chick?"

"No, I think that it will sound better coming from you."

"Did you two have a little spat?"

"Let's just say that she can be kind of flakey."

"Well geez hot shot, she's a freaking reporter! What the hell did you expect? Ok, this is what I'm going to do. Let me chew on this a while. In the meantime don't run out in front of any cars!"

CLICK.

Well the ball is now in the hands of the Lt. and Candee. I hung around my place until I couldn't take it anymore. While the Lt. was chewing on my idea, I decided to go to my home away from home. I took my favorite seat at the bar and Louie greeted me.

"What will it be buddy?"

"I'll have a gin and tonic."

While waiting I noticed that a band was rolling in equipment for a performance later tonight.

"Here you go buddy."

I motioned to the stage.

"It's nice to see things getting back to normal!"

"Amen to that brother! You know we took a small hit during the drive."

"Yeah I can imagine!"

I saw Louie looking over my shoulder at something. I then felt arms wrapping around my waist.

"I'm in love!"

I should have known! It was Carman. Louie started laughing as he walked away.

"So did you and Nurse Linda hook up in the hospital?"

"You've been watching too many dirty movies!"

"So why were you hiding the fact?"

"I wasn't!"

"Well you didn't say anything."

"Don't you have something to do?"

"Yeah I do. Come with me, I have someone for you to see!"

"What are you up to Carman?"

"Just come on dummy!"

She took me to a dimly lit area of the bar, and sitting alone at a table was Angie. I was overwhelmed to see her. She stood up and with one arm free, she hugged me.

"I wanted to thank you so much for all of your hard work! After being away for so long, I realized how much I missed you, all of you."

She then hugged me again, and I must say that she smelled great! In all of the years that we've known each other, we've never exchanged hugs. It was a strange feeling, one that I can't describe. For some reason I didn't feel the way that a man's suppose to feel when he hugs a beautiful woman. Even though there's never been any physical attraction between us, I still should have felt something. I can't put my finger on it.

"So Sherman, I hear that there's a new love interest in your life."

"I guess that news travels fast, or should I say that Carman's lips travel fast!"

"Your friend must be incredible! To put this effort into someone that she doesn't even know says a lot about her. I owe her a great deal of gratitude. By the way, what's up with you and that reporter?"

"Well aside from her helping out with the drive, she's a mistake that I'm trying to forget!"

"Well I won't mention her again."

"How is your arm doing?"

"It's doing well. I'm hoping to get this cast removed soon. My arm is itching like crazy! How are you healing?"

"I'm almost good as new."

I then raised my glass.

"Here's to a speedy recovery!"

"Here's to unfinished business!"

After our toast we sat around laughing and talking about old times. I had no idea of how fast the hours were passing. The evening crowd was rolling in and the band was ready to strike up their opening number. One of the band members stepped up to the microphone and put his hands in the air. After getting everyone's attention he began to speak.

"Thank you ladies and gentlemen. Tonight we have the pleasure of being accompanied by a special guest. She's here in the states from Costa Rica and we're lucky to have her here tonight. Without further ado, please welcome Miss Lillianna Alvarez!"

With the exception of a dim blue light shining on her, all other stage lights were turned off. She wore a long white, tight evening gown that must've been made for her, not to mention that she looked like an angel.

After a four count, the band laid down their version of the classic "Desafinado". I was blown away! Not only was the band hot, but this woman had a voice that was sexier than her body, and she sang in Spanish.

Laughing and talking with Angie, plus seeing this band was the cherry on top of my day. I could listen to Angie and the band the rest of the night, I probably will!

# THE CITY BLOCK: 39

## THE SILVER FOX THINKS OUT LOUD

Here I am sitting alone in my lavish home with the blinds closed in my study. In darkness I review the conversation that I had with Sherman. It had been eating at me since our lunch date. At my age I'm a changed man, but there was a time when I was among the powerful men that used the services of high class call girls. Not only that, but I was quite aware of what could happen to them if things got out of control. Deep inside I'm ashamed of myself.

Thirty something years ago when I was drunk and rolling around in the hay, I had no idea that one day I'd be adopting the son of a call girl. I'm no better than Carlton and Rex for what I've done. Sherman loves me dearly, and there's no way that I can reveal this side of myself to him. I'm devastated by the news that he may have a sister.

While sitting in the darkness of my study, my thoughts were soon interrupted by the ring tone of my phone. The letters on the screen spelled out Sherman's name. I didn't have what it took to pick up the receiver, but I did hear the message that he left.

"Hey Dad just checking in, I love you man!"

I dropped his head and wept.

# 39: PART II

Later that evening when I was about to step out and go for a walk, my cell phone vibrated.

"Hello, this is Sherman."

"Hi, it's Nurse Linda."

"Hi, how are you?"

"I'm in the area. Do you mind if I stop by?"

"Sure honey!"

Not ten seconds later there was a knock at my door. I still don't know how she keeps getting pass the lobby door. I opened the door and there stood Nurse Linda. I just smiled and shuck my head.

"Why should I even be surprised?"

"Is something wrong?"

"No honey, it's good to see you!"

"In that case, I brought this for you! Go put them on."

She handed me a bag and stood smiling at me. I looked in the bag as Linda went to the bedroom. I saw a remnant of what was maybe once a whole piece of fabric. From the bedroom I heard her yell.

"I want a lap dance, and hurry up!"

"You know you're a real piece of work!"

"Yeah I know!"

After being talked into putting on my imitation "Chippendale" under ware, I couldn't peel Linda off of me! It must've been somewhere around 1:00am when my phone rang. With a weary voice I answered.

"This is Sherman."

There was no response. In my mind I was thinking no, not now! I held the phone to my ear for about five minutes and then hung up. Linda rolled over and looked at me like she was waiting for an answer. After a moment she turned back over. I once believed that these calls were coming from the Lip Stick Murderer, but I've recently ruled her out. There would be no point in her leaving notes on my door. What bugs me the most is the fact that the person refuses to speak. I didn't sleep a wink the rest of the night.

Morning came and Linda got out of bed without saying a word, not even a good morning. She went straight to the shower and I went to the kitchen and made a pot of coffee. I sat trying to come up with a reasonable explanation for the phone call. While I was having a mug of coffee I heard my living room door slam closed. I went to the living room, but I was too late. She was gone. I went out on the balcony and called her name, but she ignored me.

"Damn, I can't believe that this shit is happening again! I just can't win!"

One thing for sure, I've got to find out who the hell is calling me! The first thing that I'm going to do is request phone records from my cell phone provider. Sitting on my sofa now I called customer service. Even though I was excited about the information that I would be getting, I was still a bundle of nerves. I wanted Linda back! She was smart, silly, and exciting in bed. I can't let it end like this! I got dressed and headed for my phone store. It was there that I could get a printout of my phone's recent history.

When I walked into the store I was greeted by a well dressed young man that introduced himself as Phil. I told Phil what I needed and he got right on it. Back at home now I decide to give Linda a call, but all I got was her voice mail. It gave me the same feeling that I had when Maria wouldn't take my calls.

After going through the first two pages of the printout I didn't see anything strange. On the third page I saw just what I was looking for. There was a number that was extremely long, more than ten digits. I knew right away that the call was coming from outside of the country. The problem is that I don't know anyone outside of this country.

I highlighted the number and gave the operator a call. It took her a few moments but when she finally got to me she dropped a major bomb on me. It turns out that the calls were coming from Puerto Rico. I said thank you and hung up. I grabbed my head with both hands and fell backwards on the sofa. It was Maria. It has to be! This is too damn much! Why is she doing this? I can't handle all of this shit right now! Why the hell doesn't she say anything? If she's trying to torture me, she's doing a damn good job! Now all I can do is wait for her next call.

I decided to take matters into my own hands and call the hospital. I've had enough of being kicked to curb because of misunderstandings. I asked the hospital receptionist to connect me to the nurse's station.

"Nurse's station, how may I help you?"

"This is Sherman Brothers. I'd like to speak with Nurse Linda please."

"I'm sorry Mr. Brothers, but I've been instructed not to put your call through."

"You tell Nurse Linda I said to get her ass on this phone right now!"

"I'm sorry sir, but I can't."

"You tell Nurse Linda that if she doesn't call me back in the next ten minutes, I'm coming there and I'm going to create a scene that no one there will ever forget!"

With that I hung up the phone! Three minutes later my cell rang.

"This is Sherman! If you're not Linda then hang up the damn phone!"

"Who the hell do you think you are calling my job and making threats?"

"Well what the hell did you think you were doing by walking out on me?"

"I'm not going to be your fucking booty call and another one of your whores!"

"For your information I don't do whores!"

"Well who the hell was that on the phone last night?"

"For the last few weeks I've been getting weird phone calls. The person doesn't speak. I keep the line open for 3 or 4 minutes and then I hang up the damn phone! Last night was one of those times. This morning I contacted the phone company to get a printout of my incoming phone calls for the last month."

"Well I love you Sherman, but I need to think about this."

"That's all that I'm asking for."

CLICK.

My plan now is to confront Maria the next time she calls. Maybe once that she knows that I know it's her, she'll talk. Hopefully I'll be able to put an end to this mess once and for all.

# THE CITY BLOCK: 40

The next day Linda came back out to my place. She had taken a personal holiday off. We sat down and had a very long talk which included some ground rules. While we were talking she got a call on her cell phone. She stood up and started pacing as she talked to the person on the other end. When she finished her call she flopped down on the sofa like something was wrong.

"Sherman honey you're not going to believe this!"

"What's up honey?"

"We just made medical history!"

"I'm sorry, but what are you talking about?"

"We've got a match!"

"I still don't know what you're talking about."

She just looked at me with a dumb look on her face.

"Oh, we've got a match!"

"In my entire career I've never seen or even heard of finding a match so quickly!"

"I have to admit, that does sound incredible."

"Now that we've found a donor, there are is still tests to be run. There's a possibility that the donor's blood type won't meet certain prerequisites. That means that we can't contact Angie or the donor until we know that we have the green light for sure."

"And if it doesn't pan out?"

"We're back to step one."

"Linda there's something that I want to say. I haven't discussed this case with you much, and there's a reason for that. I can't go into detail, but I have a personal connection with the murder victims, and I have to protect their privacy."

"You know something Sherman, you're just full of freaking surprises! I go to the ends of the world for you, and you still hide things from me!"

"Linda honey, please don't do this again!"

"Well how the hell does this Candee Harris woman fit in?"

"Well you see…

"Stop right there! Think before you speak!"

I told Linda everything about Candee and me, from beginning to end. I finished by telling her that Candee was a huge mistake, and now she's stuck in the picture.

"She was a mistake, and so is this! You don't get it! I'm not going to share you with that bitch! I'll be in touch with the City Block. Good luck with the freaking details that you can't give me!"

Nurse Linda took off and I said fuck it! I'd had enough! I was grateful for all that she had done regarding Angie, but this whole jealousy trip was too much for me. She needed to grow her ass up and learn to trust me! At this stage of the game I needed real love, and there was only one place that I could get it.

At the Block all of the stools were taken, so I ended up at a table for two. After a couple of minutes of waiting, Carman arrived. She stopped in her tracks with her arms folded.

"I walked all the way over here for you?"

"What's wrong with that?"

She pulled a chair over and sat next to me.

"How are things?"

"I've had better days!"

"I'm sorry honey, what can I get for you?"

"Gin and tonic please!"

"Hey, are you sure you're ok?"

Yeah, I'm ok. You know, ah that's alright."

She returned with my drink and sat back down.

"Are you going to tell me or not? It's a woman right?"

"Several!"

"Several! Let me guess. Nurse Linda and your TV pal."

"How did you know?"

"You know Sherman, out there on the street you kick ass, but on the home front, I don't know about you buddy!"

"What do you mean?"

"As long as this killer is out there and you're working with this Candee chick, any woman that comes within a hundred miles of you is gonna to be threatened by her. Use your head Sherman. Keep your pants on a while. Any woman that really wants you will wait."

# THE CITY BLOCK: 41

The next day I took off walking. My destination was the neighborhood café. While walking I wondered why I hadn't heard from the Lt. yet. At the diner I took a seat at my usual booth. The waitress came over and placed a cup of coffee and a glass of water on my table.

"Good morning sir."

Hi, how are you?'

"Do you need a few minutes to look at the menu?"

"Yeah I do."

"Ok I'll come back."

Five minutes later a huge man wearing a tee shirt, a baseball cap, and a apron came out from behind the grill. It was obvious that he was headed my way. I began to wonder what his angle is. When he reached my table he stuck out a hand so big that it enveloped my hand when he shook it.

"Around here they call me Tiny."

"Hey Tiny I'm Sherman. What can I do for you?"

"Well man I've seen you come in a lot."

"Yeah the food's great!"

"Thanks that's nice to hear. I notice that you eat a lot of burgers, fries and shakes."

"I think I know where this is going."

"Relax brother! Let me make you something that taste great, and it's good for you. If you don't like it, it's on the house!"

"Tiny you have a deal."

I couldn't wait any longer, so I called Lt. Lopez. On the first ring he answered.

"Not now hot shot, we've got a freaking mess going on down town!"

"What's happening?"

"Turn on your TV."

CLICK.

Over the counter with the old fashion round stools bolted to the floor, was a flat screen TV mounted on the wall. At the time there was one of those daytime courtroom shows on with the fools airing their personal lives! Just as I was about to get the waitress's attention, Tiny came out from the kitchen. He placed a huge salad in front of me. Now this wasn't just any old salad! For starters it had three different kinds of lettuce, sliced tomatoes, walnuts, sun dried cranberries, boiled eggs, grated pepper jack cheese, and it was all topped with jumbo tiger shrimp.

"Holly molly!"

Tiny looked at me and said, well?

"Tiny my man, I think that I've died and gone to heaven!"

"Enjoy my friend!"

"Hey Tiny, do you think that you could change that program to the local news?"

"It'll be my pleasure."

On the bottom of the screen was a ticker tape that read LATE BREAKING NEWS. The scene was down town in front of the police department. A podium had been sat up with at least ten different microphones on it. The immediate crowd was reporters with note pads, pens, and recorders. Among the crowd was my friend Miss Candee Harris.

Behind the reporters were protestors carrying signs. All of the signs had red lip stick kisses on them with various insults about the police department's failed efforts to catch the murderer.

With my eyes glued to the TV, I continued my attack on the culinary delight that Tiny prepared for me. The scene hadn't changed much, but I did notice that Candee had taken out her cell phone and was about to call someone. Moments later the strangest thing happened. Yeah you guessed it, my cell phone vibrated. What the hell was she up to?"

"Hello this is Sherman."

With all the noise in the background I could hear her yelling at me.

"Hi it's me! Turn on your TV!"

"I'm already watching! Who are we waiting for?"

"We're waiting for The Chief of Police."

"Have you talked to the Lt.?"

"No, he's clammed up. I've got to go!"

CLICK.

I hung up thinking that she must be out of her damn mind! Finally, in full uniform, the Chief of Police stepped up to the podium. On his left was a gentleman that looked more administrative than law enforcement. Lt. Lopez himself was on his right.

"Good afternoon everybody. Thank you for coming. Let me get right to the point. The police department combined with other law enforcement agencies is working diligently to apprehend this predator."

In the background one of the protestors yelled out.

"What the hell are you doing?"

"Please be patient, let me finish and then I will turn the podium over to Lt. Lopez. He will answer as many of your questions as he can without jeopardizing the investigation. The safety of the citizens is our first concern. This case has been the police department's priority since the beginning. Though they may not be giant steps, we have been making some progress. We've learned that the killer has a plan. These are not random acts of violence. The good news is that our killer has been making mistakes, and knows that we're getting closer because of these mistakes. At this time I'd like to turn the microphone over to Lt. Ricardo Lopez."

I was surprised to see the Lt. wearing a blazer over his usual attire. He must've barrowed it from someone in the squad room.

"Good afternoon, as the Chief said, the suspect has been making mistakes. For starters she's allowed herself to be captured on video surveillance. The department's computer techs have come with a rough image of the suspect. It will be made available to all of you today."

The screen was split in half and the image was shown on one side. It was then that reporters started questioning him, all at the same time. It was crazy! Candee worked her way up to the front and yelled out.

"Is it true that the department is working with an unknown private investigator?"

I could see the pissed off look on the Lieutenant's face.

"That's all that we have for right now folks. At this time I'm going to turn the podium over to Pat Weatherford, Public Affairs Administrator."

At that point I lost interest, and I guess that the station doing the broadcast lost interest as well, because they cut back to their normal program.

Tiny was right, the salad was great! I washed it down with a big glass of iced tea. The walk home was good for me. I really wanted to call the Lt. to see what his next move was going to be, but I didn't think that this was the right time. Whatever kind of mood he was in, I'm sure that Candee was the cherry on top!

Back at home I was dying for my phone to ring. I wanted to hear from

Candee, the Lt. or even Maria for that matter. The waiting was making me crazy! Finally my phone did ring but it wasn't either of them. I saw Nurse Linda's name on my phone, and I was thinking oh God, here we go again!

"Hello this is Sherman."

"Sherman this is Nurse Linda. I'll make this will quick. The lab results have come back. You're not going to believe this, but we've found two matches."

"Two matches!"

"Yes two. One of the matches is close enough to be a relative or even a sibling. The other one is close enough to be her biological father."

"What the hell! You're kidding me!"

"Sherman this is more than incredible. It just doesn't happen unless you're taking samples from the immediate family. Now before you ask me who they are, they're protected by law. I don't know who they are and there's no way that I can find out. We've contacted Angie. She's both excited and nervous. The possible biological father has agreed to the surgery under the condition that he remains anonymous. Angie will never meet, or know who he is. Those are the terms for saving her life."

"Linda I don't know what to say. I'm sorry for how things worked out, and I can't thank you enough for what you've done for Angie."

"Good luck Sherman."

CLICK.

# THE CITY BLOCK: 42

Later that evening I got a call from Rex.

"Hey dude, what's up?"

"It's the Silver Fox, he wants to see us."

"He wants to see all of us?"

"Yeah, at the firm, ASAP!"

"Did he sound pissed off?"

"No he didn't, I don't know what the hell's going on!"

"Do you think that it's his health?"

"I'd doubt it, he's in better shape than all of us put together!"

"Ok, well I guess that I'll see you guys in a little bit."

CLICK.

I locked up, jumped in my car and put the pedal to medal. I headed north for the firm. Feeling a sense of urgency I made it there in twenty minutes flat. Stopping at the entrance of the parking lot, I got out and tossed my keys to Ralph, the parking attendant and went straight to the elevator. At the twelfth floor I got off and stepped into the lobby. Everyone was there and waiting. Dad came out of his office.

"Why don't you all come into the conference room."

We all followed him and took a seat.

"I'm going to get right to the point. I'm going to be leaving town for a while."

There was a variety of emotional responses. Carlton was the first to speak up.

"You can't leave town!"

I asked Dad what was going on.

"Nothing son."

"Well why this sudden decision to get away?"

"Look damn it, I'm your father!"

He was pointing at all of us.

"I don't have to give you an explanation!"

"I'm going to take a couple of weeks, maybe longer."

Carlton wasn't happy with that.

"Can you at least tell us where you're going, and how we can contact you?"

"I'm going to Los Angeles."

"Why Los Angeles?"

"I've got business to tend to and don't dare think about asking me what!"

"But Dad...

"Don't but Dad me! If there's an emergency, leave me a message and I'll get back to you."

He then pointed at Carl and Rex.

"I assume that the two of you can keep the firm from burning down, and not get our asses sued off!"

Carlton just dropped his head.

"Yes Dad."

"Is something wrong with your tongue Rex?"

"Yes sir, I mean no sir. We'll take care of things while you're away."

"And for Christ sake, can you keep each other alive? Now that I have everyone's attention, I'll be leaving tomorrow."

All of our eyebrows rose.

"Are there any comments?"

No one said a word.

"That's all, you can all go now."

I asked Dad if he needed a ride out to O'Hare Airport.

"I've got a shuttle picking me up, and remember there's no need for anyone to know that I'm not here."

We all gave Dad a hug and headed for the elevator. During our ride down, we all expressed our opinions on Dad's news. I decided that everyone needed a little good news. I told them that Linda had informed me that their lab had found a match for Angie. Everyone gave a little cheer as we waited for Ralph to bring us our cars.

Rex and I decided to meet up at the Block and when I walked in he was already there sitting at a table with Carman. Everyone in the place had a smile on their face. It was obvious that the good news was spreading. At the bar I was greeted by Louie who told me that my first drink was on the bar.

"We're celebrating the good news."

I got my drink and joined Rex and Carman.

"Do you mind if I steal Carman for a minute?"

"Sure, go ahead, I need to get a refill."

"Hey Sherman what's up?"

"I need your opinion on something."

"You need my what? You've got to be kidding me!"

"Considering the good news that we've received, do you think that we should thank Candee Harris for her help?"

"As much as I can't stand that bitch, it would be the right thing to do."

"Maybe she could recap the story and let the people know that their efforts may be saving a life. It could be the Block's way of saying thank you."

"I have to admit it is a good idea."

"But there's a catch Carman."

"It's always a catch with you Sherman!"

"I can't communicate with Candee. One of you guys has to do it. I've already lost two women because of her. Pretty soon you're going to be the only woman left in the city!"

"In your dreams buddy!"

Rex returned and I walked away. I headed back to the bar and took a seat. After chewing the fat a little, I went home. I turned on some music, grabbed a beer and went out on my balcony. I was just starting to doze off when my cell phone rang. With all of the news that I received today I had forgotten all about Maria, and to my surprise it was her again. This time I was ready for her game.

"Hello this is Sherman."

Just as I suspected there was no answer on the other end.

"Maria, why are you doing this? Look, I know that it's you. Honey you're hurting me! Please say something!"

All I heard was a slight whimper, and then click. I took a seat and hung my head back, looking up into the sky.

# THE CITY BLOCK: 43

## THE SILVER FOX REACHES HIS DESTINATION:

At 7:00am I was reaching into the window of a taxi. I gave my driver the fair plus tip. With a small suitcase in hand, I turn and face the main entrance of the hospital. In the lobby I see a sign that directs me to Admittance.

Today I'm attempting to make amends in my life. I have a shady past because of reckless living when I was a younger man. The world had given me everything. I believed that I could have whatever I wanted and whoever I wanted. My sexual escapades produced a life, today that life is in jeopardy and I'm here to save it. Walking down the hall I arrive at a counter that has two nurses and a receptionist behind it.

"Good morning sir, may I help you?"

"Yes, I'm here to admit myself."

"Can you fill this form out for me please? What is your name sir?"

"My name is Carlton Remington."

"Oh, we've been expecting you! After you finish filling out that form, I'll escort you to your private room."

On another floor in that very same hospital, Angie is facing life changing surgery, and being counseled about the procedures and recovery. She interrupts the doctor.

"Can I ask you something?"

"Of course can, what is it?"

"Why would anyone risk surgery to save a life, but not want to know who they're saving? I would want to know if I were the donor."

"I don't know. Sometimes it's a privacy issue, and sometimes it's just guilt."

"Yeah I guess so!"

"Look, I know how you feel, and I know what you're thinking, but remember that their privacy is protected by law."

"Doctor there's something about me that you may not know."

"It can't be! We've taken very careful steps regarding your condition."

"No that's not what I mean."

"Well what is it young lady?"

"I'm a foster child, and I was given up at birth."

"Oh, now I understand. You think that you may be related to the donor. Well it is possible, but not likely."

The doctor took her hand.

"Look, you're young, attractive, and soon to be healthy woman. Why not start a family of your own and do the right thing?"

With that he smiled.

"Get some rest. I'll be back a little later."

On another floor a nurse showed the Silver Fox to his room. Inside she provided him fresh linen and a gown.

"Someone will be with you a little later to take your vitals."

"Excuse me nurse."

"Yes sir?"

"Would it be alright to wear my own pajamas?"

"Sure, please do. Later own the doctor will come to talk to you about the procedure."

"Ok."

"Sir you look a little nervous. Are you alright?"

"I'm ok I guess."

"If you need anything, press the call button.'

"Thanks."

Lying in bed now, The Silver Fox began dwelling on his life, his family, and this wonderful young woman that doesn't know her father. He knows that if he revealed himself several lives would be changed forever. He'd be crucified for what he's done. The stress moved him to speak out loud.

"God, what a mess I've made!"

Three days had pasted since he had admitted himself into the hospital. He was feeling the stress of not being in control. Back at the firm he's the man. He calls all the shots. This is the first time in years that the shoe has been on the other foot. Here at the hospital there's a whole team of people telling him what to do, when to do it, and how to do it.

Today will be the first official day of his mission. He'll be receiving the first in a series of daily injections that will prepare him for the surgery. In addition to this he'll be given the news that the decision has been made to remove the bone marrow from his hip bone.

In the lobby of the hospital Carman stands in front of a elevator. Holding flowers she presses the button. She's Angie very first visitor. She knocks on her door before entering. Leaning over she gives Angie a kiss on her forehead and hands her the flowers.

"Oh Carman these are beautiful!"

"How are you doing girl?"

"I'm ok I guess. I don't know! There's a lot on my mind."

"Well you know we're all here for you! What can I do for you? Are you comfortable?"

"Girl I'm fine! Why don't you sit down? Did you bring the stuff that I asked for?"

"Yeah hold on."

From her oversized hand bag she retrieved a box of stationary with matching envelopes. For herself she pulled out a pen and a note pad.

"Did you bring the names of the nursing staff that worked the donor drive?"

"Oh yeah here it is."

"Thanks, I want to write individual letters to each of them. How is everything at the bar?"

"Things are going fine."

"I guess you guys don't need me!"

"Girl you know that's not true! The place isn't the same without you. Everyone misses you and sends their best."

"How is Sherman doing?"

"Sherman?"

"What's wrong with me asking that?"

"Nothing, I'm just surprised, but he's doing fine too."

"Oh by the way, he was dating that Nurse Linda."

"I thought that he was seeing a Latin woman."

"The truth is he lost both them because that reporter Candee Harris."

"That's too bad, I feel sorry for him!"

"Oh boy, here we go again! Be honest with me Angie, what's wrong with Sherman?"

"There's nothing wrong with him!"

"Do you think that he's cute?"

"Yeah."

"Do you think that he's a good person?"

"Yeah."

"You know you guys do have things in common!"

"The only thing that we have in common is you pushing us!"

"So you guys have talked about this?"

"No, but I've seen you corner him at the bar."

"So what does that mean?"

"Tell me the truth, were you guys talking about me?"

"Ok, yes we were!"

"If he's all of that, why don't you go after him?"

"He doesn't like me, he likes you!"

"Oh yeah, I guess he told you that!"

"He didn't have to, I see the way you two look at each other! There's something that I can't put my finger on. It's not a romantic attraction, but something else that other people don't experience."

"Ok Carman, it's official, you're crazy!"

"Alright, let's take a scientific approach."

"Is this why you came here today?"

"No, but sense I have you cornered!"

"You know you're a piece of work! Ok, shoot!"

Carman began defending her theory.

No.1, he says I'm a piece of work too.

No.2, He avoids the subject too.

No.3, He finds you attractive too.

No.4, He needs a good person to take care of him too.

No.5, Both of you are foster kids.

No.6, Even though neither of you will admit it, you both have a longing for a family.

No.7, There's still that strange emotional connection between you.

No.8, With all of the people back home, his is the only name you asked about.

With that Angie broke down and started crying. Carman immediately got up from her chair and wrapped her arms around her.

"Ah honey I'm so sorry! I didn't mean to hurt you! You mean the world to me, you both do! I guess that's why I push you both so hard. I'm so very sorry!"

"It's not your fault Carman."

"Then what is it?"

Angie began wiping her eyes.

"You can't repeat this Carman."

Carman placed both of her hands on Angie's cheeks.

"Girl you know that you don't have to say that! Now what is it?"

"Sherman is my brother."

Carman fell back in her chair covering her mouth with her hands. After a few moments she spoke.

"Girl I love you more than anything in the world, and I know that you're going through an emotional time in your life, but you can't be thinking straight. How did you arrive at this conclusion? Honey he's not your brother!"

"Carman the lab results were incredible! They said that they found two matches that had percentages high enough to be blood relatives."

"Oh my God girl, are they sure?"

"I don't know, I guess."

Again Carman wrapped her arm around her.

"Look honey I know how bad you want this, but the donor's privacy is protected by law."

Angie began crying again.

"I know that. The doctor told me the same thing."

"I'm sorry honey, but you better try to forget about it."

"Girl I've been trying to! You know, you are right about one thing."

"What is that?"

"I do feel something when he's near, but it's not what a woman feels for a man."

Carman didn't know what to say, so she climbed into bed beside Angie and told her to try to go to sleep.

# THE CITY BLOCK: 44

It's been three days since I've heard from Dad. I guess that no news is good news! I haven't drummed up any new clients, but that's life in this business. The good thing is that none of Carlton's other brothers have been killed. I guess that means that the killer is still pulling the strings. If only the Lt. would listen to me, maybe this whole mess would be over. I guess that in his head he just can't take advice from a punk like me. Now he has the Chief of Police bending him over to take it the hard way!

With nothing else to do I made my way over to the Block for happy hour. Inside I passed Carman when she was lighting candles. I gave her a nice big warm smile and a hello. Without even looking at me she gave me a cold dry hello. I took my normal seat at the bar and Louie walked up.

"What's up with Carman?"

"She's been acting weird all day!"

"What's going on?"

"I don't know, but I've learned not to push these women! When she's ready she'll let us in on it."

While I was waiting for my cocktail I looked over at her. She shot me a look that damn near knocked me off my stool! Louie walked up just in time to see her do it.

"I can't take anymore Louie!"

I then approached her.

"Carman is everything alright?"

"Yes, everything is fine!"

"Well in that case, can I have a hug?"

"No Sherman, you can't have a hug!"

"Ok, what did I do this time?"

She ignored me and kept moving around like I wasn't even there, so I went back to my stool.

"I told you Sherman, just let it be."

"I guess I have no choice."

A couple came in and sat down next to me. We exchanged greetings and laughed it up for a while. Still thinking about Carman, I turned around to take a look and she was coming my way.

"Sherman you're so stupid!"

I took a deep breath and let it out. I didn't say a word as she walked away. Thirty minutes later she reappeared, and I still didn't say anything.

"I'm sorry, and no, you can't have a hug!"

With that she walked away again and I turned my attention to Louie.

"Have you guys heard from Angie?"

"Well I haven't, but Carman took her some flowers yesterday."

"Did she say anything about the visit?"

"You know now that you mention it, she didn't say a damn thing! You know what else? That's when she started acting weird!"

"Ok, now I get it!"

"You get what?"

"This thing is all about Angie and me. I can't believe that Carman is this pissed off because we're not together. I think that tomorrow I'll take a trip out to the hospital and put an end to this nonsense!"

"You know Sherman, it's none of my business, but I don't think that that's such a good idea. Angie is under a lot stress and you don't know what was said between the two of them. It had to be serious enough to make Carman disrespect you like this."

"You know Louie, sometimes I hate talking to you!"

"Well they tell me that that's what bartenders are for!"

Louie reached under the bar and pulled out two shot glasses and a bottle of Don Julio.

"Here's to love and happiness!"

We both downed our shots.

"That was good Louie, thanks!"

"A night off would really be good. Things have been hectic around here without Angie. Maybe I'll talk to Carman about bringing in a sub."

After a couple of more hours of suffering Carman's wrath I headed home.

# THE CITY BLOCK: 45

I went straight to bed when I got home. I only got up once, and that was to go to the bathroom. About 2:30am I heard my doorbell ring.

"Who the hell could this be?"

Before going to the door I grabbed my pistol. After finding notes from the Lip Stick murderer in the mornings when I wake up, I wasn't taking any chances. I buzzed whoever it was up and stood with the door open and my pistol pointed toward the hallway. Moments later I got the shock of my life. Standing in the doorway was none other than Carman. The first thing out of my mouth was what the hell!

I lowered my pistol and invited her in.

"Will you put some damn pants on?"

I guess my pistol didn't scare her! I left the living room and came back dressed.

"It's 2:30 in the damn morning! What the hell are you doing here? Haven't you given me enough hell for one day?" You've been giving me the shit all evening, and for what I don't know! I can't take anymore of this shit! You're supposed to be family to me, and right now I don't like you very much! Now it's your turn!"

"First I want to say how sorry I am for coming here this time of night. You know Sherman, you are family to me. I love you like a brother. Maybe that's why I'm so hard on you. You're the only man that I know that's a stand up guy. I feel the same way about Angie."

"Is that what this is all about?"

"Please Sherman, this isn't easy. Please let me finish. I promise that tonight, or today will be the last time that I ever say a word to either of you about being together. I realize now that I've been wrong and out of line all this time. I've made two of the dearest people in my life miserable. It was my dream, not yours. I treated you horribly earlier today. Yesterday at the hospital I brought Angie to tears. Can you believe that? If you want to kick me out, now would be a good time!"

There was a long moment of silence.

"Say something please Sherman!"

"Can I have that hug now?"

With tears in her eyes she rushed into my arms.

"I think that I'd better go now."

"Hey, it's too late for you to be riding around alone. Why don't you stretch out here on the sofa?"

"Are you sure?"

"Yes I'm sure, we're family right?"

She smiled and took off her shoes and got comfortable on the sofa. I went back to bed. When the morning came Carman and I had coffee together and she took off.

The past few days had been emotionally draining. Between the blood drive, Linda ending up being another disappointment, Dad taking off, and Carman appearing at my door, I needed some alone time. And this time the lake front wasn't going to cut it! I decided to take advantage of Dad being away and take his boat, "The Firm" out on the water.

Once I had made up my mind, I wasted no time. I grabbed a duffle bag, my cooler, and headed for the grocery store. After a little shopping I hit Lake Shore Drive and headed north for the harbor. It was another custom made day for driving with the top down. It wasn't long before I had the harbor in view. Sometime when you're stressed out your mind can play tricks with you.

As I pulled into one end of the harbor parking lot, I could've sworn that I saw a red Porsche headed for the exit on the other end. I quickly told myself that it couldn't be. I made my way through the parking lot looking for a spot fairly close to where the boat was docked. It took me a couple of trips back to the car, but finally I had everything onboard the boat. I debated taking The Firm out for a spin and decided to uncork a bottle of wine and stretch out down below for a while. I poured myself a glass, switched on the radio, put my feet up and closed my eyes.

"Now this is living!"

Fifteen minutes later I heard the sound of tires screeching on the parking lot pavement. Some place nearby I heard the car come to a sudden stop, followed by the closing of a door. Finally there was silence again. All I could hear now was the sound of the radio and the water splashing against the docked boats.

Over the mellow sounds of jazz music filling the air, a voice came from outside of The Firm.

"Ahoy there!"

Oh my God, my mind wasn't playing tricks on me! With my glass in my hand, I went up on deck. Sure as hell it was Candee in cut-off jeans, a sports bra and her cat eye shades. It was just like the first time that I saw her.

"That glass of wine looks good! Permission to come on board?"

"Ok, I'll bite!"

"Ah Sherman, don't be like that!"

"So how did you find me here?"

"Well actually I was already here. A friend of mine has a small yacht here."

"A small yacht, I didn't know there was such a thing!"

"I saw you unpacking. It looks like you're going to be here a few days."

"Maybe."

"How about a glass of that wine?"

"Sure, why not."

"So where's your girlfriend today?"

"I don't have a girlfriend anymore. Why do you ask?"

"I was making small talk. We haven't talked in a while."

"Well I've been working."

"You know that all work and no play make's Jack a dull boy!"

"I've heard that somewhere before! Did you and the Lt. kiss and make up?"

"He would have to get over himself before that could happen!"

"I'll drink to that!"

"Now that I have your attention Mr. Brothers..."

"Yes."

"You never did let me drive that car of yours."

"You know you're right!"

"Wow, you've changed!"

"Not really, I just realized that there are things that I don't need in my life right now."

"Does that include me?"

"Well you never were part of my life. You were just passing through on your way to your life."

"Does that mean that we can't be friends?"

"I'm sharing my wine with you, aren't I?"

"Are you trying to get me drunk or something?"

"Candee please tell me that you're kidding!"

"If I didn't know better, I'd think that you hate me."

"Let's just say that I'm a bit disappointed in you."

"So I guess that I'm yesterday's news!"

"If it makes you feel better, I still remember what it was like."

"So I can come and see you while you're here?"

"You're seeing me now!"

"I remember a time when you enjoyed my company. What happened?"

"You happened. I had a lesson to learn and you were a great teacher."

That was it! Candee threw her glass of wine in my face.

"Go to hell Sherman!"

She tried to leave, but I grabbed her wrist and wouldn't let go.

"Let go damn it!"

"Are you sure that you want to leave? You can sit back down, I'm done."

We sat quietly drinking wine until Candee broke the silence.

"So, are you going to kick me out of here drunk, or can I stay?"

"Let me think about that!"

"You humiliated me already, plus I think that you want me to stay."

"I'll tell you what, pick a spot and get comfortable. I'll see you in the morning."

Candee had fallen back down to earth, and I had discovered a new useful power. Maybe I had changed.

# THE CITY BLOCK: 46

It was morning now and the sun was rising over Lake Michigan. Candee obviously was awake before I was. I came up from below deck and she was gone. I found a note that she left me in a wine glass.

"Thanks for letting me stay."

I made myself some coffee and took my time getting my act together. Now that Candee's out of my hair I have the day to myself. After enjoying my coffee I squeezed into the tiny shower. I got dressed, locked up and went for a walk along the pier. As I walked along the pier I could see that others were enjoying a lazy morning without rushing into the day. The thought occurred to me that I should start a new regiment of doing this every weekend. That is if Dad's not using the boat. After all, it is his!

I had walked so far that I lost sight of The Firm. By now it was going on 10:30am. When I turned around to head back, my cell phone vibrated. At first I thought twice about answering it, but I saw the City Block's name appear. Due to Angie's circumstances I couldn't avoid the call.

"Good morning, this is Sherman."

"Hey this Louie, you sound like you're having a great morning!"

"You would be right my friend! How can I help you?"

"Well actually you wouldn't be helping me alone, but us. We could use your help. "Can you come in when you get a chance?"

"It sounds like a small emergency, is everything alright over there?"

"It's nothing to worry about, but the sooner we can talk the better."

"Ok, I'm down at the harbor on my Dad's boat. Give me a little time to get things together and I'll drop in."

"Thanks Sherman."

I walked into the Block just before their noon day opening. Near one of the tables Louie was standing and shaking hands with an attractive young Asian woman. He saw me and excused himself, leaving the young lady with Carman.

"Thanks for coming in Sherman."

"Sure, what's going on?"

"We decided to bring in a part time bartender during Angie's absence. We were just finishing up with the interview."

"So how is it going?"

"Well I like her, but you know that Carman's got to have something to say!"

"Yeah I know what you mean! So what did you guys need from me?"

"I'd better wait for Carman. Come on let me buy you a drink."

When the interview was over Carman came and sat beside me.

"So what's up Miss Carman?"

Before she could answer, Louie spoke up.

"Sherman we need a doorman that can slowly be trained to cover the bar every now and then."

"You guys must be crazy! Louie did you let her put you up to this?"

"The truth is buddy we need you!"

That's when Carman put in her two cents.

"Don't go that far Louie! His head is going to get so big he won't be able to get it through the door!"

"I don't know about the bar, but what would I have to do at the door?"

"You would have to check ID's, work the crowd and give the jerks 86 warnings."

Carman then started laughing.

"What's so funny?"

"You can have all the phone numbers that will fit in your dirty little pockets!"

"For your information I've decided to go solo!"

"If that's true, I want to be the first person to throw my twenty bucks in the pool!"

"So, do I start tonight?"

"Nope, you been drinking, and we don't want to get sued dummy!"

"Carman, have I told you that I don't like you?"

Carman smiled, gave me a kiss on the cheek, and walked away.

"Hey Carman, did you hire the Asian girl?"

"I swear Sherman, if you put one damn finger on her…

"I was just asking!"

# THE CITY BLOCK: 47

It's been two weeks since I started working the door at the Block. I let Louie and Carman know that there would be times when I'd be working a case, and that would be priority.

Dad came home with a little surprise. He was walking with the aid of a cane, and favoring his right hip. He said that he fell getting out of a pool. As usual we weren't allowed to ask any questions. His biggest concern was who had been on his boat. Opps!

I've had the chance to take a closer look at Mai, the new bartender, and I must say that she's quite a classy lady! Even though Carman threatened to kill me, I took it on my own to look, but not touch. Besides, if I wanted to get into trouble, this place is crawling with women.

I've been well on my own and even getting used to it. Nurse Linda and I have texted each other, but that's about all. Carman has spent more time at Angie's place than her own. She's been preparing for her arrival back home. She's even received instructions from the doctors for Angie's recovery period. Her apartment has been stocked with groceries and medical supplies.

I spoke with Angie to see if there was anything that I could do. She said no, but she was grateful for me bringing Nurse Linda and Candee into the picture. Despite everything I've been through with those two ladies, they both were professionals at the right time. For that I am grateful. Speaking of Candee, I haven't heard a word from her, the Lt. or the killer.

Angie herself wasn't doing that great. The doctors say it will take time before we know for sure that the surgery was successful. According to Carman she has good days and bad days. Sometimes she even looks like she has one foot in the grave.

It's getting close to my 7:00pm report time, something I'm still getting used to. When I got there the usual crowd was rolling in. It was a good night, without any incidents. After locking up, Louie, Mai and I took a seat at a table. After a little small talk Louie left us alone. Mai was a little curious about me.

"Can I ask you something Sherman?"

"Sure, go ahead."

"Well I don't want to pry."

"We're all family here, don't worry about it."

"You look familiar to me."

"Yeah I get that a lot."

"I used to work at a piano bar down town. I think that I've seen you there before."

"Well I've been known to hit a piano bar or two."

"I'm pretty sure of it, because you're a hard guy to forget!"

"I know how this is going to sound, but I think that I should be going!"

"Wow, you scare easy!"

"Well it's not you that I'm scared of! Do you mind locking up behind me?"

I would find out later that Mai had quite a night after locking up. In her Honda Civic, she made her way west on Cermack Road. She slowed down for a red light just before the I-94 underpass. With her mind on the City Block, she was unaware of her surroundings. Suddenly her passenger window was smashed in. A guy reached in and grabbed her purse off the seat. On her side of the car another guy stood with a pistol pointed right at her face, and was told to get out.

She quickly locked the door, but her assailant busted out the window with the butt of his gun. He then reached in, grabbed her and dragged her out of the car. The two thugs then jumped in her car and drove away, leaving her lying on ground in broken glass.

On the corner an attendant at an all night gas station saw the whole thing unfold and called the police. He then locked up the station and ran across the street to help her. He helped her cross the street to the station. Before they reached the station, a blue and white squad car rushed into the station. It was being followed by the Fire Department Paramedics. After being treated for cuts and minor bruises, she was interviewed by two police officers.

She gave them a description of her car and they put out an APB on the vehicle. She described the thugs as being Asian. One of them wore a Mohawk hairdo, and the other one wore a red bandana. Through tears and heavy breathing, Mai added that they both had neck tattoos in Chinese letters. She also said that the one wearing the Mohawk had rings in his lip and eyebrow.

After making the report the officers offered her a ride home, but she was reluctant because the thugs now knew her address. She asked to be taken back to the City Block. Mai was a smart girl. She kept her key to the bar separate from her car keys. She entered the bar and turned off the alarm right away. In the rear office was a rolodex. She found Louie's number and dialed it right away.

Lying in bed, Louie was startled by his phone ringing so late. The screen on his phone indicated that the call was coming from the Block.

"Who is this, and what the hell are you doing in the bar?"

Mai was crying uncontrollably and trying to talk at the same time.

"I'm sorry Louie, it's me Mai!"

"Mai, what are you doing at the bar? What the hell is going on?"

"I was mugged and car jacked! I didn't know where else to go!"

"Oh my God, lock the door and don't leave! I'm on my way!"

Knowing that I was closer than he was, he called me immediately. Not ten minutes later I was slamming on my breaks in front of the Block. Not waiting for Louie I entered using my key. When I first walked in I didn't see anyone, but I heard movement. Looking behind the bar I saw Mai on the floor wrapped in a fetal position. She trembled as I lifted her in my arms. I sat her down lightly on a nearby chair and gave her a cocktail napkin. Wiping her eyes she began telling me what happened. The more I listened, the higher my blood pressure went.

Just as I was about to explode Louie came in and calmed me down. He pulled up a chair beside Mai and wrapped his arms around her.

"Everything is going to be alright! Remember, you're family now!"

She looked at Louie through teary eyes.

"Is this what you meant when you said that I'd catch on?"

He looked at her with a warm smile.

"Yes it is, and you need to get some rest, but this isn't the place. Do you mind Sherman?"

"It'll be my pleasure!"

Louie helped me get Mai into my car and we took off for my place. At home I prepared the sofa for an overnight guest.

"Is there anyone I can call for you Mai?"

"I'm sorry, but no." "Well I'm going to say good night."

"Thank you Sherman."

"Ah honey, you're so very welcome!"

"I'm not thanking you for your sofa."

"Then what are you thanking me for?"

"I'm thanking you for being my family. I needed it one!"

Mai didn't know it, but she had just sat up camp in my heart. I hadn't felt this way since I met Rebecca.

# THE CITY BLOCK: 48

Morning came and I gave Mai fresh linen and a bar of soap. In the kitchen I made a pot of coffee while she showered. She was rather quiet when she joined me at the kitchen table.

"Are you feeling a little better this morning?"

"A little I guess."

"What can I do to help you this morning?"

"I don't know, I mean, I feel so ashamed!"

"Ashamed for what, you haven't done anything wrong!"

"Here I am sleeping in your home, bathing in your shower, and I don't even know you. If my family back in my country knew of this, they'd disown me. I'd be an embarrassment to the family."

"I'm sorry to hear that Mai, but I think that there's a way to make this a more honorable experience."

"How can we do that?"

"Why don't we spend the day getting to know each other? That way you'll never have to feel this embarrassment again."

Before she could comment, my doorbell rang.

"Excuse me Mai."

I went to the intercom by my door.

"Yes, who is it?"

"Just buzz me up dummy!"

I should've known! I pressed the button and waited. Moments later I opened the door to find the City Block's own Florence Nightingale! In her arms she held a pair of jeans, a tee shirt and a small toiletry bag.

"Good morning Carman."

"Look me in the eyes Sherman!"

"No Carman I didn't and you need to get off of that!"

"Yeah well I'm watching you! Where is she?"

"She's in the kitchen."

I stepped out of her way as she passed by. In the kitchen she put the things down and hugged Mai.

"Girl, are you alright?"

"Yes, I'm fine now!"

"Are you sure?"

"Louie and Sherman have been very good to me."

I gave Carman a look, and she just rolled her eyes at me!

"Can you ladies excuse me a moment? I have a phone call to make."

As soon as I left the kitchen Mai began to cry and Carman wrapped her arms around her.

"What's the matter honey?"

"You guys really are family, aren't you?"

"Of course we are honey, and now you're part of us!"

With my bedroom door closed I sat on the bed and dialed up Candee's number.

"Good morning Candee."

"It's kind of early, but what the hell, I can come right over!"

"It's not that Candee, but I do need a favor."

"Oh, so you actually do need something from me!"

"Look, a friend of mine was mugged and car jacked in the wee hours of the morning."

"Let me guess, it's a woman right?"

"What difference does it make?"

"It just feels strange to me Sherman!"

"Look, I know that you keep up with crime in this city."

"So what is it that you're looking for?"

"The mugging took place in the China Town area near the I-94."

"I can check my sources and get back to you. Give me some more details."

"I think that it was a routine night for these punks! They were Asian, and one sported a Mohawk with rings in his face. The other wore a red bandana. They both had neck tattoos in Chinese lettering."

"That's not good Sherman!"

"Why, what have you got?"

"Those guys have struck before. They've been strong arming and carjacking in that area for the last three months."

"Why hasn't it been publicized?"

"Look Sherman, this kind of thing happens every day all over the city. If we put it all on the air, people will be afraid to leave their homes, and the police department will catch hell. It's not the message that we want to send."

"So what can I do now?"

"Nothing, your friend need's to move on with her life!"

"You know I'm not going to sit for this!"

"Sherman you need to stay out of it this time!"

"You I can't do that!"

"Have it your way! I'll be in touch if I hear something."

"Thanks Candee."

"Don't thank me honey! This ain't free, you owe me!"

"Oh yeah right!"

"Now you can do me a favor."

"What would that be?"

"Don't get yourself killed before I can collect!"

"Goodbye Candee!"

CLICK.

I immediately started making plans to roll out to China Town tonight when I get off duty at the Block. It's time to pick up another rental car. Back in the kitchen Carman had managed to make Mai smile and laugh a little.

"How would ladies like a real breakfast?"

Carman grabbed Mai's hand.

"Come on girl, Sherman's buying! The sky's the limit!"

"Where are we going?"

"You'll see, and we're walking!"

"Well just so you'll know, we're two classy chicks, and we don't eat at greasy spoons!"

"Don't worry, just trust me!"

On our way to the Café, we stopped at the phone store to pick up a new phone for Mai. When we arrived at the Café we were greeted by the waitress Jerri. She was soon joined by Tiny.

"These ladies are my friends Carman and Mai."

Tiny put his now famous big smile on and greeted the ladies like the gentleman that he is.

"Sherman my man, I want to be like you when I get big!"

We all laughed and were then escorted to a booth. The food was great as usual and the ladies were impressed. During our meal I got a call from Candee and excused myself from the table. Apparently Candee overheard the cops on her police scanner, and it looks like Mai's car had been recovered. I thanked her for the tip and went back to the ladies.

"Hey ladies, I've got some good news!"

Carman but her arm around Mai and asked what?"

"Mai your car has been recovered! We can pick it up when we leave here if you like?"

Mai was overcome with emotion by the news.

"How did you find out about it so quickly?"

Carman answered her for me.

"Girl you've got to get used Sherman! He's got eyes and ears all over the city! I imagine that no one has told you, but he's a Private Investigator, and it's the only thing that he's good at!"

Mai started laughing and got a real kick out of how Carman and I get along. After Carman finished flirting with Tiny we dropped her off at her car and headed for the police pound. Aside from the busted windows in the car, it was alright. Even her purse and keys were still inside. We immediately took the car to a body shop, and then I took her to the Block. It wasn't quite opening time yet and Louie was sitting at a table doing some paperwork. He saw Mai and dropped what he was doing.

"Mai, how are you doing? Do you need anything? What can I get for you?"

Mai put two fingers over his lips and then wrapped her arms around him.

"Thank you for everything, I'm fine, and I want to work today!"

"Mai you really don't have too!"

I broke into the conversation.

"Look honey, Louie and I need to run a little errand."

"Sherman I don't know if I can run this place by myself!"

"Carman's on her way, and you'll be fine until she gets here."

Outside of the Block I told Louie about my late night plans. I also requested a ride to the car rental. In addition to that I asked that he not tell the ladies about what I'm doing. He understood and we were on our way.

# THE CITY BLOCK: 49

Later that evening things were going well and Mai looked good behind the bar. The regulars were beginning to take to her well. As the hours went by I kept looking at my watch. I was eager to nail the punks that jacked her. About 30 minutes before closing I went to Louie and asked if I could take off. He knew what I was up to and was fine with it.

"Do your thing brother, but be careful! I'll see you tomorrow."

With that I was out! My first stop was home. Under the circumstances I'd feel better if I didn't ride alone. From the shelf in my closet I removed Mr. Smith and Mr. Wesson. I put the pistol in the glove box of the rental and started the engine.

I decided to zigzag through China Town and the surrounding area. I figured that I'd go from east to west between Cermak Road and Western Ave., and north to south between 47th Street and Roosevelt Road. Before driving away I remembered something and turned the engine back off. I had forgotten my duct tape, or should I say my poor man's hand cuffs! If things go as planned, I'll need it.

For the first hour or so things were rather quiet. I'm not sure what street I was on, but I came across a bar that was letting out. All I knew is that I was just east of Western Ave. and just south of Cermak Road. In front of the bar stood five punks that looked like they weren't going anywhere too soon. They definitely had the look. Their pants hung down around their ass, baseball caps turned sideways, the whole nine yards! I decided to park in the shadows and watch for a while.

I started getting the feeling that these punks ran the place. Everyone that came out avoided them like a virus! Among the crowd coming out was Dumb and Dumber in living color! I saw the Mohawk and the red bandana, this was too easy! I don't know what the hell the cops have been doing! They kicked it for about 15 minutes and then crossed the street to a brand new BMW.

They took off and I followed until the car pulled over and let the passenger out. From there the driver went to where I thought was his house. He went inside and didn't come back out. I wrote down the address and headed home.

The following night after getting off I was right back out there. This time I knew where I was going. My first stop was the house where the BMW parked last night. Sure as hell, there it was, and wasn't long before Mr. Bandana came out and got into the car. He led me to his buddy's place where he jumped in.

I followed them throughout the night as they hit Chinese Restaurant after Chinese Restaurant. They were taking turns doing smash and grabs. These no good assholes were jacking their own damn people! After a while I followed them to last place in the world that I thought they'd go to. These idiots went right back to Cermak Road and the I-94 underpass.

They pulled over behind a old pick-up truck and parked. I watched as they sat smoking a cigarette. I pulled into the all night gas station across the street. I took my pistol from the glove box and stuck my duct tape inside my jacket. I then crossed the street and went into my role. I started staggering like a drunk. When I got about 30 feet from the pick-up truck I turned my back to them and bent over pretending to be throwing up.

I wanted them to see me. I stood up and started staggering toward them again. I walked right up to the driver's window and he gave me a nasty look.

"Get the fuck outta here!"

"Give me a smoke man."

"Fuck you, get outta here!"

That's when I stuck my pistol in Mr. Mohawk's ear.

"No, fuck you!"

Mr. Mohawk froze, but Mr. Bandana started reaching for the glove box.

"I hope your buddy is reaching for a Q-Tip, because he's going to need one to clean your brains out of his ear!"

Mr. Mohawk said something in Chinese. I don't know what it was, but his buddy froze. I then made them get out of the car. I walked them to a street light post and had Mr. Mohawk put his arms around the post. He didn't like the idea so I had to encourage him by slapping him in the side of his head with my pistol. I removed my duct tape from my jacket and gave it to Mr. Bandana.

"Tape his wrist together!"

He started, but not to my satisfaction. With my free hand I grabbed his pants, which were already halfway down, and pulled them all the way down. I then put the barrel of my pistol between his cheeks.

"If you don't stop fucking around and wrap it tight, I'm going to stick this gun so far up your ass that bullets are gonna come flying out of your mouth!"

When he was done I took the tape away from him.

"Now it's your turn!"

I had him wrap his arms around the same post. With one hand I wrapped the tape around his wrist. I put my pistol back in my belt and began wrapping extra tape, extra tight around both of their wrist.

"Have a nice night assholes!"

Back at the gas station I used a pay phone to call the police.

"I have a package that you've been looking for. It's tied to a light post on Cermak Road near the I-94 underpass. Oh yeah, you'll also find a brand new BMW parked there as well."

CLICK.

I went to my rental car and waited for the cops to show up. While waiting I gave Candee a call and she answered on the second ring.

"Not now Sherman, I have a headache!"

"That's real cute! Grab a pen and paper. Write down these two addresses and turn on your scanner. At these two addresses the police should find plenty of stolen property, firearms and cash. You can thank me tomorrow!"

CLICK.

Five minutes later the cops showed up and I took off.

# THE CITY BLOCK: 50

The next morning after sleeping late I headed for the Block just before opening to share the good news. Everyone greeted me as they were busy getting ready for opening. While I was waiting to place my order, my phone rang. It was Candee.

"Good morning Sherman. You might want to catch the noon day broadcast."

"I was hoping that you would say that!"

"Oh yeah Sherman, thanks!"

"You don't have to thank me, catching those punks was like fishing in a barrel!"

"I've got to go!"

CLICK.

Finally Carman came to take my order.

"Hey Carman, why don't you have everyone gather around and turn on the TV."

"Why, what's going on?"

"Just do it, you'll see!"

Everyone gathered around the bar while commercials held them in suspense. Finally there was Candee standing across the street from the all night gas station.

"Good morning, I'm Candee Harris with the WLOK news crew, and we're coming to you live from the China Town area."

I could see that Mai was getting nervous all over again so I took her hand.

"I'm standing at the intersection of Cermak Road and the I-94 expressway. This is just one of several locations where strong arm robberies and carjacking have been taking place over the last three months. The police department's gang task force unit has been monitoring this community, and in the wee hours of this morning as arrest was made. The police say that they got a tip from a concerned citizen."

While Candee was speaking the faces of MR. Mohawk and Mr. Bandana was shown on the screen and Mai started to freak out. Carman quickly put her arms around her.

"It's alright honey! It's all over!"

Candee went on to say...

"The police were shocked when they arrived at the scene. Not only did they find a brand new stolen vehicle, but the bandits were tied to a street lamp post."

Louie slapped me on the back and started cheering!

"The police department also wants to stress to the public not to try to do police work. If you have a tip, please call them. I'm Candee Harris with the WLOK news crew."

Carman jumped up in the air and Louie gave me a high five and yelled out.

"You're a bad man Mr. Sherman!"

Carman came over and gave me a big hug and a kiss. Mai was completely lost.

"What's going on? What did I miss?"

Carman had to tell her what was going on.

"Honey the story we just saw was complements of Mr. Sherman Brothers!"

"Oh my God, you're the concerned citizen!"

I smiled at her and stuck my arms out. She jumped right in my arms and Louie popped open a bottle of champagne. After filling four flutes he made a toast.

"Here's to the good guys!"

The rest of the day was filled with joy and happiness. We all needed the lift and I was glad to be part of it.

It was Saturday morning. In south suburban Homewood the Mallory family was sitting in the breakfast nook of their 5,000 sq. ft. estate nestled in a wooded area of town. The kids were talking about their weekend activities. Frank was telling his wife about the worst two weeks of the year. She tells him that he has two days to prepare himself.

The task that he has before him is spending the first week visiting five of the corporation's multiplex theatres. His goal is to make sure that they're meeting industry standards, as well as corporate expectations. The directors are powerful people. They can make or break an entire region of theatres. In any case, the welfare of his family is directly impacted. He has every right to be concerned about the upcoming two weeks.

Back in Chicago Angie's riding a bumpy road to recovery. She's on the sofa and propped up on several pillows. In the kitchen Carman is preparing a breakfast that she may not be able to keep down. She enters the living room carrying a tray.

"Here you are honey. This is oatmeal and fruit it'll be good for you. It's comfort food."

Angie sat up straight and Carman placed the tray on her lap.

"Look at the bright side girl, at least there's no prunes in it!"

"Yeah I think that I have that area covered myself!"

While Angie ate Carman brought her up to date on what's been going on at the Block. After she finished eating they both drifted off and took a little nap. As the days go by Angie has good days and bad days, but Carman doesn't let up on her. What she really wanted was some fresh air. Knowing her physical capabilities outside would prove useful in the upcoming days.

# 50: PART II

## ANGIE MAKES A PLAN:

I decided to stop fighting Carman. The secret to the success of my plan was to get Carman to trust me to the point where she'll drop her guards. In addition to that I'll take advantage of the times that she's asleep, or not there. In my bedroom closet I'm putting together a kit that I'm going to need when I put my plan into action.

I love Carman dearly and I hate to use her this way. It's not by any means personal, but in my mind this has to be done. These bastards have to pay for what they've done. I can't go on with my life with this hanging over my head. I want to learn how to love men. My body will be filthy and contaminated as long as these men walk the streets like nothing happened. I don't think that this is a necessary evil, but justifiable and anyone would understand. I don't like having to live two lives because it isn't fair to those who love me. More than anything I want it all to be over.

As I sit looking out the window, I put together a mental list of items I'm going to need for my kit. I picture an oversized football jersey, a pair of shades, a baseball cap, a bottle of water, a small box of rat poison, a tube of red lipstick, a retractable cane, and most of all, a needle to inject the deadly venom! One thing that I learned during my weeks in the hospital is patience. It will prove to be my strongest weapon.

# THE CITY BLOCK: 51

Today is my day, and I intend to put my culinary skills to work. I stood in front of the refrigerator with the door open. Will it be seafood, beef or poultry? Before I could decide I heard the doorbell ring. Damn, I can't win! Who could this be? I pressed the intercom button.

"Yes, who's there?"

"Hi Sherman, it's me Mai."

I buzzed her up. Now I was getting scared! Why would she be coming here?

"Hey, you caught me about to test out my culinary skills. What brings you here?"

"I'm sorry for not calling first. I just feel like I'm the only one that still doesn't really know you well."

"Well why don't you come into the kitchen and we can talk while I move around."

Mai followed me to the kitchen and took a seat at the table.

"You know Mai, there's still a lot I don't know about you."

"I don't know where to start."

"Well, were you born and raised here?"

"No, I was born in Beijing to a very poor family. I was raised to be a servant. Not being born male was not in my best interest. My total worth was no more than that of a calf. When I reached my teen years, my parents sent me away to avoid a life of prostitution."

I was now using every fiber in my body not to reveal to Mai that she was tearing my heart out!

"So Mai, did things improve for you?"

"It's kind of a matter of opinion. I only avoided one kind of prostitution."

"What do you mean?"

"For starters that was the last time that I had contact with my parents. It wasn't allowed in my new home. I was still a servant, but I was being taught to speak English. At that age I didn't know why. Not only that, but I had never heard of America. As a kid, servants aren't educated about worlds outside of their own."

"That's incredible Mai!"

"When I was sixteen years old I noticed that every now and then, one of the older girls would go away and never come back. When I asked about them I was told to be quiet and keep working. At the age of eighteen I found out where they'd gone. I was told that I was being groomed to become an American bride."

I couldn't hold back anymore. I took her hand in mine.

"Mai I'm so sorry!"

"The other girls all hated me."

"But why did they hate you?"

"It was believed that my new American husband would give me a life of wealth. When my time came I was given a photo of a much older American man. That's when I learned that men were the same all over the world. They all lusted for young women."

I just looked down at the floor, because there was nothing that I could say.

"I was escorted to the airport and left alone. I had been told to be on my best behavior when I meet him. We met and boarded the plane for America. When we arrived a wedding had been prearranged. We lived in a huge house, and all around were people doing all the things that I used to do. He was very nice to me. He even hired tutors to teach me so that I could pass the GED exam. He told me that as long as he lived, that would be the only education that I would need. It wasn't long before he wanted me to do wifely duties."

"Mai, you don't have to do this!"

"That's nothing, it gets better! Four years later he passed away in his sleep. His biological family, who never approved of me, showed me the door."

That's when I put my arm around her shoulder.

"I then made my way to China Town. I felt that the best place for me was around my own people. I've worked in restaurants and bars every since."

I gently took her face in my hands.

"Oh Mai, I'm so very sorry! You deserved so much better."

Tears ran down her cheeks.

"Now you know why I'm so blown away by you guys taking me into your family."

"Look at my eyes Mai. I promise you that we're going to love you forever!"

"Now you know why I came here today."

"I have to say, you're the strongest person, man or woman that I've ever met!"

Mai stayed and shared lunch with me. During her visit I couldn't help but think about Rebecca's words of wisdom once again. Maybe this was one of the educational experiences that God was giving me.

# THE CITY BLOCK: 52

It's been days since Mai and I talked. As hard as I try, I can't help but see her through different eyes. I never said anything to the others. I didn't think that I should have. She'd already been accepted and things were going well. Not only that, but I was beginning to think that they were going to keep her around, even after Angie returns.

Over at Angie's place, things were going well also. The reports that I was getting from Carman were encouraging. Things were going so well that Carman felt like she could leave without worrying about her. It was a positive sign that Angie was healing.

# 52: PART II

## ANGIE RESEARCHES HER TARGET:

It was late afternoon and Carman was napping. That gave me the chance to go online. I began thinking to myself. I recalled research that I had previously done informing me that Mr. Mallory managed at least two movie theatres within an hour's drive. My problem would be finding out which one he'd be at, and when. Since I'm under Carman's care, I can't go to his home and follow his movements. I hoped that going online would help me a little. The only thing that I knew for sure was that the theatres were called the CMJ Multiplex Cinemas.

I typed in the name and boom, there they were! I scrolled a listing of states and clicked on Illinois. I then clicked on the Chicagoland area. Just about then Carman woke up and I dumped the screen.

"What are you doing?"

"I was just killing some time."

I now had a head start on my plan. Carman went to the bathroom, and when she came back she curled right back up in the easy chair. It wasn't long before she dozed off again. I went right back to the web site, clicked on the search box and typed in the word management. Five photos appeared, one of which was Mr. Mallory himself.

I called both of the area locations and got just what I wanted. At the second theatre I was told that he wouldn't be in until Thursday. After hanging up I found that Carman was still fast asleep.

I had two days before I could pay Mr. Mallory a visit. My kit was just about complete. The hard part was going to be working around Carman. It had been a while since I had driven a car, and I really didn't know if I was strong enough to do it. However my mind was made up and nothing was going to stop me. I thought about taking Carman's car, but didn't want her dragged into this mess if things went wrong. The only other choice I had was using my own car. I planned to take off Thursday morning, and I knew that Carman would be at work prepping for opening at the bar. Not having to look at Carman's face before leaving to do my dirty deed made me feel better.

It was Wednesday night and Carman was at the bar working. I was sitting at home alone. It's the eve of my next mission. I went over my plans in my mind over and over again. I double checked the details, not wanting to overlook anything.

It's 10:30pm and I'm lying in bed watching TV. Just like clockwork, Carman calls to see how I'm doing, just as she's done each night this week.

"Hi Carman, I'm doing fine. I was just about to go to sleep. I was thinking about getting some fresh air tomorrow."

"Are you sure about that honey?"

"Yeah I'd like to catch a matinee."

"Well why don't I go with you?"

"First let's see how I feel in the morning. I'll give you a call."

"Ok honey, sweet dreams!"

CLICK.

I hung up thinking that I couldn't let Carman change my plans. I got up out of bed to go to the bathroom one more time before calling it a night. When I stood I felt amazingly hot and dizzy. I then felt a strange feeling in my stomach. In a rush I barely made to the toilet before throwing up. When I finished I gargled with mouthwash and washed my face with cool water. Once I was stable I made my way back to bed. While lying in bed I remembered the doctor telling me that this would happen. I hated the timing, but tomorrow I have a date with Mr. Mallory.

# THE CITY BLOCK: 53

## ANGIE LOCKS AND LOADS:

A warm breeze off the lake swirled around my bedroom. Off in the distance, I could hear the sound of the Ell train making its way along the elevated tracks. Rubbing my eyes I looked at the clock radio on my nightstand. It was 8:17am. For a few minutes I just laid there in bed.

I closed my eyes again and my mind took me back 14 years. I was a young foolish and drunk little girl trying to attract attention. Tears began to run down my cheeks. Suddenly I began feeling that same filth that I felt the morning after the horrible deed had been done to me. Not being able to stand it, I dashed to the shower and began scrubbing my body! After soaping and rinsing repeatedly, I finally redeemed my dignity.

Back in my bedroom I began getting dressed. I put on a pair of jeans, white tennis shoes, and a white sports bra. I tied my hair up in a bun and then sat down to relax. Not only did I have time, but I wanted to be calm when I talked to Carman. Sticking to my routine, I had a couple of slices of toast and a glass of juice. I needed something in my stomach before I could take my meds.

It was now just past 10:00am, and the matinée didn't start until 12:15pm. I had about a 35 minute drive. There was time to kill. After a while I start-ed getting nervous and fidgety. From my closet I removed the kit that I had so carefully put together. I had stuffed everything into a kid's sized back pack. I then went out to the building's parking lot and put everything on the floor of my car.

Back in my apartment now I stood before a mirror looking at myself. It was then that I decided not to call Carman. I'll make some excuse and call her when I get back.

The time had come. I took a deep breath and let it out. I slipped on a pair of dark shades and took off. In my car now, I headed west for Cicero Ave. in the City of Hometown. When I reached Cicero, I made a left turn heading south bound.

When I got within a block of the theatre, I could see the large marquee on the corner of the lot, CMJ Multiplex Cinemas. As I scanned the other nearby businesses, my heart began to race. Directly across the street from the theatres was one of those 24 hour restaurants that served breakfast around the clock. I thought that it was the perfect spot to park, and walk across the street. By time I pulled around to the rear of the restaurant at was 12:15pm and the matinee was starting. I remained sitting in my car allowing the movie goers to get settled.

## CARMAN'S DISCOVERY

Here at the City Block we had just opened for business. I realized that I hadn't heard from Angie, so I took a break to give her a call. When she didn't answer, I began to get nervous, but calmed myself down because she could've been in the bathroom. 15 minutes later I tried again and still didn't get an answer. This time I freaked out and screamed out Louie's name! Both Louie and Mai came running.

"What's going on?"

"Angie is missing, and I can't reach her by phone! I'm going to her place! Call Sherman and tell him to contact me!"

When I got to Angie' place the first thing that I noticed was her car missing. Once inside, she was nowhere to be seen. I remembered her talking about a movie, and the other night she was on the internet looking for something. I speed dialed Sherman and turned on the computer at the same time. He immediately started asking questions.

"Is she there?"

"No, I think she may have tried to drive herself to a movie."

"To a movie!"

"I'm checking the history on her computer right now. Hold on. There it is Sherman!"

"What, what!"

"That stupid girl!"

"What! Where!"

"Have you ever heard of the CMJ Multiplex Cinemas?"

"Yeah, there's one out on Cicero Ave. Stay by your phone. I'm on my way out there!"

CLICK.

ANGIE PUT'S HER PLAN INTO ACTION

I got out of my car and went to the passenger door to remove the back pack. I slowly walked to the corner where I waited for the walk sign to cross the busy street. Once I was inside of the theatre lobby I began walking around and looking. The most important thing that I saw was a sign on a door that said employees only. Diagonally across from that door was the ladies room.

It was time for me to put my plan into action. Just as I turned to go into the ladies room, Mallory himself stepped out of the shadows of a long corridor that led to one of the theatres. I lowered my head as he passed right by me. He went into the office marked employees only, and I went into the ladies room.

Inside I entered a stall and closed the door. From the back pack I removed the jersey and the baseball cap. I then let my hair down from the bun style that I walked in with. That was followed by putting on the jersey and cap. When I was sure that I was alone, I came out of the stall. I then took the top off of a trash can and poured lighter fluid into it that I had in the back pack. Along with the fluid, I took out a pair of white framed shades, a book of matches, the poison filled syringe, and my tube of lipstick.

I no longer needed the back pack. I stuffed it into the can along with the remainder of the fluid. I then dragged the can under a ceiling mounted smoke detector. Using one match I lit the whole book and dropped it in the can. While waiting for the alarm and sprinkler to go off, I applied the red lipstick to my lips. I then tossed the tube into the fire. Moments later the alarm went off and the sprinkler started spraying water.

Peeking out of the door, I waited until it was total chaos. Huge crowds were being led outside by the theatre attendants. Across the hall I saw the employees only door begin to open. With the syringe in my hand, I broke through the crowd heading for Mallory, but then something went terribly wrong. I started getting hot and dizzy again, but kept on going. I stumbled my way over and when the door opened completely, I ran right into Mallory with the syringe. He collapsed to the floor taking me down with him. As his muscles began to lock up I broke away from his hold.

For a few moments I looked him in the eyes. There was terror in them as his body became motionless. I then leaned over and kissed him on the cheek. In my own pain I struggled to get to my feet. I put on the white framed glasses and turned to leave. During the excitement I failed to see that his arm was sticking out of the office into the lobby. I mixed into the crowd and struggled to maintain myself.

I was screaming down Cicero Ave. in my Vette! As I approached the theatre I saw crowds of people storming out of the front entrance. Off in the distance I could hear the sound of fire department sirens getting closer. I wondered what the hell was going on. All the time I was scanning the crowd for Angie. My cell phone was ringing off the hook! I knew that it was Carman, but now wasn't the time to talk to her.

Back inside the theater, a security guard had seen a woman leaving the employees officer during the chaos. Running, he worked his way through the crowd. He saw Mr. Mallory's arm sticking out of the door. He checked for a pulse, it was faint, but there. On his radio he called for help. Back on his feet he ran for the front door, but the crowd was hampering his movement.

As I drove slowly by, I saw a woman removing a baseball cap and a jersey. The heat and the smoke were too much for her. I saw that it was Angie and slammed on my breaks. Jumping out of my car, I ran around and picked her up. As I did so she passed out right in my arms! While putting her into my car I yelled at her.

"Jesus Angie, what have you done to yourself?"

There were fire trucks, EMT units, and squad cars all over the place! I burnt rubber leaving the parking lot. In my rear view mirror I saw a security guard talking to a plain clothed cop. I could've sword that it was Lt. Lopez, but it could've been.

As I drove I shuck Angie on the shoulder.

"Please Angie, please, hang in there!"

I must've broken every traffic law there was trying to make it over east to the I-57 Expressway. I finally hit Halsted and was heading for the 99th Street expressway entrance ramp. That's when my cell phone rang again. This time it was Candee. I clicked it off, and then back on. Two minutes later it rang again.

"Shit!"

"Yes Candee, what the hell is it?"

"Sherman that woman that you're with...

"What about her, and how the hell did you know?"

"Damn it Sherman! The Lt. thinks that she's the Lipstick Murderer!"

"The hell with the Lt. This woman is dying and I've got to get her to the emergency room!"

"Sherman you don't understand! They've got the entire police department and half of the state troopers on your ass! I'm in the air in a chopper covering the whole damn thing! Please stop Sherman! I don't want anything to happen to you!"

"Candee call the City Block and tell them what's going on!"

CLICK.

I floored the gas pedal and hit the expressway ramp headed south. As I weaved through traffic I could hear the sound of helicopters. Overhead about a car length behind me were two of them on either side of me. One had the WLOK news logo on it, and the other one was the Chicago Police Department.

I couldn't let them stop me now! All I cared about was keeping Angie alive. Once I cleared the Chicago city limits, just south of 127$^{th}$ Street, my whole world came crashing down on me! Just about five blocks ahead of me, the entire expressway was blocked off. There were Illinois State Trooper squads blocking the way in both directions. Standing behind the squads were officers with shotguns and rifles, pointed right at me. My mind was racing in all directions! Coming up behind me was Chicago's finest with their blue lights flashing. There was no way out!

I couldn't believe this was happening. Angie was still out cold. I could see that she was breathing, but nothing else. Suddenly sixty feet above me, on my right a third helicopter screamed by me. At about half the distance between the troopers and me, it did a 180 degree turn and landed facing me. About one hundred feet away from it I decided to give it up. I let up off the gas and slammed on my breaks.

I went into a skid and turned the wheel trying not to hit the helicopter. When I finally came to a stop I was sitting horizontally across the expressway, maybe 20 feet from the helicopter. I turned off the engine, threw my keys out on the pavement, and stuck my hands up in the air.

By now the air was filled with helicopters from every major television network in the city. For that I was grateful, because the next thing that I saw was the passenger door on the police helicopter open up and Lt. Lopez jumped out. He walked over to Angie and touched her neck. I assumed that he was checking for a pulse. He then took the radio off of his belt and called for a Medivac helicopter. Even though he may have had his own little nasty reasons for doing it, I thanked God that he did!

Now standing directly in front of the hood of my car, he folded his arms and stood there for a few moments. He then walked over to my door.

"Well well, well, hot shot! What the hell am I going to do with you?"

"You can take my dying friend to the emergency room and let me drive away from here."

"In your freaking dreams! Dying friend my ass! Get the hell out of the car!"

When I got half way out of the car, he grabbed me by my shoulder and spun me around, which didn't do shit for my rips! He then slammed my face down on the trunk of the car.

"Hey, what the hell are you doing?"

"You're under arrest hot shot! I told you that you knew this bitch, but you wouldn't listen!"

"She's just my friend!"

"You still don't get it do you? She's the Lipstick murderer!"

"Lopez, you've lost your mind this time!"

"Maybe, but I'm going to nail her ass, and yours too!"

"What the hell for?"

"Aiding and abetting a fugitive, accessory after the fact, and about a dozen or so traffic violations. Whata ya say to that hot shot?"

He then slapped the cuffs on me and pushed me back down on the trunk.

"Stay put! If you move, I'm going to think that you're trying to escape, and I'll have to put a couple of 40cal slugs in your ass!"

He then laughed and walked away.

"You know good son of a bitch!"

"What was that?"

I ignored him. Just about then the Medivac unit landed on the other side of the expressway. Two medics got out, one pulled out a gurney, and the other carried what looked like a toolbox. They put Angie on the gurney and began to examine her. I yelled out that she had just undergone a bone marrow transplant, and one of the medics signaled that he heard me. They then rolled her over to the helicopter, loaded her up and took off. I closed my eyes and prayed.

# THE CITY BLOCK: 54

Lopez took me by the arm and shoved me into the back of a squad car. As we drove away a flat bed tow truck went past us. I was taken to Cook County Jail for processing. When the officers walked me into the lobby, Dad, Carlton and Rex were already there waiting. I yelled out to them.

"Dad, get me out of here!"

"Don't worry son, I'll have you out of here in a couple of hours!"

During my processing, I couldn't help but wonder why Candee and the police were so bent on Angie being the Lipstick Murderer. What did I miss? Did my love for her make me blind? I still think that they've got the wrong woman, and soon I'll find out.

I prepared myself mentally for being locked up. I was forced to strip and was then searched, and I mean everywhere! I then showered with the help of a guard and water hose. After drying off I was given a prison uniform to put on. Once again I was hand cuffed and taken to a cell.

It was a large cell with about ten guys in it. All of which had been arrested on the same day as I. Most of them kept to themselves and some were talkative. I backed up to a wall and sat down. I didn't know how long I'd be there, but I had to keep an eye on everyone. The smell of the place was horrible. I guess that that was part of the punishment.

You get a strange feeling when you're locked behind bars. It's not just a feeling of hopelessness. You tend to think about the simple things in life. I thought about how easy it was for me to sit on my balcony, or feel Nurse Linda's soft flesh against mine. At this point I'd give anything to be at home with my ribs wrapped in bandages.

It seemed like it took forever, but finally a guard appeared at the door of the cell.

"Brothers!"

"Yeah!"

"Over here. Turn around and put your arms behind you."

I did as I was told and he hand cuffed me. He then unlocked the door, took me by the arm and led me away. We walked until we reached a door where we had to be buzzed through. I was then allowed to put my own clothes back on. Once I changed, we had to be buzzed out again. In the lobby I was greeted by Dad, Carlton and Rex.

"Come on son, let's go home and get some rest. Tomorrow we've got a lot of work to do!"

"Thanks Dad, but can we stop and get my car out of jail too?"

"You and that damn car! Sure son, we can do that!"

Rex and Carl laughed as we walked out the door. On the way home I asked Dad about Angie.

"She's still in the hospital under guard son, and sense she's been accused of murder, there's no possibility of making bail."

"So what are we going to now Dad?"

"You know me son, I've always got something up my sleeve!"

Once we got my car out of jail I finally had time to myself. As I made my way home two things occurred to me. One was that this wasn't a dream. Two was people on the street proved it by pointing at my car. Obviously they had seen the coverage on TV. The first thing that I did when I got home was pour myself a double shot of scotch. I took a shower to get the jailhouse residue off of me and laid down in darkness.

Again I asked myself what I had missed about Angie. Despite what the police thought, I wouldn't allow myself to believe that she's involved. One thing for sure, that strange feeling of closeness between us was creeping back into my head. After a couple of hours of lying in the dark, my doorbell rang. I knew that it was either Candee, or my family from the Block. I didn't bother to ask who was there, I just buzzed them up.

To my relief, it was my family, and not Candee! I was greeted with hugs, and Carman immediately broke down in tears.

"Sherman I'm so sorry, it's my fault. I should've been there!"

"No honey, it's not your fault."

"If I had been there, she never would've tried doing something stupid like going to a movie. Now she's in the hospital, and you went to jail!"

"Look honey, she made the decision to go there on her own, and I did the same thing that I would've done for any of you. Relax it's not your fault."

Mai offered to make some coffee, which was a good idea. I asked who was running the bar and Louie said no one.

"We closed up as soon as we found out what was going on. We watched the coverage and as soon as it was over, we went to the hospital."

"How is Angie doing?"

"She's stable now, but heavily sedated. She has one hand cuffed to the bed rail and there's an officer outside her door."

"Damn, I was hoping they wouldn't do that!"

Mai came back with a tray of mugs and a coffee earn.

"Help yourselves guys."

"I know that I'm new here, but I was just wondering. What are you guys going to do now?"

The three of us just looked at each other until I spoke up.

"I'm meeting with my dad at the firm tomorrow, and I suggest that you guys work out something for Angie. I've already been told that due to the murder charge, she can't make bail."

That's when Carman blew up!

"So what the hell are we supposed to do?"

"Carman for starters you've got to stop going off like that!"

"You're nobody's damn boss!"

That's when Louie stepped in.

"Look guys, we're not going to get anywhere by biting each other's head off! Carman please let Sherman finish."

"What I was going to say was my dad's got something up his sleeve. Why don't we just wait to see what it is, and in the meantime let's be prepared in case she is released and allowed to come home."

"That sounds good to me Sherman. Can we all agree with that?"

It was hard for her, but Carman finally agreed. As I sat sharing coffee and fighting with my Block family, the Silver Fox sat alone in his study.

## THE SILVER FOX PICK'S HIMSELF APART

I stared at an old photograph of my wife that I keep on my desk. I sipped on rare brandy from a snifter and thought about the horrible thing that Carlton and Rex had done years ago. I couldn't stomach it and in a rage I threw the brandy snifter against the wall shattering it.

What I hated the most was that my son, like me, had made a hor-rible decision that will haunt him the rest of his life. It appeared that sex had taken us both for a ride that wasn't over yet. I feel responsible for ev-erything that was happening in Angie's life. I wondered if this very same young woman was the one that was abused years ago, and the same woman that's committing these revenge murders. I wish that I could hold her in my arms like a real father. I'd tell her that she could kill the beast, but not the memory. Heaven knows that I've tried.

Tomorrow morning will be the first day of a new mission. Like all missions, a strong experienced ally is required. The livelihood of this young woman is at risk. I only know one person that was up for the task, and that's my good friend Oliver. My plan is to call him first thing in the morning.

# THE CITY BLOCK: 55

As I drove down the highway en route to the firm, every flashing light and turn signal that I saw gave me the creeps. I kept thinking that the cops were on my tail. I couldn't wait to get to the firm. I pulled into the parking lot and left my car in the hands of the parking attendant.

Inside the building I went straight to the elevator, and when I stepped out I was greeted by the firm's receptionist.

"Good morning Sherman. They're all waiting for you in the conference room."

Great, I caused this mess, and yet I'm the last to get here! In the conference room the first thing that I noticed was a pot of coffee, mugs, a pitcher of water and some glasses. Oh boy, this is going to be long one! Everyone was there, including Abbigale. Dad wasted no time.

"Let's get down to business, time is important. First of all, Abbigale honey, I love you like a daughter, but there's something that you should know. This case is a huge mess. There is no doubt in my mind that it'll be anything less than a media circus, and this firm is going to be in the center ring! There will be no privacy for any of us. It's in your best interest not to be around. The less you know, the better off you're going to be. Please honey, don't think ill of me, but I suggest that you visit a friend or family for a while. Trust me Abbigale the media is going to relentless!"

She had seen this look on his face before, and she knew that she couldn't reason with him.

"I understand Dad."

She stood, excused herself, gave Carlton a kiss, and said goodbye. After she left Dad stood and started pacing the floor. The room was so quiet that you could almost hear the wheels turning in his head.

"Fellows starting now, I want you to chancel everything that you have going. I mean everything! Normally at this time I would ask if everyone is committed to the end, but I've already taken the liberty of making that decision for you! Are there any comments?"

Rex spoke up right away.

"Are we going to be representing Angie?"

"No we're not Rex."

Both Carlton and I raised our eyebrows. Dad then continued.

"We're too close to her. Thanks to the good people at the City Block, we've all given blood samples on her behalf. Anything we say or do is going to look like we're just trying to keep our friend out of jail. Any first year law student would rip us a new one! Just the personal relationships alone would make us sitting ducks. not to mention the media, thanks to Sherman! Now that I have everyone's attention, Sherman I don't care how you do it, but you'd better put a damn muzzle on your friend Miss Harris! I'm sure that she's going to be in this mess up to her pretty little neck! Do you hear me son?"

"Yes Dad, I hear you."

"Good!"

Dad then gave Carlton and Rex a stern look.

"Ok, let's stop dicking around here! Do the two of you really want some new punk who's trying to kiss the D.A's ass to go digging around and find a connection between you and Angie? Yeah, I didn't think so!"

Both Carlton and Rex dropped their heads. That's when I spoke up.

"No disrespect intended Dad, but Angie doesn't stand a chance in hell with a Public Defender."

"Well like I told you yesterday, I've got something up my sleeve. Carlton!"

"Yes sir."

"Tomorrow afternoon at 2:14pm you're going to be at Union Station."

"Why will I be at Union Station?"

"I've got a gun slinger coming in on a train from Texas."

"Texas!"

"That's right. He's boarding a train this morning in San Antonio. Apparently he doesn't care for flying. In any case you'll pick him up and bring him straight here."

"Is there anything else you can tell me about this guy?"

"Well, he only represents women."

Rex spoke up again.

"What is this guy's full name?"

"Oliver Wendell Cartwright."

"I've heard of this guy. Isn't his wife a Female Activist?"

"Not anymore, she's no longer with us. The down side is that the good people presiding in our superior court system, hate's him like a bad rash!"

"Why is that?"

"He's been accused of putting on courtroom theatrics, and using his southern charm on the jury."

"Yeah I could see how that would piss a judge off."

"There's also another thing. He loves the media, and they love him! I can't stress to you guys enough not to judge him. He's as sly as a fox and capable of striking like a snake at a moment's notice! We will support him in any way that we can. Is everyone clear on that?"

The three of us all answered yes sir.

"Dad I have one more question."

"What is it Sherman?"

"What's going to be our first move when Mr. Cartwright gets here?"

"He and I are going down to the D.A.'s office and try to get the charges against you dropped. There's one more thing that you all should know. Once he makes an appearance at the D.A.'s office, the cat is going to me out of the bag! Everyone is going to know he's in town, and more than likely, they'll know why!"

# THE CITY BLOCK: 56

When I got home the first thing that I wanted to do was contact the guys at the Block. I know that it's against what Dad said, but I've got to make sure that they don't screw things up. I dialed the Block and Louie answered.

"City Block, this is Louie speaking."

"Don't talk, just listen. Get everyone together and go into the office. I'm going to call back in five minutes. Put me on speaker phone when I call back."

CLICK.

Five minutes later I called back.

"Are you ready?"

"Yes, we're ready."

"Listen carefully and don't interrupt. This will be the last time that you hear from me for a while. Don't call me, and don't attempt to see me. From this point on Angie and I are off limits. I mean this Carman! No phone calls or visits to Angie. "I'll find a way to update you on her condition." Each one of you will be watched and recorded. At the bar, at home, you name it! Investigators working for the D.A, the media, and the cops are going to be all over us! Do not discuss anything between yourselves over the telephone. Remember that any new customer at the bar could be an informant. If anyone asks you anything about me, Angie, or the case, you must play stupid. This also includes Rex as well. Do I make myself clear?"

They all answered yes.

"Hey Carman."

"Yeah."

"Don't go anywhere near Angie's place, and if any of you get a phone call from her, or anyone claiming to be representing her, hang up immediately. I've got to go now."

CLICK.

The rest of the day I sat around going crazy. I couldn't go to the Block for a cocktail, and I couldn't go for a drive because my car sticks out like a sore thumb! I no longer had Nurse Linda to keep me company, and Candee was out of the question.

The following day at 2:00pm Carlton was already sitting in Union Station. He kept nervously checking his watch. On a large TV a news broadcast was recapping the story of my arrest. Carlton turned away and started people watching, but that wasn't good enough. It was starting to drive him crazy!

He looked at his watch and saw that it was now 2:16pm. He decided to take a walk just to get away from the people. Just as he started walking an announcement was made over the PA. The train from San Antonio, Texas was now arriving on track number 16. As he waited, people of every race, size, and age started piling off the train and making their way up the platform. As he watched, not one of them matched the description of Mr. Cartwright.

The lobby turned into a sea of people hugging, kissing and crying. The scene was like that of military soldiers arriving home from overseas duty. Across the huge lobby a man was making eye contact with him. He was overweight, had big bushy eyebrows, and wore a cheap suit with cowboy boots. As he got closer Carlton began to wonder who he was, and what the hell did he want. When he got within hand shaking distance he put his bag down.

"Well I'll be lassoed and hog tied! You must be Carlton's little colt!"

It all hit Carlton at once.

"Mr. Cartwright?"

"That'll be son. I'm as guilty as a rooster in a hen house!"

Carlton shook his hand.

"How did you know who I was?"

"Well you're a dead ringer for ya daddy."

He smiled and grabbed Mr. Cartwright's bag and they started making their way through the crowd. The ride back to the firm was entertaining to say the least. Carlton thought that if nothing else, it was going to be fun having Mr. Cartwright around. When they got back to the firm he was given the royal treatment right from the start. Carlton stopped the car right in front of the door and they were greeted by the doorman and the parking attendant.

"Good afternoon Mr. Cartwright. Welcome to the firm. Please allow me to secure your bag sir."

"Why thank ya son!"

The welcoming committee stood just inside the lobby, shoulder to shoulder. There was Dad, Rex and Dad's personal secretary with pen and pad in her hand, and of course, me. Dad immediately stepped out of formation to give Mr. Cartwright a hug.

"Why Carl, you ole rodeo clown you! How's that chapped hide of yours?"

"Oliver old buddy it's good to see you!"

Mr. Cartwright turned to the rest of us.

"How yall doin?"

He then shook hands with all of us with the exception of Dad's secretary. He bowed and kissed her hand.

"Carl, yall been hidin this delicate rose from me?"

"You're still the same old Oliver! You still think you can charm the horns off of a bull!"

"Ah naw come on, don't go gettin jealous. Hey boys, yall know ya daddy always did hate competition!"

"Come on cowboy, let's head upstairs."

On the way up Dad asked Mr. Cartwright if he needed to take a rest, or get right to work.

"Why hell, we can start this roundup right naw!"

In the conference room Dad's secretary had already set up a laptop to project images on the wall.

"Oliver we're going to start from the beginning to bring you up to speed. What you're about to see is news footage of the murders our client has been accused of. The local media has named them the Lipstick murders."

"Why they name em that?"

"All of the victims were found with a red kiss on their cheeks."

Seeing the old footage was a bit unnerving for Rex and Carl. It was like pouring salt into an open sore. Seeing the faces of their dead frat brothers was too much.

"Freeze it right there. Who's that lovely flower reporting all these here stories?"

Dad rolled his eyes.

"She's no damn flower! She's more like damn Venus Fly Trap!"

"I take it that she ain't no cowgirl in yo dreams!"

"A pain in the butt is what she is! She gets in the way of law enforcement and the court system with that camera of hers!"

"Well I guess we gone have to lasso that little philly!"

"Yeah you've got that right!"

"Ok yall can go ahead naw."

During the review of the footage it was stopped periodically to explain what was going on.

"Who is that ole bald guy keeps on showing up?"

"Dad, do you mind?"

"Sure Sherman, go ahead."

"Mr. Cartwright, that's one of Chicago's finest."

"Oh really naw."

"That's Lt. Ricardo Lopez."

"Naw he looks like a real gun slinger!"

"He's a legend in his own mind!"

"Sounds like yall got some history."

"Yeah we go way back! His favorite hobby is riding my ass!"

"Did that ole boy ever get physical with yall?"

"Why don't you ask me how many times he didn't?"

That's when Rex spoke up.

"Mr. Cartwright I personally interrupted this Lopez guy attempting to use Sherman as a punching bag."

"Why that's good stuff son, but according to ole Carl here, it wouldn't be in our best interest to put yall on the stand."

"Mr. Cartwright there's something that Rex and Lt. Lopez don't know."

"What's that son?"

"This incident was recorded by a security camera that I have access to."

"Naw that we can use! What else yall got on this ole boy?"

The footage was fast forwarded to the story where the Lt. was being investigated because of the evidence found in his squad.

"Naw wait a minute, Yall tellin me that that ole boy was accused of being the murderer himself?"

"Yes sir Mr. Cartwright."

"Naw I don't believe he did it, but that's good stuff! I think that the tomorrow morning I'm just gone pull my boots up, and ya daddy and me is goin down ta that D.A.'s office. "Yeah we gone have a good OLD fashion Texas bar-b-q!" Ya see son, yo Lt. Lopez done been a thorn in yo bonnet far too long. In my neck of the woods we call that harassment. One thang that all D.A.'s hate is losing, especially when they get embarrassed by they own law enforcement. Don't yall worry, we gon get those charges against you dropped. In fact I might have some fun wit that ole boy down the trail a bit!"

It was getting close to 6:30pm, and Mr. Cartwright suggested taking a break.

"What yall cal chow around here?"

Dad offered to take him out to dinner.

"Thank ya Carl old buddy, but that French chow yall city boys eat don't rightly fill my plate! I need something that sticks to the ribs, like some bar-b-q sauce, if yall know what I mean."

"Same old Oliver, still trying to kill yourself!"

"Excuse me Dad."

"Yeah Sherman."

"I may be able to help out here."

"What did you have in mind?"

"Well let's just say that I have a secret weapon!"

"Well hell cowboy, don't just sit there, putta saddle on that puppy!"

With a smile on my face, I asked to be excused for a moment. I stepped out into the hall and dialed 411 to reach Tiny. After saving the number I pressed the call button. On the first ring Jerri answered.

"Hey Jerri, this is Sherman. May I speak with Tiny?"

"Sure, hold on."

"Hey buddy, we've been worried about you down here. Is everything alright?"

"I'm good man, thanks. I can't talk right now, but I need a favor."

"What did you have in mind?"

"I've got a good ole Texas boy in town, and I need something that'll make him feel right at home."

"You know Sherman, a meal like that may take a while."

"Can you deliver too? I'll make it worth your wild!"

"Like I said, it'll take a while!"

"There's one more thing. Can you throw in a Chef's salad for one?"

"You've got it baby! What's the address?"

"Ok Tiny, there are some conditions. When you get here, you'll be greeted by the doorman. He will escort you to where I am. Whatever you see or hear doesn't exist, and your visit here never happened."

"What visit?"

"Thanks man, you'll be well taken care of!"

CLICK.

# THE CITY BLOCK: 57

Dad thanked and excused his secretary. The rest of us waited for the meal to be delivered. While waiting, Dad left the room and returned with a bottle of wine, four glasses, and a beer for Mr. Cartwright. The two of them kept us entertained with stories from their past. Time was flying, and it wasn't long before there was a knock at the door. I opened the door to see Tiny holding a large box with the doorman standing beside him.

When Tiny entered the room, the aroma from the box filled the air and got Mr. Cartwright's attention.

"Na that's a big ole boy! Son yall come right on over here! We gon get along just fine!"

Tiny smiled and sat the box on the table. He leaned over and whispered in my ear. I then whispered back into his ear. He then reached into the box and pulled out the Chef's salad and handed it to Dad. Dad opened the container and was pleasantly surprised.

"Thank God son!"

He then shook Tiny's huge mitt. In the meantime Mr. Cartwright was opening containers like a kid on Christmas morning! Once again, Tiny had out done himself. He prepared baby back ribs, bar-b-q chicken, collard greens, corn bread, baked beans, and corn on the cob. He even threw in an apple pie. All of our eyes lit up like fireworks! Tiny then smiled.

"Gentlemen, enjoy!"

I walked out into the hallway with him and laid two big ones in his hand.

"Right on Sherman!"

"You got it big man!"

"Take care of yourself Sherman."

I went back into the conference room and looked at Mr. Cartwright.

"How did I do Mr. Cartwright?"

"Son, if it was beef out there in that parking lot instead of BMW's, I'd think I was right at home! Why don't ya park yo hide, and let's pig out!"

An hour later we all sat around the table loosening our belts and holding our stomachs. For the sake of time and convenience, Mr. Cartwright stayed at Dad's place. It also gave them the one on one time that they needed. That night before turning in the two of them relaxed on the patio.

"So tell me Carl, what's the story on this little ole girl? Is she guilty?"

"I don't know. I don't think so. She's a sweet kid, well loved in the community, and a business woman without a record."

"Well Carl, I done known ya far too long, and I can tell when something is eating at yo hide. What is it?"

"Well it's the cops. They seem to think that these murders aren't serial or random."

"Are we talking revenge?"

"It could be! Look, these guys are being found with their pants down around their ankles, and a red lipstick kiss on their cheeks."

"Well it sure as hell sounds like revenge! The pants down and the lipstick have to be a humiliation tactic."

"There's one more thing Oliver. Tomorrow I want you to meet her by yourself."

"Ah Jesus Carl, don't tell me there's something between you and this little philly!"

"No, it's not like that!"

"Well what the hell is it?"

"It's Sherman. He's a Private Investigator, and before this thing became a media mess, he was nosing around and, well, hold on to your boots buddy! Some time ago he found a hand written message taped to his door."

"What kinda damn message?"

"It was from the murderer."

"What the hell! You mean that he knows the killer?"

"No, but she knows him."

"How do yall know it's from the killer?"

"She put a red lipstick kiss on it."

"Jesus Carl, yall ole boys got mo cow patties around here than the whole state of Texas! Is there any mo?"

"Yeah there's more."

"How could it possibly be mo?"

"She hit him with her car."

"You mean this little ole philly tried to kill em?"

"No, we think that she wanted to put him on the bench for a while."

"It sounds like to me that yo boy was doin a better job than that Lt. fella."

"Yeah, but it damn near got him killed! You can see why I don't want any contact with the girl. We're your team and you're the captain. Whatever you need, we'll dig it up."

"Carl ole buddy, I think I'm gon call it a night."

"Sure buddy, have a good night."

By 9:00am the Silver Fox and Mr. Cartwright were leaving the house. They had quite a day ahead of them. Their first stop will be the D.A.'s office. Their mission was to get the charges against me dropped. After their arrival they were escorted to a small conference room. A few minutes later Assistant District Attorney Margret White entered the room. The gentlemen both stood up. Oliver attempted to give her his card.

"That won't be necessary Mr. Cartwright, I know who you are. The question is what are you doing in my city?"

"Well Ma'am…

"You can save the charm too!"

"Ok then. I'm here to represent Mr. Sherman Brothers."

"I know you're not here to cut a deal Mr. Cartwright!"

"No Ma'am I'm not."

"Then what do you want?"

"I want the charges against him dropped."

"You're kidding right? Perhaps they don't have TV's in your neck of the woods! Why would I drop the charges?"

"Well, to answer yo first question, we do have TV's in my neck of the woods. I do have to admit one thang though. You people in this fine city sure do have some great surveillance cameras."

"So what's your point?"

"Perhaps yall should take some time to watch this here little ole footage that I done brought wit me."

"Why would I do that?"

"Well Ma'am yo lead detective has quite a history wit my client."

"Lt. Lopez, that's baloney!"

"I thought yall might say that. Why don't yall take a look right here."

Mr. Cartwright opened his laptop and started the footage that Louie had recorded at the City Block when Lopez was punching me.

"Well Ma'am, whata ya think?"

"Well he probably asked for it!"

"Ma'am I got witnesses that'll disagree wit ya."

"You call this history?"

"Oh Ma'am, there's plenty mo! Did yall know that yo detective and my client done been working together for months on yo so called Lipstick murders?"

"That's ridiculous!"

"Well let me show yall some mo."

The next scene was that of Candee covering one of the murders. ADA White looked at the laptop.

"Na I'm sure that yall know who this lovely little flower is. I hear that in this neck of the woods, law enforcement just loves her right down to her pretty little toes!"

"What are you getting to Mr. Cartwright?"

"This little ole lady is the third member of yo investigative team. That's right, she's in it right up to her pretty little ole neck! Na this here is what I wanta say Miss White."

"Go ahead."

"Na the truth is that my client was just aiding a dear friend who had just had major surgery. Na against the doctor's orders, she decided to put her life in jeopardy by going out for a little fresh air, and he may have just saved her life."

"Is that all Mr. Cartwright?"

"Well we all know that he's not guilty of anything, besides, yall got the big fish locked up."

"Well Mr. Cartwright, I'm going to say goodbye for now, and I'll give it some thought."

"Well Ma'am, na that's all I'm asking fo! Oh yeah Miss White?"

"Yes Mr. Cartwright!"

"I'd hate fo the good people in this fine city to see all this here ugliness come out on their TV's. We would all look so bad!"

Oliver then dropped his business card on the table and they turned to leave. Behind them they heard ADA White slam the door. When they got back inside Dad's car, he looked at Mr. Cartwright.

"You know Oliver, you're a real bastard!"

"Why hell, that little ole cowgirl in there was ridin backwards! That ain't my fault."

As they drove away, they felt confident that they had accomplished their mission.

"You know Oliver that ADA is going to hate you with a passion when she finds out that you're representing Angie."

"Yeah, I have to admit that I don't look forward to ridin that ole bull."

"I'm sure that Miss White has a trick or two up her own sleeve."

They were now in route to the hospital so that Mr. Cartwright could visit with Angie.

"So tell me mo about Angie Carl."

"Well aside from Sherman and the guys at the City Block, she doesn't have any family. In fact those guys are her only family."

"That's a shame!"

"She's strikingly beautiful, quiet and intelligent."

"So what's this City Block place?"

"It's a bar in the community where Sherman lives."

"Sounds interesting, maybe I should drop in there."

"Well if you decide to, make sure that you let Sherman know first."

"Why's that?"

"Let's just say the he has them on a gag order. These guys are tight. They won't say a word to you!"

"Well maybe later I'll saddle up and take a little ole ride over there."

When they arrived at the hospital Dad dropped Mr. Cartwright off at the main entrance and waited in the car at the parking lot. Mr. Cartwright went straight to the counter and asked to visit Angie.

"I'm sorry sir, but she has restricted visiting rights."

"Oh I'm sorry darling, here's my card."

The nurse read his card out loud.

"Oliver Wendell Cartwright, Attorney at Law."

"Yes Ma'am, that's me alright!"

She got on the phone and called the nurse's station near Angie's room.

"I'm sending up a Mr. Oliver Cartwright. Here's your pas sir, please pin it on."

"Thank yall Ma'am!"

He turned and went straight to the elevator. At Angie's door he was greeted by a uniformed police officer. He stepped inside and closed the door behind himself.

"Well my, my, you're bout as pretty as a butterfly on a sunny day!"

"I'm sorry sir, but I don't think that I know you."

"Oh I'm sorry darlin! My name is Oliver Cartwright. Here's my card. I'm a friend of Sherman's."

"You're an attorney?"

"Yes Ma'am."

"Well sir, I love Sherman to death, but I can't afford you!"

"Na don't you worry yo pretty little head bout that! It's taken care of. How are you this lovely afternoon? Is there anything yall need?"

"I'm fine, but are you sure that you're supposed to be here?"

"Look darlin, Sherman's very special to me, and you're very special to him. We gone get you outta this here mess. Do you mind if I ask yall a few questions?"

"No sir."

"Angie, do you remember what happened?"

"Well I wanted some fresh air and went to the theatre. Something happened and they made everyone leave, but I got real hot and dizzy, and then I woke up here."

"Do you know why there's a lawman outside yo door?"

That's when tears started running down Angie's cheeks.

"No one will tell me, but on the news they're saying that I killed a man."

Oliver grabbed a box of tissues from the nightstand and gave them to her.

"Here ya are darlin, wipe ya pretty little ole face!"

"Is Sherman in jail because of me?"

"He's not in jail, and everything is going to be alright. Look honey, yall get some rest, and I'm gone be in touch with ya, I promise!"

"Thank you Mr. Cartwright."

"Darlin from now on, yall call me Oliver! Na you get some rest."

When Mr. Cartwright got down stairs to the lobby he called Dad.

"Carl ole buddy, I'm bout done here."

Dad could see the lobby entrance from where he was parked, and pulled right out heading that way, and just he was about to pull over, he was cut off my another car that stopped right in front of Mr. Cartwright.

"Hey Cartwright!"

Oliver looked up and a flash went off. The car then sped away. Dad pulled up and Mr. Cartwright jumped right in. Dad was pissed off!

"Son of a bitch!"

"Why hell Carl, it was just a matter of time before the whole world knew I was in town!"

"Yeah well, you can bet the farm that Candee Harris is behind this stunt!"

"Well Carl, all we have to do is find the silver lining in this here ole cloud!"

# THE CITY BLOCK: 58

They drove away from the hospital, but Dad didn't think that Mr. Cartwright wasn't quite listening to him.

"Oliver I know that you're running the show, but I'm telling you that this woman Candee Harris is bad news!"

"Well buddy, that's just what I'm depending on! I'll tell ya something else too. That ole gun slinger Lt. Lopez, we gon dress him up like a rodeo clown and put his ass to work! Yeah I think we gone have us a lil ole game of cowboy poker!"

"What the hell is that?"

"Man you city slickers! What we do is take four cowboys, a card table, a deck of cards, one mean ass bull, and put em' all in the middle of a coral."

"Let me take a guess? The four cowboys are you, Lopez, ADA White, and Miss Harris."

"That's righttt! Then we gon slap that ole bull on the ass and set em' free! Yeeee ha!"

"So where do we start?"

"Well I'm thinkin that before the day is over, I'm gon get a lil ole nasty gram from that Miss White. Why don't ya get yo boys together and tomorrow we gon have us a lil ole meeting."

"Ok, consider it done."

"Why don't we stir up this here pot of chili and have it in the public?"

"You're kidding right?"

"We've got to do some ridin in rough country Carl!"

"Where did you have in mind?"

"Well I kinda took a likin to that Tiny fella."

"It figures you would!"

"How bout a nice lil ole country breakfast? Hell, live a little!"

"More like die a little!"

"In the meantime why don't yall take me back to yo ranch and let me freshen up a taste. Maybe later yall can get me a ride down to that lil ole saloon yall call the City Street."

"Jesus Oliver! It's the City Block!"

"Yeah thattt."

That night Oliver did indeed make it down to the Block. When he entered the bar, the trio all saw him at the same time. Red flags went up like the I.R.S. was on a hunting spree! When he made his way over to the bar he stuck out like sore thumb. He was definitely out of his element. He climbed up on a stool and Mai welcomed him to the Block.

"What can I get for you sir?"

"Well I'll take a scotch and water if yall don't mind darlin."

"It's coming right up."

"Thank ya."

Mr. Cartwright then reached into his pocket and took out his cell phone. Mai returned with his drink and sat it down in front of him. It turns out that Mr. Cartwright was calling me.

"Hey buddy, how yall doin?"

"I'm good Mr. Cartwright."

"Well I'm resting my hide down here at the City Street, I mean the City Block."

"Ok, I get it. Can you give your phone to Louie?"

"Hang on cowboy. Excuse me darlin."

"Yes sir."

"Yall gotta ole boy here ya call Louie?"

"Yeah why"

"Well this here call is fo him."

Mai motioned to Louie to join her at the bar.

"This gentleman says he has a phone call for you."

Mr. Cartwright gave the phone to Louie.

"Hello."

"Louie it's me Sherman. The guy sitting at the bar is Angie's attorney. His name is Oliver Cartwright. He's good people! My dad brought him in to represent Angie and me. He may want to talk to the three of you."

"Ok, thanks Sherman."

CLICK.

Louie gave the phone back and called Carman over to join him and Mai.

"I just finished talking to Sherman. Ladies this is Oliver Cartwright. He's an attorney representing Angie and Sherman both. He's on our side."

"Well how yall doin?"

"Hi, I'm Louie, this is Mai and this is..."

"Oh I know who this lovely lil ole flower is! She's that lil ole philly yall call Carman."

"What did you call me?"

"Oh I'm sorry darlin, I didn't mean to rain on yo bonnet. That ole boy Sherman told me you was a wild flower."

Both Louie and Mai busted into laughter. Carman then shook his hand.

"Welcome to the City Block. How can we help you Mr. Cartwright?"

"Well fo starters, I want yall to know that I sat a spell wit Miss Angie today."

"You did, how is she?"

"She's doin just fine! That pretty lil ole butterfly is just lying in the sun, getting some rest. Na don't yall worry none, we gon get that lil ole philly outta this here mess. Carman darlin, ya mind saddling up right here next to me?"

"What?"

Louie started laughing.

"For crying out loud Carman, take a seat!"

"Oh, ok."

"Na I hear that you and Miss Angie is like two peas in a pod."

"Well Mr. Cartwright, she's like a sister to me. I've known her for years, and she wouldn't hurt a flea!"

"Have yall ever known her to have some ole cowboy ridin around in her stable?"

"Do you mean a boyfriend sir?"

"Yes'm."

"No, she's kind of shy. I think that she's waiting for Mr. Right."

"I find it hard to believe that out of all the cowboys that hitch up at this here saloon, that they ain't takin a likin to her."

"Well Mr. Cartwright, I think that...

Louie interrupted her.

"Carman, don't go there!"

"Don't Carman me Louie!"

"Whoa whoa, slow down darlin! What's itching yo hide?"

"For years now I've always thought that her and Sherman should be together."

"Na why is that darlin?"

"I don't know, it's weird, it's like there's some kind of connection between them."

"Well that's might interesting! Mr. Louie, what do yall think about that?"

"I think that she's happy with her life."

"Na Miss Mai, I hear that yall the newest angel in this lil ole slice of heaven."

"Yes sir, but before you ask, I haven't had the pleasure of meeting Angie."

"Well tell me what ya think of Sherman."

She immediately blushed, but Mr. Cartwright didn't let on that he caught it.

"I think that he's a real standup guy. I can see why everyone here loves him."

While Mai focused on Mr. Cartwright, she didn't know that Carman noticed her blushing too. At that time Louie came over and got everyone's attention. With the remote control in his hand he pointed to the TV and turned up the volume. On the screen were Candee and ADA White. They were standing in front of the building that houses ADA White's office.

"Hi, I'm Candee Harris with the WLOK news crew. I'm standing here in front of the D.A.'s office to bring you an update on this week's high speed chase that's allegedly connected to the Lipstick Murders. Joining me is Assistant District Attorney Margret White. ADA White can you tell our viewers the latest?"

"Thank you Candee. Due to new developments in the D.A's office, we've determined that the alleged murder accomplice, Sherman Brothers, will have all charges against him dropped. After further investigation, the D.A's office has found that he was only trying to get a severely ill friend medical care before she expired."

"Are there any new developments regarding the Lipstick murders?"

"At this time I can't comment."

"Thank you Margret. Well folks, there you have it. Now we're going to swing over to a south suburban hospital where we believe that the alleged murder suspect, Angie Cruz is being treated."

Right away a picture of Mr. Cartwright coming out of the hospital appeared on the screen.

"Do you know who this man is? He's the famed Oliver Wendell Cartwright known all over the country for defending women. Rumor is that he had a private visit today with Miss Cruz. Stick around folks. This is going to be good! I'm Candee Harris with the WLOK news crew."

The trio all turned to Mr. Cartwright and gave him a high five for clearing my name. He then raised his glass.

"One down, one to go!"

Mr. Cartwright was pleased with the guys at the Block. He felt as though they trusted him. He knew that Dad was waiting for him with baited breath, so he took off.

# THE CITY BLOCK: 59

Before Mr. Cartwright could ring the doorbell, Dad opened the door.

"Howdy Buddy, ain't you got something to do instead of waiting on an ole tin horn like me?"

"Come on in Oliver. How was your evening?"

"Well them folks pour a mean ole glass of scotch and water! You shoulda came wit me!"

"Yeah, I can just imagine!"

"Carl buddy, we gotta find a way to get them bugs outta yo bonnet!"

"Ah just come on in the kitchen! I'm having a cup of coffee and some pie."

"Na ya talkin cowboy!"

"So how did it go Oliver?"

"Well that bunch down there show did make me home sick for my family! I really gotta kick outta that lil ole philly they call Carman."

"Yeah I hear she's a real fire cracker."

"I'll tell ya one thang. Those folks down there sho do think the world of yo boy!"

"Yeah he has a way with people."

"If I was ta put any one of that bunch on the stand, I'd have the judge cryin like a one leg cowboy in a onion field!"

"So what did you find out?"

"Did yall know that lil ole reporter gal, that Lt. fella, and yo boy done been meeting at the City Street?"

"No I didn't."

"That ole boy Louie done recorded it all on his camera. Hell, I got a copy on one them disc in my bag."

"Well I'll be damn!"

"That ole gun slinger Lopez is gone be pulling thorns outta his hide long enough to spike down a tent!"

"So what's next?"

"Well tomorrow morning we gone put them boys of yours to work. It's bout time fo them ole boys to saddle up and shake the dust off they hide!"

"Yeah I couldn't agree more. Why don't we, how do you say, get some shut eye?"

Before Dad went to sleep he gave me a call to get the directions to Tiny's place. He wanted to meet at 9:00am. I couldn't help but ask what brought this on.

"Well it seems that Oliver has taken a liking to Tiny."

I started laughing.

"Don't laugh son! Good night."

CLICK.

The following morning we all met at the entrance of the Café. Jerri the waitress greeted us and showed us to a large family size booth. Between the five us we must've ordered one of everything on the menu. Mr. Cartwright got right down to business.

"Na boys I had a talk wit ya daddy last night, and we decided that it's bout time we get yall boys saddled up. Na Sherman we gone start wit you. I'm show yo daddy is gone be against this, cause it's dangerous."

"What do you need sir?"

"Well I need ya to charm copies of the murder scene news coverage from that lil ole reporter friend of yalls"

I looked at Dad and he just shook his head.

"Just do it son, but please be careful!"

"Na junior, I hope ya don't mind me callin ya junior?"

"No sir, that's fine."

"Well son, in this here fine city, don't yall have them ole temporary hiring services?"

"Yes sir we do."

"Well we gone need us some lil ole phillies just about Angie's height and weight. Na after yall find these flowers, we just gone put em' on call. Na Mr. Rex."

"Yes sir."

"I understand that yall got one of them ole 24 hour restaurants where Miss Angie parked her car on the day in question. I want ya ta take a look outside and see if they got one of them ole cameras mounted on the building. If so son, I want ya to go inside and make them folks an offer they can't refuse. Get any footage they got from that day. Talk to some of them teenagers they got workin in there. See if they know that ole security guard that claim he done seen everything, and find out if he wears glasses."

"Yes sir."

Dad then spoke up.

"What do you need from me?"

"Carl old buddy, you just keep that ole check book of yours warmed up!"

"Yeah it figures!"

Just as we were about to wine things up, a car slammed on the breaks right outside our window. The driver jumped out and came running inside. He held a clipboard in his hand as he was greeted by Jerri. We could hear him say the name Cartwright. That's when Mr. Cartwright stood up.

"Yall lookin fo lil ole me?"

"Oliver Wendell Cartwright?"

"That's me alright!"

"Can you sign right here please"

He was given an envelope which he opened and read.

"Well we done got us a lil ole invite from ADA White."

What did she say, asked Dad?

"It seems that Miss Angie done been charged wit four counts of Premeditated Murder and one count of Attempted Murder."

That's when I sparked up.

"What do you mean one count of Attempted Murder?"

"It looks like that ole boy down at the movie house is still alive."

The news was a major shock. This guy could be the mother of all witnesses!

"Na fellas, don't yall go sellin the farm just yet! Let's just let Miss White say her piece. Hell, all she's got is that Lt. fella, and he ain't got no mo chance than a hog in a butcher shop! If that ole movie house boy could talk, that pretty lil ole reporter gal would have her microphone so far down his throat it would be sticking outta his hide!"

Rex and Carlton didn't have a word to say. They both looked like the cat that swallowed the canary! It was obvious to me that Dad hadn't brought Mr. Cartwright up to speed about their connection to the victims, and it would be a cold day in hell before I said anything!

Like they say, when it rains, it pours! My cell phone vibrated and I held it under the table to look at it. It was a text from Nurse Linda. Angie had taken a turn for the worse, but she was hanging in there.

"Damn it!"

Everyone looked at me. I didn't realize that I spoke out loud. Dad saw my phone in my hand.

"Sherman what the hell is going on, and who are you talking to?"

"I'm sorry Dad, but I just got a text from Nurse Linda. Angie has taken a turn for the worse, but she's hanging in there."

"Na son, do yall think that I need to talk to this lil ole nurse?"

"Well it's possible that she could explain to the jury how difficult it would be for Angie to commit these murders."

Mr. Cartwright then turned and looked at Dad.

"Carlton what do you think?"

"Well she's been here since the beginning. In fact she engineered the blood drive for Angie's bone marrow transplant."

While sitting there Mr. Cartwright noticed that Rex and Carl were rather quiet.

"Yall boys done been quieter than a church mouse on Sunday morning! There ain't nothing we need to chew on is it?"

No sir answered Rex.

"Well why don't yall boys take off. Me and yo daddy gone sit a spell. Sherman I wanta see that lil ole nurse, and don't yall make this ole thin horn wait too long."

"Yes sir."

The three of us took off and left the two of them alone to talk. The ride back home in Carl's car was extremely quiet. I knew that Carl and Rex were being haunted. I also knew that Mr. Cartwright is sharp as a tack, and there was a good chance that he smelled a rat, possibly two rats.

# THE CITY BLOCK: 60

When I got home I was faced with the requests that Mr. Cartwright had made of me.. I had to contact two people that I really wanted to avoid. I decided to send Nurse Linda a text first.

"Hi Linda, thanks for the update on Angie. Forgive me for dragging you into this, but Angie's attorney would like to meet and talk to you."

Ten minutes later she texted me back, and I was surprised at her response.

"Let's meet at 7:00pm. You know where."

That went smoothly, but I didn't expect the same from Candee. Before calling her I sent Dad a text to pass the word to Mr. Cartwright about the 7:00pm meeting. I then took a deep breath and called Candee.

"Hi Candee, it's me, and I need another favor."

"Well, if it's not Speed Racer himself!"

"Please Candee, not now!"

"You know Sherman you've been asking for a lot of favors lately, and I always play nice. The lease you could do is show a girl a good time, if you know what I mean!"

"Candee we need to talk, but not on the phone. Why don't we meet at the harbor later?"

"Sherman I don't have time right now! How about 10:00am tomorrow?"

"That'll be fine."

"Should I wear panties?"

"Goodbye Candee!"

CLICK.

After that nerve wrecking conversation I decided to take a walk. As I walked through the community I noticed two kids on either side of the street passing out flyers. I wondered what they were all about. I kept walking until I came across one of the flyers posted in the window of a shoe repair shop. I was shocked at what I was reading. Someone was organizing a protest rally in support of Angie.

"Oh my God!"

The rally was scheduled for 8:00am on the morning of Angie's hearing in front of the court building down town. On the bottom of the flyer was bold letters.

FREE ANGIE CURE THE SICK! Below that it read: LIPSTICK DIPSTICK, COPS GET A CLUE! LIPSTCK DIPSTICK COPS GET A CLUE!

Just about then one of the kids came up to me.

"Here you are Mister."

It was clear to me that this was going to be a far bigger media circus than I've ever dreamed of. I took a seat on a nearby bench and gave Dad a call. This time a text wouldn't do!

"Hello son. Please tell me that you have some good news!"

I could tell that he had been dragged through the wringer by Mr. Cartwright.

"I'm sorry Dad, but it's not good."

"Ok son let me have it."

"Dad I was just out for a walk and came across some flyers that are being posted in the community."

"What kind of damn flyers?"

"Dad there's a protest rally being organized in support of Angie."

"Ah Jesus, that's just what we need! It's bad enough to have the media covering our every move, but now the whole freaking city is going to be camping out!"

"I'm sorry Dad!"

"Ok son, I'll talk to you later."

CLICK.

I continued my walk until I came across a small appliance shop that had a TV in the window. I had to do a double take when I saw myself on the expressway handcuffed and bent over the trunk of my car. I couldn't belief it, but there I was in all my glory! It was then that I decided to take my ass home and wait to hear from Linda and Mr. Cartwright.

By time 6:45pm rolled around I had gotten bored with waiting, so I took off for the Block. To my surprise both Linda and Mr. Cartwright were already there. Linda sat at a table, and Mr. Cartwright was at the bar. They both caught my eye when I walked in. I motioned for Mr. Cartwright to hold on a minute.

I went and sat across the table from Linda. I had forgotten how in-credibly hot she was. For a few moments neither of us said a word. We just sat there looking at each other. This was exactly what I was afraid of. Finally she broke the silence.

"How is my little speed demon buddy?"

I just dropped my head and she reached over and grabbed my hand.

"I'm sorry!"

"This is hard for me, so why don't we get down to business."

Still silly as ever, she mocked me using a deep male voice.

"Ok Mr. Brothers!"

"Will you stop it?"

"Loosen up some Sherman! It wouldn't kill you if we shared a smile!"

"Are you ready to meet Mr. Cartwright?"

"I guess that I am. The truth is I'm a little nervous."

"Trust me you're going to love em! In fact he's going to sweep you off your feet!"

"Not if he's the guy that they showed in front of the hospital on the news!"

I waved at Mr. Cartwright and motioned for him to join us at the table. When he reached us I stood up because I really wanted to leave them alone to talk.

"Mr. Cartwright this is Nurse Linda."

He immediately grabbed her hand, bowed and kissed it.

"Darlin I must say that you're as lovely as a honeysuckle in full bloom! Mr. Sherman I had no idea yall had such precious creatures in this here fine city! Ma'am it would be my absolute pleasure to join ya."

"Please Mr. Cartwright, have a seat, I'm going to leave you two alone. If you need me, I'll be sitting at the bar."

When I turned to walk away it dawned on me that Mai had been looking straight down the throats of both Linda and me. I wondered what that was all about, but I took a seat at the bar anyway.

"Hi Mai, how are things going?

I spun around on my stool to see if anyone else had noticed Mai's reaction to Linda and me. The first person that I saw was Carman. Great! She motioned for me to follow her into the office.

"What's going on Carman?"

"I know that you're not going to belief this because I'm always on your back."

"Now what did I do?"

"Mai has a major crush on you!"

"Carman you know I don't need this right now!"

"The other day when Mr. Cartwright was interviewing us, she damn near had us all in tears talking about you!"

"So what am I suppose to do?"

"Sherman, Linda isn't a ten, she's freaking twelve, and the two of you were just sitting over there looking at each other all goofy and stuff! You need to nip this in bud!"

Carman took off and I walked behind her to find Mai had been replaced at the bar by Louie. I then looked around to see that Linda and Mr. Cartwright had been joined at the table by Mai herself. Not only that, but he had them both laughing like two drunken sailors! I couldn't belief my damn eyes! It was then that Carman walked over to me.

"How in the hell do you always manage to land on your damn feet?"

I just looked at her and smiled. I don't know what Mr. Cartwright said or did, but I learned years ago not to look a gift horse in the mouth! I decided to take off and get the details from Mr. Cartwright tomorrow.

When I got home I threw a bag of popcorn in the microwave and turned on the TV. I found a classic black and white movie and stretched out on the sofa. This was the most relaxed I've been in the last few days. About an hour into the movie I was thinking that I deserved these moments. It wasn't long before I heard a annoying familiar sound.

DING DONG!

"Ah hell, please don't be Candee!"

I pressed the button on the intercom and asked who it was.

"Are you going to buzz me up, or am I going to stand here all night?"

I don't know why, but it was Linda. I buzzed her up, opened my door, and stretched back out on the sofa. She walked in and kicked off her shoes.

She then pushed my feet out of her way and sat down. But that wasn't good enough! She had the nerve to pick up my bowl of popcorn and put her feet up on the cocktail table. I couldn't belief my damn eyes! She began eating my popcorn.

"So what are we watching?"

At first I just looked at her like she had lost her mind.

"This is Twelve Angry Men."

"That sounds good! Do you know what this is?"

"What?"

"This is your punishment."

"What, punishment for what?"

"This is for misleading Mai."

"You don't even know Mai!"

"We're going to need more popcorn Sherman."

"I swear when this is all over, I'm never going to speak to that crazy ass Carman or you ever again!"

"Sherman."

"Yes Linda."

"Do you remember the last time we made love?"

"What?"

"Do you?"

"Yes."

"Do you remember the time before that?"

"Yes Linda I do!"

"Good, I've got to go now!"

She then got up to leave.

"You know what? You need to stay the hell away from that damn Car-man!"

The two of them ruined my damn night, but I guess that's what their plan was! Never in my wildest dreams, that I think that the two of them would join forces. On second thought it does make sense, because in my book, they're both nuts! The only fear that I have now is that they become running buddies. I hope the world is ready!

# THE CITY BLOCK: 61

My main priority this morning is to meet with nut case number three, Candee! Today will be the first time I've driven my car since my arrest. Hopefully things have died down enough that I won't stick out like a sore thumb. As I drove along the only looks that I got appeared to be from car freaks, which was normal.

I pulled into the parking lot of the harbor and a red Porsche came zipping in beside me like a bat out of hell! That's it I'm convinced they've all lost their damn minds! I guess it won't be long before they all start hanging out together at the Block just to screw with my head!

"Good morning Mr. Brothers. Why don't we take a walk?"

"Ok, that's cool."

"I thought that we might take a spin on that boat."

"There's no time for that right now."

"Well I guess it's a good thing that I wore my panties!"

We both got out of our cars and she stopped to look at me.

"What is it?"

"What is what?"

"You got me out of bed instead of into bed! What's the favor?"

"I know how this is going to sound, but I need copies of the footage that you guys shot at the murder scenes."

"I know that you didn't just ask me what I thought you did!"

"It would be a major help to me, and I promise never to ask you for another favor!"

"Sherman I shot that stuff, but you know that I don't have the rights to it! You're asking me to jeopardize my career by stealing from the network!"

"Candee I know the risk you'd be taking, but I also that you could easily do it because you're working the case anyway. No one at the studio will know the difference. I'm begging you please!"

"Excuse me, but did I just hear Sherman Brothers say please?"

"Yes I said please."

"Ok, this is what you're going to do!"

"Oh God!"

"You're going to spend the night at my place."

"What?"

"Don't interrupt me! There will not be any sex, but I promise you that I'm going to make you climb the walls all night long, and I mean all night long! That's the deal! You can take it, or you can walk away empty-handed!"

Before saying anything I paced back and forth a bit. I then stopped and stuck my hand out to shake on it.

"You've got a deal, but you promise to keep your panties on?"

"I'm not promising that! So where do you want to meet so I can give you the disc?"

"I'll make it easy for you and meet you at the studio."

"I'll give you a call when it's ready. By the way, cheer up it's going to be fun!"

She then got in her Porsche and brunt rubber leaving the harbor. I stood there wondering who had the hardest punch, her or Lt. Asshole! I sure hope that Mr. Cartwright gets what he's looking for from the footage.

Across town at the D.A.'s office, the Silver Fox and Mr. Cartwright sat waiting in a briefing room for A.D.A. White. Mr. Cartwright looked at his watch.

"That ole gal's runnin late!"

Just about then a legal assistant entered the room and handed him an envelope. He opened it and read it.

"Na ain't that something! Look's like we gone have this here lil ole meeting in the judge's chambers! That ain't the only rooster in the hen house either."

"What else is it?"

"The presiding judge is none other than the honorable Phillip T. Evans."

"Do you know him?"

"Well he ain't ready to take me to the big dance, if that's what ya mean!"

"Yeah well, let me tell you something about your honor. He holds the record in this state for handing out the most life sentences. Not only that, but rumor is that he's being groomed to run for governor, and what he does today adds up to votes tomorrow. Let's face it Oliver, everybody in this city wants to see someone fry for these murders. As far as the judge is concerned, if all he has to do is fry some bastard, you can damn bet he's going to do it!"

"Well I can see ya point, but I gotta tell ya, they ain't nothing worse than a politician serving on the bench! All we can do naw is pull up our boots and go sit a spell wit that ole boy."

In the court building they were escorted to the judge's chambers. A.D.A. White was already there.

"Why good morning Ma'am, it sho is a beautiful day in this here city."

"Mr. Cartwright I prefer that you address me as A.D.A. White."

"Yes Ma'am."

Just as they were sitting down the judge walked in.

"Good morning A.D.A. White."

"Good morning Judge."

"Oliver Wendell Cartwright. You have no idea of how moved I am to see you again!"

"Well I must say that it's mighty fine to see yo honor again too!"

A.D.A. White just shook her head.

"Let's get down to business people. I have a lot on my plate this morning."

"Well Ma'am I do belief that ladies go first."

"Judge we have the state versus one Angie Cruz."

"What's the charge?"

"Four counts of Premeditated Murder, and one count of Attempted Murder."

"Na hold naw! Yall done let the horse out ta barn! Four counts Premeditated! Yo honor!"

"That's right, and it should be five!"

"Ok that's enough! You both can save it for the trial! What's the status on the attempted murder victim?"

"He's been left in a vegetative state, and his breathing is currently being supported by machines."

"Ok that's enough. Today is Wednesday. The hearing will be held one week from today at 9:00am. Good day people."

The judge got up and left and A.D.A. White gave Mr. Cartwright one of the nastiest looks he's ever seen, and then walked out.

"Na that ole gal got a bee in her bonnet that just won't quit!"

"Come on Oliver let's get the hell out of here!"

"Yeah I guess we better be getting our posse together."

As they were leaving the building, the Silver Fox could see the wheels in Mr. Cartwright's head turning.

"What's on your mind buddy?"

"Well I been tryin to turn over every bale of hay in the barn to sho we ain't missing nothing, and well, I think we gone have ta send one of yo boys on a mission. Don't yall have them ole drug rehab centers here?"

"I don't know, you need to talk to the boys. Oliver I've been meaning to tell you that I got a call from Sherman yesterday."

"What did that ole boy have ta say?"

"It appears that someone is organizing a protest rally in support of Angie. Flyers are being passed out in the community. I thought that he would've told you at the bar."

"Well he left the barn door open on that one! I'll say one thang doe, that lil ole Nurse Linda can make a dead cowboy ride a bull!"

"Was she informative?"

"I think that she's gone be downright handy. You know them ole protest rallies can work fo ya, or against ya. We don't need no help pissing Miss White off!"

On their way home Dad contacted all of us and requested our presence at the firm this afternoon. When the time came Mr. Cartwright opened the meeting on a sad note.

"Boys I have something I wanta say to yall. I know that I done been all gung ho bout cleaning this mess up and clearing that lil ole gal's name. I need yall to know that murder is murder, and I don't like it! Na as yall know, Miss Angie done got herself one count of Attempted Murder. Reason is that ole boy done been left in what they call a vegetative state. As of right na his life is sustained by machines. Na I don't know ha yall feel, but I reckon that's a damn sight worse than death! Anyhow, I just wanted to say my lil ole piece on that. Na junior, was ya able to round up them Phillies like I asked ya?"

"Yes sir, they're ready and waiting."

"Na Mr. Sherman. Did ya get that lil ole reporter gal to help ya out?"

"Yes sir, I'll get copies of the footage later today."

"Good, we gone need you and junior to get together and make some still photos offa that footage. Na junior, them Phillies ya done got is gone have to look like everyone of them so called murderers on that footage. You can take em on a shopping spree, I mean outfits, hair color, accessories, and every thang! Ya know boys, there's a demon that's been sticking me in my hide wit that ole fork of his! It's done dawned on me that we's about a flea's ass away from going to trial wit nothing! I done reached the conclusion that all we got is the A.D.A.'s evidence. So na that that ole gal done did all the work, we gone use it against her. We gon start out wit them ole Phillies that junior done rounded up. Na yall get the picture?"

We all got a smile on our face and Dad spoke up.

"Oliver you're a piece of work!"

"Rex ole buddy, how did it go down at that ole restaurant?"

"I struck out because they had dumped the footage, but I had better luck across street at the theatre. I talked to a kid working at the ticket window. The security guard in question, a Mr. Charles Lancer, does indeed wear corrective lens."

"Why ain't that nice! This just keeps getting better and better! Yall boys done did a fine job. Na there's just one mo thang we gone need befo we can fry this kettle of fish. I was talkin to yall daddy, and he say there might be one of them ole rehab centers around somewhere. What we gone need is a expert witness that can say how easy it is fo any ole cowboy to get one of them ole needles."

That's when Rex spoke up.

"That shouldn't be too hard to do. I think that an Aids Prevention Center would be easier. They've been known to give out fresh sterilized needles to addicts to help prevent the spread of AIDS in the community."

"Why hell, get on it! Find us one of them ole administrative boys and cut his ass a check, cause we gone need em!"
After the meeting we all went our separate ways.

# THE CITY BLOCK: 62

At home at had to take a quote from Mr. Cartwright, and pull my boot straps up and face the enviable by meeting with Candee. It was time for me to take one for the team. I got in my car and headed for the WLOK studios. I parked right outside the guard's booth and waited for Candee to come out. It wasn't long before she stepped out of the building wearing her cat eye shades and a shit eating grin. She walked up to my car door with a disc in her hand.

"Here's your footage Mr. Brothers."

"Thank you Candee, I really appreciate it."

"Sure you do! By the way, you should get as much rest as you can. I get the feeling that you're going to need it!"

"Candee you could have any guy in the city. I'm sure that some would kill to be with you!"

"Yeah, but they're no fun! Just look at it as a scavenger hunt that I designed."

With that she blew me a kiss.

"Bye bye Sherman!"

She went back inside and I took off. Back at home I thought that I'd take a shot at the still photos myself. I have a photograph program in my lap top that I've never used before. Sitting at my kitchen table I had my lap top, printer and a cup of coffee. After all the bells and whistles were activated, I slipped the disc in.

A few clicks of my wireless mouse and bang, the footage began to roll. The murder scenes ran back to back. I could start and stop them, but I couldn't freeze a single frame. I knew that the program I was using was capable, but I was stuck in a world of operator error! As much as I hated to admit it, this seemed like a good time to read the program manual.

After reading and rereading, I stumbled across just what I needed. A few simple key strokes and I had mastered it. Once I found the frames that I wanted, I took advantage of the program's offer to save it to my hard drive. It took me quite a while, but I managed to play around with the brightness and contrast. I ended up with full body shots as well as portraits. I saved them all to one fresh disc and printed out a set for Carlton. My mission was accomplished. I now only hoped that everyone else was having success.

With time on my hands, I decided to take a nap. I stretched out for about two hours or so. When I woke up I decided to give Carlton a call. I figured that this would be good news sense he has his hands full with the models.

"Hey buddy I've got good news. The still photos are ready for you."

"Oh yeah, I guess that is good news."

"You sound kind of down buddy. What's going on?"

"It's the shopping spree with those models. Shopping ain't really my thing."

"Yeah I know how you feel dude." Let me tell you what you need to do."

"I'm all ears!"

"Get your girls together and go to the mall, any mall. Give them each a photo and say this is how I want you to look. Find yourself a restaurant in the mall, have a nice lunch, and a couple of glasses of wine. When the girls are done, call it a day!"

"Sherman brother, you're the man! We should've traded missions."

"I don't think so! You wouldn't believe what it's going to cost me for that footage."

"What do you have to do?"

"I may have to sleep with the Devil!"

"Would Abbigale approve?"

"Are you kidding me? Dude, Rex wouldn't even approve!"

"Well good luck! I'll talk to you later."

CLICK.

# THE CITY BLOCK: 63

When the Silver Fox and Mr. Cartwright entered the courtroom they could see that A.D.A. White and her team were already there. When they reached the front of the courtroom, Mr. Cartwright smiled and tipped his imaginary hat to A.D.A. White. In return she gave him a look that said go to hell! The two of them took a seat at a long table opposite of the A.D.A.

Nine a.m. had come and gone. Both the prosecution and the defense were repeatedly looking at the clock on the wall. A late arrival seems to be typical for a judge of this status. The tension in the courtroom was getting thicker by the moment. It was just about 9:15am when the judge entered through a side door.

The courtroom bailiff spoke out.

"All rise! The honorable Phillip T. Evans now presiding."

Every one rose and sat back down after the judge.

"This hearing is now is session."

"Good morning everyone."

Mr. Cartwright naturally was the first to speak up.

"Hi yall doin this morning yo honor?"

The judge just looked at him and rolled his eyes.

"Ok people, let's get this over with. The documents before me indicate that we have the State of Illinois verses one Angie Cruz. A.D.A. White, let's have it."

"Your honor, the state intents to prove that without a doubt the defendant is guilty of four counts of Premeditated Murder and one count of Attempted Murder."

"Na come on yo honor, she ain't nothing but a delicate lil ole flower!"

The judge slammed his gavel down.

"Save it for the trial. You'll get your turn!"

A.D.A. White then spoke up.

"Your honor, unfortunately the victim is unable to be here today because he's been left in a vegetative state. The state request that no bail be allowed."

"Ok ok, you've had your say!"

A.D.A. White reluctantly took a seat.

The judge took a deep breath and let it out. He then rested his face in both hands for a moment.

"Now Mr. Cartwright, it's your turn."

"Thank ya yo honor. Well fo starters, this lil ole flower's lying in bed wit mo tubes running in and outta her body than a French horn! There ain't no way on God's green earth that she's gone jump bail!"

"Mr. Cartwright, can you please move it along? How does your client plead?"

"Well yo honor, she's just a lil ole business gal frighten fo her life!"

"Please Mr. Cartwright!"

"Not guilty on all counts yo honor."

"Thank you Mr. Cartwright."

"Oh yall welcome!"

The judge just looked at him for a few moments.

"This is the biggest mess I've seen in my courtroom in a long time."

He then took another deep breath.

"As much as I hate to say this, I have to agree with Mr. Cartwright. Under the circumstances, I don't believe that Miss Cruz is going to be running anywhere soon. Therefore, bail or no bail what's the difference?"

Mr. Cartwright immediately smiled at A.D.A. White. Her eyes turned into daggers and pierced his heart simultaneously.

"Alright people, take out your calendars. For the sake of time, cost, and my own personal sanity, let's go for two weeks from today at 9:00am. Does anyone have a problem with that?"

"Well yo honor, if it don't ruffle A.D.A. White's feathers, it's just fine wit this ole boy!"

The judge put his face in his hands again. At the same time he said Jesus Christ!

A.D.A. White then spoke up.

"The state doesn't have a problem with it your honor."

"Thank you A.D.A. White. The court is adjourned."

The judge then slammed down his gavel and the bailiff said all rise. The judge then left the courtroom. A.D.A. White immediately made a beeline for Mr. Cartwright.

"You're a real bastard!"

"Na Ma'am, that ain't no way to treat a visitor in yo fine city. It's a beautiful day, why don't yall enjoy it!"

She then stormed out of the courtroom being followed by her team. In the courtroom alone now, the Silver Fox turns to Mr. Cartwright.

"Look, you've got to let up on that woman, and stop pushing the judge!"

"Na calm down Carlton, it's only the hearing. Hell, I was just havin a lil fun! Come on, let's get outta here. The drinks are on me!"

"Yeah well, it's about time!"

When they got outside A.D.A. White had a mob of reporters around her. Once the two of them were spotted, the mob immediately ran to them. One of the reporters wasted no time asking questions.

"Mr. Cartwright, is your client innocent?"

"Why of course she is! She's just a lil ole flower lying in the hospital fighting fo her life."

"A.D.A. White says the state has a good case."

"Well it seems to be that the burden of truth lies in ta lil ole delicate hands of the lovely Miss White."

"Mr. Cartwright is it true that you have a reputation for courtroom theatrics?"

"Na na yall, I'm just a good ole boy from Texas! Na I'd love to stay here and talk ta yall, but this here is a right fine city, and I wanta do some sightseeing."

All of the reporters started laughing as Mr. Cartwright and Dad made their way through the crowd to the waiting Towne Car. Once inside the car Mr. Cartwright made a comment.

"Mission one complete."

"What do you mean?"

"Come on Carl, don't go getting old on me! We done got them ole reporter boys eaten right outta our hands! It's just what we need."

"You think so?"

"Heck yeah! Look Carl ole buddy, it's far better ta have them ole boys on our farm, than the neighbors. Na we got us two weeks to line up our ducks. I say we go home and yall can open up that ole bottle of scotch ya been hiding from this old tin horn!"

# THE CITY BLOCK: 64

With all of the media coverage of the hearing yesterday, I made it a point to go out to my nearest news stand today. There it was, but not exactly what I expected.

On the front page were two large color photos. On the left was Frank Mallory lying in a hospital bed looking spaced out. On the right was Angie with an IV and tubes going into her body. Above the two photos was the caption, LIPSTICK DIPSTICK.

"Wow?"

On the second page were comments from the brief interviews outside the court building with A.D.A. White and Mr. Cartwright. There were additional pictures in black and white of the protesters with the riot geared cops in the background.

Not that it made a difference, but I found it interesting that Angie's door was guarded by a cop, and Frank Mallory was surrounded by his family. It wouldn't hurt to have Angie surrounded by her love ones. I put my head back together and headed back home. When I got there I received a message from Dad.

Due to the two week window before the trial, Mr. Cartwright decided to take a week and go home. He also suggested that we all take some time and not let the upcoming trial eat us up. Two weeks is a long time and Mr. Cartwright is lucky to be able to get away from the city for a while. I could go down town and get a room for a few days, but I'd still be surrounded by media coverage.

I even thought about taking a road trip, but didn't want to put the mileage on my car. In a desperate move I picked up my news paper and turned to the travel section. This was an absolute first for me. As soon as I opened it a scene on Bourbon Street in New Orleans caught my eye. They have history, night life, and good food. Not to mention I've never been there before. I was sold!

I grabbed my lap top and started banging away. It took a lot of work, but I landed at a hotel on Canal Street. The rates weren't the cheapest because of the location, but I went for it anyway. There was no point in booking a flight if I didn't have a room to stay at. Now that that was out of the way I started stroking away in search of reasonable air fare on short notice. After making all of my arrangements, I sent Dad a text informing him of my plans. I have an 11:00am flight tomorrow morning. I ordered a shuttle pick-up at my place for 8:00am. All I had to do was keep my nose clean for the rest of the day.

I popped open a beer and found myself watching reruns of the Antique Road Show. Aside from being in New Orleans, I couldn't get any further away than watching old geezers trying to flip junk they found in the attic. What the hell, it was entertaining, plus it was killing time. When the show ended I went to the kitchen and poured myself a shot of scotch.

After flipping from one channel to another I started getting drowsy. It was still early and I tried to fight it, but I lost. I woke up on the sofa just before midnight. I turned off the TV and headed to bed. 6:00am came a lot faster than I was expecting. When my alarm went off I had to get up moving fast.

I grabbed all of the essentials and put them in a bag. After jumping into the shower I got dressed. I then had a few minutes to catch my breath before the shuttle was due to show up. The ride to the airport was nice, mostly because I didn't have to do the driving. I only had one bag to check in, making my experience passing through security a breeze.

After locating my terminal, I stopped in a magazine shop. One magazine, one roll of breath mints, and I was almost ready. I needed to make one more stop, and that was the nearest cocktail lounge. I had about an hour and 15 minutes to kill before boarding. Between the people watching and the two cocktails that I had, the time went by quickly.

The boarding process began and I stood to one side and waited because I was in boarding group B. It looked as though the plane wouldn't be full, which was fine with me. When I got onboard I headed for the rear. I like to be 4 or 5 rolls from the end. That way it's a short walk to the john.

Once the big bird was in the air I ordered a cocktail and started reading my magazine. It wasn't long before I drifted off to sleep. About 20 minutes before landing I woke to the sound of an announcement telling passengers to return their seats to the upright position. During this time I couldn't help but notice a handsome Black couple sitting across the aisle from me. The woman was slender with big brown eyes. Her hair was in long cornrows. Her skin was a luscious cocoa color.

When she saw that I was taken by her, she smiled. I smiled back and quickly turned my head.

"Slow down cowboy! You haven't even touched ground yet, not to mention that she's with someone."

When we touched down I felt as though a burden had been lifted, at least for the next four days. Once inside the airport I was surrounded by the traditional sound of New Orleans jazz. The taxi ride to my hotel was interesting. Everything had an old and historical look. The hotel that I booked was fabulous. My room was on the 29th floor. I had a view of the mighty Mississippi River, and right down below me was Canal Street with trolley cars going in both directions. Now I feel like I've gone somewhere!

The humidity here is off the chain, and was I about to take my second shower of the day. After getting dressed I sat out for some of the great culinary pleasures that I've always heard about. Along the way I came across every kind of street entertainer or hustle that there was. After stuffing myself to a ridiculous point, I headed over to Bourbon Street where I was bombarded by both jazz and blues.

Outside of one club the doorman was working the crowd. I asked him about their lineup and told him that I'd catch him later. Not only did I need a nap after eating so much, but I was almost due for another shower. After taking my nap I woke up to darkness. When I looked outside my window I immediately noticed two things. The city had transformed into a different world, and the streets were a non-stop party!

I got dressed and headed out. A funny thing happened when I reached the hotel lobby. For a split second I made eye contact with someone directly across the hall in another elevator that was closing. It was that incredible woman from the airplane this morning.

"Whata ya know, it's a small world after all!"

On my way to the blues club that I saw earlier, I couldn't get her big brown eyes off of my mind. As I walked I bumped into two college girls that were drinking from tall green decorative plastic bottles.

"Excuse me ladies, but what is that that you're drinking?"

"Dude, this is a hurricane, you should try one!"

With that said one of them took two steps back and threw up. That's when I decided to let the hurricane blow by! As I approached the club the doorman saw me coming.

"My man, I knew you would be back! Come on in but be careful!"

"Why's that?"

"Because my man, women get the blues too!"

I just laughed and walked on in. I took a seat at a table and before I could get comfortable, a waitress was at my side. After placing my order I started checking the place out. It was definitely my kind of place, at least age wise. Over the bar was a 14 to 16 foot alligator wearing a New Orleans Saints football helmet. The band was already jamming, and I must say that they were hot.

My waitress returned with two drinks on her tray, which puzzled me a bit.

"Don't worry honey, we have two for one drinks."

As the night kept rolling, she kept bringing me cocktails. I could now see why the streets were a non-stop party! I enjoyed the rest of the band's set, and half way through their second set. It was then that I started walking back to my hotel room. On the desk in my room was a magazine that advertised different entertainment in the city, which was just what I needed. I figured that there's got to be more to in this city than eating and drinking. After ear marking a few pages in the magazine, I jumped in the sack.

Morning came and I was a little shocked at first. It took a moment for me to realize that I wasn't at home. I wasn't looking for anyone, and no one was looking for me. I loved it! Around 11:00am I finally got my butt in gear. The one thing that I wanted to do today was visit the local aquarium. According to the map in the magazine, it was in walking distance, but the map also showed the trolley route going the same way.

I figured that I'd take the trolley down to the river, hit the aquarium and see what happens next. It was nearly 1:00pm when I crossed the street to the trolley stop. While waiting I noticed that there was a totally different crowd on the street this time of day. The trolley car experience was kind of rickety, but cool. It made me feel like a tourist.

The Mississippi River was huge. I could see why they call it the Mighty Miss. The aquarium was right there, but I wanted to check out the river front a little. The river was bordered by a park. It kind of reminded me of home. It was the kind of place where you could read a book, or just collect your thoughts. After picking out a couple of points that I wanted to come back to, I headed for the aquarium.

Once inside I felt right at home. This is my kind of place. I could stay here all day. I've always been fascinated by underwater life. The aquarium wasn't really big, but they had done a lot with the area they have. In one section there was tanks that could be viewed from all sides.

I was checking out some jellyfish when I got a visual that that blew my mind! It was my mysterious friend from the elevator. When she saw that I had finally noticed her, she smiled. What could I do, I smiled back. She stepped around the tank to my side and once again I was taken by her beauty.

"Are you following me Mister?"

"I was going to ask you the same thing!"

"Hi, my name is India."

"A beautiful name for a beautiful lady! Oops!"

I quickly turned to look around.

"I'm sorry you're with your husband!"

"You mean the guy you saw me with on the plane?"

"Yeah."

"That was my agent."

"Oh my God, can we start over?"

"Sure, do you want me to go back to the other side of the tank?"

"And you have a sense of humor! My name is Sherman. Are you an actress?"

"No, I'm a model."

"I should've known!"

"It's just something to hold me over until I finish school."

"Let me guess, you're studying law."

"How did you know?"

"Well you look like you have the brains for it."

"My, you're full of compliments! So Mr. Sherman, what made you leave the windy city?"

"I just needed to get away for a while. What brings you here?"

"I'm doing a photo shut here."

"That sounds exciting! When is it, if you don't mind me asking?"

"It's tomorrow morning. Have you ever been to one?"

"No, I can't say that I have."

"Actually it's going to be right here at the river."

"Is that an invite?"

"Well I don't know. I'm not accustomed to inviting strange men into my world."

"I understand Miss India, but there's a silver lining in this cloud."

"Oh yeah, what's that?"

"We have the rest of the day to convert me from a stranger to a friend."

"Is that an invitation?"

 I bent my elbow and extended it to her.

"You're a handsome man Mr. Sherman, but if I take your arm, I may be sending you false signals."

"Well I guess that a girl can't be too careful. It was a pleasure meeting you. I'm sure that I'll be seeing your face again. Enjoy the rest of your day."

"You sure do scare easy Mr. Sherman!"

"The truth is that I believe that the future is brighter with someone that's naturally interested in me."

"So you're a cautious man."

"Well, if you do enough living you learn to be. I am a little confused though."

"Why is that?"

"You don't appear to be a woman starving for attention, but yet you invited me to your photo shot."

"You're right, but I've made some bad decisions in the past with men like you."

"What do you mean, men like me?"

"The kind that's good looking, intelligent and physically fit."

"We've been talking for a few minutes now. It would have far more pleasant if we were walking along the river."

Miss India stood surveying my eyes.

"Trust me, I don't bite! Let me put it this way. Remember the first time that you stepped into an agency, tying to get that first photo shut?"

"Oh God yes, my emotions were up and down the charts! Why do you ask?"

"That's how I feel right now. Instead of things happening naturally, I feel like I have to audition for you. Anyway, it's been an absolute pleasure, but I think that I should be going now."

The incredible smile on India's face turned into a blank look as I turned to walk away. Perhaps I was barking up the wrong tree to begin with. My recent history with women hasn't been good to say the least. I still want companionship, but not at any cost! I left the aquarium with a picture of India in my head.

# THE CITY BLOCK: 65

I made my way along the river and through the park. At the end of the park I came across a path that led across the trolley tracks. The other side led me back into town. I found a restaurant that had a dining area on the patio. It seemed like as good a place as any to have a late lunch. The host escorted me to a table. I asked him where I could wash my hands, and he directed me to the men's room.

On my return I saw the back of some woman's head sitting at my table. Not only that, but she was giving the waiter an order. Confused, I walked up behind her.

"Excuse me, but this is my table."

The woman turned around and shocked the hell outta of me! She was none other than Miss India!

"Like I said earlier, I've made some mistakes. Do you mind if I join you?"

I took a seat without saying a word.

"Can we start over? My name is India. I'm a model and a law student. Tomorrow morning I'm doing a photo shut, and I'd love to have you there."

"My name is Sherman, I'm a Private Investigator, and I've made my share of mistakes also. I love my career, but my personal life is a mess! I accept your invitation, but I can't make any promises about the future."

India stuck her hand out and we shook on it. After a great lunch and stimulating conversation, we sat out walking. We ended up riding the trolley throughout the entire route. I learned that India wasn't at all how she appeared on the outside. I hadn't had this much normal conversation with a woman in a long time. There were no games, no tricks, and no mind bending!

Finally we got off the trolley in front of the hotel. For a moment we just stood there looking at the hotel. We both turned to each other and started to speak at the same time.

"You go first."

"No. Sherman, you go first!"

"Ok, now what?"

She put her super soft hand on my face and I could smell her perfume.

"Sherman my dear, I know that it's still early, but I have to get my rest, or I'll look horrible in the morning."

"That's fine, business comes first. I have a two more days here, who knows?"

We laughed, held hands and crossed the street. Once inside the hotel we stopped like we had ran into a brick wall.

"Do you feel kind of strange?"

"Yes, and I'm glad that you asked first."

"I don't want to make a bad impression, but I don't recall ever parting with someone in the lobby of a hotel."

"Yeah, you took the words right out of my mouth! Let me make it easy for both of us. I had a great time and I'll see you in the morning. Sweet dreams!"

She gave me a short warm embrace.

"Thanks for a great day!"

She then turned and walked away.

The next morning I stepped out of the hotel to find another beautiful humid day. As I walked toward the river it dawned on me that India never gave me a time or location of the shut. Once I got to the park they were pretty easy to find. I saw large white umbrellas and all kinds of lighting equipment. Off to the side was a large tent. I imagine that it was being used for a dressing room, among other things.

After a while a little girl about seven years old stepped out of the tent. She wore a long dress with a floral print on it. She also held a floral arrangement of flowers in her arms. Following her was India wearing the same outfit. After being fussed over by makeup artist and hair stylist, the shutting began. The outfits and scenes changed throughout the morning. When it was over I managed to get India's attention and waved good bye. I imagined that after a long morning of work, she would need a break, so I took off walking.

Back at the hotel now, I decided to hang out in the lobby and just lounge around a bit. Not only was the lobby beautiful and had a bar, but there was lots of activity all around to keep me from getting bored. After an hour or so, I went up to my room where I noticed the red light blinking on the telephone. Someone had left me a message. To my delight, it was from India.

She thanked me for showing up this morning, and hoped that I wasn't bored. I hung up the phone only to see it still blinking. I pressed the button again, and it was her once more.

"Hi, it's me again. How about dinner? I'm in room 3312. We can go out, or order room service. Let me know. Bye!"

Wow, now that's what I call an invitation! The problem is that jumping into the sack early has proven to do me more harm than good. I'd love to lounge around with her eating good food half nude. It would be a lot easier if we just go out for dinner.

As I sat trying to make a decision, the phone rang again. It had to be her again.

"Hi Sherman, before you say anything, can you come to my room?"

"Sure, see ya in a couple of minutes."

This should be interesting. I was nervous, but I went anyway. India came to the door looking like the girl next door instead of a model. She wore a pair of shorts and a sweat shirt that had the sleeves cut off.

"Hi Sherman, please come in."

She got right to the point.

"About dinner…

"Yeah, I'm glad you brought that up."

"Please let me finish, this is hard for me. I can imagine what you thought when I suggested ordering room service here in my room. The problem is that I'm afraid to be alone with you. You've been nothing but a gentleman, but it's been a long time."

"You can relax India. I was worried also. I even made myself believe that we couldn't spend these hours together alone in your room."

"Why can't we Sherman?"

"Have you taken a good look at yourself?"

"Well it's not easy for me either!"

"So now what?"

"Come in, I've got to get this over with!"

With that she pulled me into her arms and gave me the biggest, sweetest, and softest kiss I've ever had! Every bell, whistle, and nerve ending in my body went off!

"Now do you think that we can do this?"

"After a kiss like that, I'd be crazy not to try!"

"Are you sure Sherman?"

"Yeah I guess, I mean what if…

"Stop right there! We'll worry about what if later. The first thing that I need you to do is take off that shirt. I've been dying to see you without it!"

I started taking off my shirt, but India couldn't wait, and started helping me. I noticed the large holes on her sweat shirt where the sleeves used to be, and I could see her breast.

"Don't you think that we're going about this the wrong way?"

She took a deep breath and let it out.

"Yeah you're right! What do you want for dinner?"

While waiting for room service we kept reasonable distance between us. After dinner things began to get a little crazy. The outcome was that the following morning India was alone in bed. It had been a tough night, but we managed to do the right thing. The rest of the day I spent trying to keep myself occupied. I knew that if I found myself alone with India again, the inevitable was going to happen. All I had to do was survive until my departure flight tomorrow morning.

I didn't know what the future held for us. Even though I may have been running away from the best thing that's ever happened to me, it's all been happening too fast. Even if I never see her again, she'll be on my mind for weeks to come. The funny thing was that I couldn't wait to get back to the misery at home.

I'm now sitting in the airport waiting for the boarding call. It's taking every fiber in my body not to call the hotel and ask for India's room. After about 30 minutes of waiting, a public announcement was made.

"Attention passenger Sherman Brothers. Please go to the nearest white courtesy phone."

It's always surprising to hear your name announced in a strange place, but I had no doubt of who was calling me. I picked up a phone that was mounted on a nearby column.

"Hello, this is Sherman Brothers."

"I'm sorry, but I had to hear your voice just one more time!"

"I needed my last day alone. I hope you understand."

"I was just hoping that I didn't disappoint you."

"No you didn't. In some ways I feel like a fool for not spending my last day with you."

"In that case, why don't you stay one more day?"

"We both know that one more day will lead to another day, and another."

"Well how about this? Why don't I come to Chicago after I'm done here?"

"Do you mind if I think about it on the plane, and give you a call when I get home?"

"I don't want to push you away, so no, I don't mind."

"I don't know what to say right now, so I'm going to hang up."

CLICK.

# THE CITY BLOCK: 66

My flight back home was restless to say the least. When I did get home I had to check in with my people. First up was Dad. I dialed him up and he sounded rather weary.

"Hey Dad, I'm back home."

"Hi son, how was your trip?"

"Dad it was great! I had no idea of how much I needed it."

"Yeah I can just imagine. Well things are still quiet around here, with the exception of the media. It's good to have you back son."

"Ok Dad, I'll talk to you later."

CLICK.

Even though I had promised to call India when I got home, I still hadn't made a decision about her visiting me. Putting her off, I decided to call the City Block first.

"City Block, this is Louie speaking."

"Hey Louie, it's me Sherman."

"Sherman, where the hell have you been? We've been going crazy down here!"

"I went to New Orleans."

"New Orleans? What the hell drew down there?"

"The truth is I just needed to get away."

In the back ground Carman overheard Louie say my name and New

Orleans. She then took the phone away from Louie.

"What the hell were you doing in New Orleans? You didn't ask anyone if you could go there!"

"If you must know, I was taken care of business missy!"

"Yeah I'd bet! I'm sure that it was monkey business!"

"I've got to go, I've got things to do!"

"Yeah I can just imagine player!"

"Good bye Carman!"

CLICK.

For about an hour I questioned myself and picked myself apart. I looked at every possibility of what could go wrong, and what could be so right. In the end I told myself that I had to find out. I took a deep breath and dialed India's number.

"Hello Mr. Brothers, how was your flight home."

"It was ok."

"At the risk of pushing my luck, I have to say that I miss you."

"Well I've been thinking that I don't want to spend the rest of my life wondering who's holding you in their arms."

"I've been thinking about going to visit my parents in New Jersey. It would be easy for me to stop in Chicago for a couple of days on my way."

"Would you be offended if I booked a room downtown? It's not that I'm ashamed of you or anything, but I think it's a little soon for you to meet my people."

"I understand, and I'm so excited that I'm going to start packing a bag right now!"

"Why don't you book your flight, and I'll book a room for tomorrow afternoon."

"Ok Sherman, I can't wait to see you!"

CLICK.

My mind shifted to the thought of driving out to O'hare Airport. Just the fact that I'm thinking about it at a time like this tells you how much I hate it. I had the rest the day to kill and my choices of things to do were slim. I could bring myself up to date on the case by use of the media, which I'm sure that nothing's changed. I could pay my debt to Candee, which is totally out of the question right now, or I could hang out at the Block, which meant I'd get grilled about my trip by the Wicket Witch of Hyde Park! None of my choices were very encouraging right now. However I could use a bite to eat. There was only one person that could put a smile on my face without judging my character, and that's the big man himself, Tiny.

It was a beautiful day in the Windy City, and for some reason I was really appreciating be here. It wasn't at all the feeling I had before taking my trip. While walking over to the Café, I thought about the two college girls that I ran into on Bourbon Street drinking the Hurricanes and laughed to myself. Even though I'm facing another intriguing challenge in my life, I did have some moments in New Orleans that weren't of the sexual nature. I'd definitely go back again.

When I stepped into the Café I was greeted by Jerri, and it was really nice because she made me feel right at home. I took a seat in my usual booth and the big man came out to say hello.

"Tiny my man, how's the grill treating you?"

"What can I say Sherman? We have a love hate relationship! I love burning it, but I hate cleaning it!"

All I could do was laugh. I noticed that Tiny was looking outside the window, and following something going by. I turned around to look and saw what had caught his eye. On the side of a passing bus was a lovely model advertising some cologne.

"Are you alright big man?"

"Yes indeed, but I could sure be better!"

"You like the girl on the side of that bus?"

"Are you kidding me brother?"

"How would you like to meet her?"

"No, you're kidding me right?"

"I'm serious."

"You know Sherman there hasn't been a dull moment since I met you!"

"I would take that as a complement, but they haven't all been good."

"Well to answer your question, of course I want to meet her!"

"I'll see if I can make that happen."

Lunch was great as usual. When I left I just bumped around the neighborhood. It occurred to me how much I was taking for granite the ability to walk around freely without the aid of a cane. My rips were back to normal and the memory of nearly being killed when I was hit was just about gone forever. There was a possibility that when the case is finally over, India might change my life in ways that I've never imagined. At least that's what I'd like to believe.

I found myself wondering over to the lake front. I was hoping to run into Rebecca and Barney. However it wasn't in the cards for me today. Once again I was walking the tight rope without a net. You would think that through all of the lessons taught to me by Maria, Linda, and Candee, I'd be used to it.

After taking in the beauty of the down town skyline, I found myself a bench and watched the sun set. It took a while to reach the horizon, but when it did, it dropped out of sight in seconds. It was my cue to start walking home. It's funny how we think of ourselves so much, as if the world revolved around us. Here I was dwelling about the effects that a woman may have on my future, while Carlton and Rex very well may be at home dwelling on the effects that they put on a young innocent girl.

If misery should walk into my life, I can take a powder on it and walk away, but for Carlton and Rex, misery will be their friend for the rest of their lives. They'll never be able to fail and start over again like I can. Because I love them, I pray for the safety of their lives, but the choice that they made as young men will always reveal an ugly scare that will never go away.

Back at home I sat out on my balcony and watched the neighborhood settle into night time. After getting tired of sitting up, I went to my room, turned on the TV and climbed into bed. It seemed like only moments had passed when I heard the annoying sound of my alarm clock radio going off. It's never fun being summoned out of bed by an electronic device that you've actually paid money for, but I was a little bit excited. Being one hundred percent all American male, I did have a vision of India's big brown eyes and sleeveless sweat shirt exposed breast on my mind. I may have fears about moving forward, but I'm not crazy!

After getting my act together, I hit the expressway thinking positive. As I drove along the highway I wondered if India and I could exist in separate worlds and still feel the same about each other. Her living in Atlanta and traveling the world doing photo shuts, and me living in Chicago seeking out the worse human beings that nature ever gave life to. It occurred to me that there are many topics that we need to discuss. As much as I hate having meaningful conversation with a woman, now was the time to do it. Will it actually happen, that remains to be seen.

Seeing air traffic increase overhead let me know that I was getting close to the airport. If I've timed this right, India should be waiting outside of the baggage area about ten minutes before I get there. I'm hoping that I don't have to do circles multiple times. I swear that everybody and their brother must've been picking someone up! When I finally got my chance to pull into the passenger pick-up lane, I could see her from a half block away.

When I got four car lengths away she saw me and lit up like a Christmas tree! I stopped right in front of her and she froze in her steps. She had a look of fear on her face. It was as if she feared for her life by coming near me.

"India come on, get in! What's wrong honey?"

That's when a traffic cop walked up to my window.

"Come on buddy, move it along!"

That's when it dawned on me. It was my car. She had seen the news broadcast of my arrest. I'm sure that she thought that I was some kind of maniac, and wondered what she had gotten herself into. I got out, went around, took her bag and opened the door. The whole time this cop was threatening to write me a ticket.

"India please honey, I can explain just get in!"

She was reluctant, but she got in, still with fear on her face.

"You're the guy that helped that woman that killed those poor men! I saw them handcuff you and throw you against this car. Oh God, what have I got myself into? Is that why you were in New Orleans? You were running from the police! So what are you going to do to me?"

"First of all you've got to calm down! Second of all, all I'm going to do is try to love you the rest of your life, but before I can do that, you're going to have to forget about that garbage you saw on TV!"

"How do I know you're not going to hurt me?"

"Do you want me to turn around and take you back to the airport?"

"That depends!"

"That depends on what?"

"Were you really going to try to love me the rest of my life?"

"I don't know. It seemed like the right thing to say at the moment."

"You better not hurt me!"

When she said that I couldn't hold back any longer, and started laughing my ass off!

"So now you're laughing at me!"

"Honey, obviously you've been living quite the sheltered life!"

"So what's that's supposed to mean?"

"India if I was running from the cops, I would've used my identification to buy a plane ticket, and I would've used it to book a room, and I damn sure would've come back to this city!"

"Well I want to know all about it, especially that woman, but first I want to take a shower!"

I couldn't help but start laughing all over again. That's when she punched me on my arm.

"Don't laugh at me! I could be a bad woman for all you know!"

"Are you saying that laughing isn't helping my case?"

"Just take me to the hotel Mr. Sherman!"

"Ye Ma'am!"

"I'm not old either!"

It wasn't long before we were on the expressway headed down town. I didn't tell India but I guess I'm a creature of habit, because without thinking I booked a room at the same hotel that I stayed at the night I met Maria. I hate to start a relationship with secrets, but this one I had to keep to myself.

India had calmed down considerably during the drive. She even laughed about her behavior herself. When we checked into the room I thought that she was going to jump my bones right away, but she headed for the shower. While she did that I opened a bottle of wine, undressed and put on a monogrammed hotel robe.

I poured two glasses of wine and waited for her. She stepped out the bathroom freshly wrapped in a towel. She then took both glasses from me and sat them down. She let her towel fall to the floor, untied my robe and wrapped her warm moist body around mine.

"Ok that's enough! Tell me about this woman and why you were with her!"

With that she climbed into bed and padded the spot beside her, indicating that she wanted me to join her. I told her the whole story about Angie's illness and both our relationships to the Lipstick Murders. It was her first introduction to what I do for a living.

"I can see that this woman Angie is dear to you, but you didn't say where you know her from."

"Oh that!"

"Yes, that!"

"You know, that's a funny story."

"Oh yeah, I'd bet it is! Tell me anyway!"

"Well, she's part of my extended family, and I should tell you that I'm a foster child."

"Oh Sherman I'm so sorry! Ok that's enough I'll feel sorry for you later. Go on."

"Like I was saying, when I'm not working I hang out at a little jazz bar called the City Block. I've known the owners for quite some time now. Angie is one of them. Over the years they've become family to me, and hopefully if things work out with us, they'll welcome you into the family."

"Is there anything else I should know about you?"

"Yeah, in the upcoming days you'll see the media portraying me and my family as horrible human beings."

"Why would they do that?"

"My dad's law firm is representing Angie, and a lot of people believe that she's guilty."

"Is that what you meant when you told me that you needed to get away for a while?"

"Bingo!"

"I bet that you weren't expecting me huh?"

"Isn't this where you start feeling sorry for me?"

"Yeah come here!"

That was when we threw caution out the window and made love for the first time. Throughout the day we stretched out the fibers of passion to the thinnest point. It was then that I realized that I was having a first time experience. All my adult life I had been having sex and now I was captivated by the sensual wrath of making love. I had crossed a threshold and promised myself that I'd never go back.

The clock was turning quickly as we lay together. Morning came and I thought it was going to take the Jaws of Life to pull us apart. At this point we were looking down the barrel of reality. The notion of trying to nurture two careers in two different cities was starting to set in. We had opened Pandora's Box!

# THE CITY BLOCK: 67

The days had gone by slowly, but it was now time for business as usual. Mr. Cartwright had returned to town and I'd soon learn that some decisions had been made. Even though the subject matter was nerve wrecking, it was still good to be back in the company of Dad and the guys. Every detail of this mess, from beginning to end was covered. Just as I had suspected, Dad did bring Mr. Cartwright up to date regarding Carlton and Rex's involvement. Due to that detail, it was decided that Dad wouldn't accompany Mr. Cartwright at the trial. It wasn't worth the risk of his name being connected to Carlton.

Dad's personal secretary was chosen to accompany Mr. Cartwright at the trial. He asked me to get an update on Angie status. His goal was to finish the trial before she was strong enough to be called to the stand. A.D.A. White hates him so much that she'd stop at nothing to rip Angie apart piece by piece! I sent Nurse Linda a text message. Moments later replied.

"She's holding her own, put not out of the woods yet."

The ball was now in the hands of Mr. Cartwright. Even though Dad had complete confidence in him, it was obvious that he hated sitting on the bench. I think it pissed him off even more knowing that he wasn't in the starting lineup because of Carlton and Rex. I get the feeling that when this is all over, if we land on our feet, Carl and Rex will be hating life for a long time!

The phone at the end of the table rang and Dad answered it knowing that it was his secretary.

"Ok, bring it in. Well gentlemen, it appears the D.A.'s office has sent us another envelope."

"Well ain't that nice! I thought that that ole philly was gone take fo ever!"

Dad opened it.

"It's the A.D.A.'s witness list. It reads as follows.

Lt. Ricardo Lopez – Lead Investigating Officer

Doctor Lewis Finkle – Forensic Specialist

Doctor Michael Conrad – Chief Medical Examiner

Charles Lancer – Theatre Security Guard

Note: Surveillance footage as well as still photos will be presented. We also reserve the right to call to the stand any family member of the victims that is willing."

"It sounds like to me that ole gal ain't got much."

"Yeah but this woman's meaner than a junkyard dog! Let's not under estimate her. Cases have been won without a bus load of witnesses. By the way, I'm sure that she's waiting to receive our list."

"Well we gon have ta round em up and get em to that ole gal by morning. Mostly what I want ta do is use Miss White's witnesses ta get inside ta jury's head. Once we give them fine folks a belly full of reasonable doubt, that's when the real rodeos gon start! Wit that ole Nurse Linda hell, all I gotta do is wine her up and let her go! We still got that boy from the Aids Clinic. Hell, I been thinkin why not find us a doctor that can give that ole security guard an exam right there in the courtroom. Hell, if that don't work, I got some special plans for that gun slinger Lopez. Na I know Miss White is gon put up one hell of a fight, but the judge ain't got no choice but let it fly!"

Dad looked over at Carlton.

"I want that list put together immediately, and during the trial the four of us will be together. I don't care if it's here or somewhere else. Oliver will give us daily reports. We have a few days left to get this show on the road. That's going to be it for today. Oliver is there anything you want to say?"

"You boys better hold on tight, cause this here is gon be one wild hay ride!"

Carl, Rex and I got a serious look on our faces as we stood to leave. With nothing but time on our hands, the three of us decided to drop by the Block for a cocktail. Inside we took a seat at a table and Mai came over to greet us. She was followed shortly by Carman. Of course she moved right in on Rex. Carl and I headed for the bar where we struck up conversation with Mai.

For the moment everyone was at peace. Carman was focused on Rex instead of me, and that gave me peace. I could tell that Carlton had discovered what most of us had, and that was that Mai is quite the delightful young lady. After a while Carl and I decided to take off, leaving Rex behind.

Later that night I lay in bed thinking about the day. Overall it was good. With the lights off and the radio playing softly, I was totally relaxed. Now if I could just find something to do with myself for the next few days. I hadn't heard from India. I guess that she was enjoying the stay with her parents. As I lay thinking my cell phone rang. It was a text from her.

"Stop thinking so loud, you're keeping me awake!"

I texted her right back.

"Ain't that the pot calling the kettle black! Good night sweetie."

The next two days completely dragged by. Minutes seemed to last forever. There wasn't a TV station on the air that didn't have a story running throughout the day and night giving their opinion on the upcoming trial. They all seemed to be experts on murder investigations and the legal system. A couple of them even had interviews with law professors from nearby universities.

After flipping through different stations, it occurred to me that if you took one of each of the so-called experts and put them together, you'll get the trial being fault on national television. I wondered what these people do when there's no hot topic in the media. The most interesting of all the experts was one that put together a profile on the murderer.

Another thing that I noticed was the constant picture of Mallory lying in his hospital bed. It was being flashed on every network. From my point of view, if the media was the jury Angie would get life in prison. I really feel for this guy's family. I can only pray that they're escaping the media.

I took as much as I could stand, and then turned to my good old standby, the Motor Channel. They were in the middle of a custom built Chevy short bed pick-up. Now this is my cup of tea! About an hour later I started getting bored again. I did manage to get the trial off of my mind, but that was only replaced by thoughts of India. I wanted to call her but I didn't know her schedule. Trying to be cool was proving to be difficult. After finally giving up on the idea, believe it or not, my phone rang. I didn't know if it was faith, God, or magic, but I didn't care.

"Hi Sherman!"

"Hello Miss India! You know I saw you the other day."

"Well what did you think?"

"Honey it doesn't take an ad on the side of a bus for you to know what I think."

"What's happening to us Sherman?"

"I don't know, but I'm doing all I can to stay busy. How are your parents doing?"

"Don't try to change the subject."

"Honey we both know that it's going to take time to make it right."

"Yeah but someone has to take control."

"Oh yeah, I've seen you in control!"

"Now that's not fair!"

All I could do was laugh.

"When can I see you?"

"I don't know. The trial starts in two days. My life is going to be on hold until it's over. Even when it is over, there's people who's dear to me that may be destroyed forever. I hate to admit it, but they've got skeletons coming out of the closet and walking right down Main Street! This whole thing is a huge mess, and I don't know what I'm…

"Hold it right there! I'll be here if you need me. I can even be here quietly if that's what you want!"

I paused for a moment to collect my thoughts.

"Well you know what they say about every good man, don't you?"

"No I don't. What do they say?"

"There's a good woman behind him."

"Thanks honey, I just wanted to hear you say it."

"I guess that means that everything is going to be alright?"

"That depends on if you stop stalking women in elevators!"

"I wasn't stalking you! You're the one that was flirting on the airplane!"

"Sherman, I think I'm ready to say it."

"Why don't you do us both a favor and hold that thought."

"Is it ok if I show it, instead of saying it?"

"That works for me in more ways than you know!"

"I've got to go now. Goodbye!"

CLICK.

# THE CITY BLOCK: 68

The last two days have been a roller coaster ride. I've either been up because of India's incredible confidence in whatever we do, or down because of dwelling on the upcoming trial. Well the time has come for someone to pay the piper! I'm now sitting at my cocktail table at 6:30am having a cup of coffee. I have the TV on and the outside of the court building is being shown. There was already wall to wall cops and crowds gathering.

For now I'm just waiting to hear from Dad. Being impatient, I decide to give Carl a call to see if he's heard from Dad.

"Yeah I just talked to him. He wants to gather at your place."

"That's fine with me. I'll see you guys in a little bit."

I hung up and went to the kitchen. I took all of the breakfast odds and ends that I had. I came up with a little bit of this and a little bit of that. It turned out to be more of a brunch. It was enough to get us through lunch, but I didn't know about dinner.

A half hour later Rex showed up, and the others followed one by one. I told everyone to help themselves to the food in the kitchen. The trial was set to start at 9:00am, and it was 8:00am as we all gathered in the living room. I didn't know about the court house, but the tension here was off the charts! I turned the volume up on the TV and the crowd was chanting "LIPSTICK DIPSTICK, COPS GET A CLUE!

I glanced over at Dad and he was shaking his head. It wasn't long before Candee appeared giving her opinion of what's to come. Behind her was other reporters doing live broadcast as well. We could see that something was taking her attention away from the camera. As she turned her head, the camera panned to her right.

The crowd was rushing in the same direction. At the end of the block there was two motorcycle cops escorting a black Towne Car that was be-ing followed by a SUV with tinted windows, and two more motorcycle cops bringing up the rear. The two vehicles stopped right in front of the path cleared to enter the court building. Out of the Towne Car stepped Mr. Cartwright and Dad's secretary. They were followed by Carlton's models and two men that I didn't recognize. I imagined that one of them was the eye doctor, and the other was from the Aids clinic. The group made their way into the building ignoring the questions being fired at them by reporters.

At that point the crowd and the reporters ran back down to the street. A.D.A. White and her crew had arrived. When she stepped out of her car, unlike Mr. Cartwright, she was happy to give an interview. One of the reporters yelled out.

"Madam Prosecutor, can you prove that Angie Cruz is guilty?"

"Yes I can. The state has very sufficient evidence against Miss Cruz. We'll prove that she's guilty beyond a reasonable doubt."

"What about her accomplish that attempted to help her get away?"

"That's all for right now."

She and her crew then headed into the court building. That's when Dad turned to me and gave me a pad on my back.

"Thanks Dad!"

"Don't thank me son. Thank your friend Lt. Lopez! I'm sure that A.D.A. White gave him a large piece of her mind as well."

The scene changed to photos of Angie and Mallory lying in their hospital beds. We could hear Candee's voice in the background.

"The Prosecutor and Defense has arrived and appears to be ready for battle. A.D.A. white is quite confident that the state is going to win this case hands down."

Dad then grabbed the remote and turned the TV off.

"Well gentlemen, it's now a waiting game. Oliver's going to give me a call as soon as they break for recess."

"Jesus this is nerve wrecking Dad!"

"Well son, get used to it! Welcome to the world of law."

"I'm starting to like my job more and more! What do you think is going on right now?"

"Well it's not 9:00am yet, but once they get settled, A.D.A. White will present the state's case against Angie to the jury. Oliver will follow by presenting the defense's case. Once the BS is over with, A.D.A. White will call her first witness to the stand."

After a while we started talking about anything and everything just to pass the time away. I got a text message from Nurse Linda.

"Angie is back on her feet now."

I sent her a text back right away.

"Does the cop outside her door know it yet?"

"No he doesn't."

"Don't tell him or anyone else! Keep her in bed in the same fashion as she was. Thank you. Keep me posted."

I told everyone about Angie's new status. Dad was worried, but he was glad that I had given Linda instructions.

"Now let's just hope that this remains quiet. I'll inform Oliver when he calls me. All we need is that cop outside her door to go shutting his mouth off!"

It was before noon when Dad's cell rang.

"Hold on Oliver, I'm going to put you on speaker phone. Ok go ahead."

"Well first off, yall was right. That ole gal is hell on wheels! She produced evidence that was found at a couple of them ole murder scenes. She even produced lipstick tubes and needles."

"How is the jury reacting Oliver?"

"Theys eating it up right na, but they also look like a sharp bunch. Look yall, it's still early in this here rodeo. The best cowboy ain't saddled up yet. This afternoon I'm gon putta bee in Miss White's bonnet! By 4:00pm I'm gon have that jury cleaning out my barn! Na I'm gon get me some lunch. Yall should do the same."

"Hold on before you go!"

Dad took him off speaker phone.

After lunch the afternoon session of the trial was under way. Outside of the court building things were starting to get out of hand. Small fights between opposing sides were breaking out. Rumors of what was happening inside was starting to spread. Protesters were being arrested for disorderly conduct. The police were putting on their riot gear and preparing for the worse. Police barriers blocking the corners were being knocked over. The size of the crowd was growing in leaps and bounds.

Many of the networks that had been reporting from ground zero had packed it up and were now broadcasting from the shelter of their helicopters in the sky. Candee no longer reigned as the queen of network news broadcasting. At this point she was a speck on the face of the globe. Her safety was in jeopardy just like the others. For the first time in her career she was the story, instead of reporting the story.

We were all in awe as we watched it unfold. The Silver Fox was pulling his hair out! Not being part of the action was killing him. This is what makes his blood flow. In the courtroom A.D.A. White had just finished questioning Lopez. Mr. Cartwright was now on the stage and Lt. Lopez was still on the stand.

"Good afternoon yo honor and jury."

He pissed the judge off right from the start.

"Mr. Cartwright I'm going to tell you right now. This is not a circus and you're not the ring leader!"

There was laughter throughout the courtroom. The judge then slammed down his gavel.

"Get on with it Mr. Cartwright!"

"Thank ya yo honor. Lt. Lopez, yall stated earlier that you don found some specific items that was left behind by the so-called defendant."

"Yeah that's right."

Mr. Cartwright walked over to the evidence table and picked up two plastic bags labeled exhibits A and B. After displaying the bags to the jury he turned around to the Lt.

"Are these here the items in question?"

"Don't play games with me, you know that they are!"

"Yo honor can yall remind the witness that he needs to answer my questions directly?"

The Lieutenant's bald head was beginning to turn red.

"Yes, those are the items."

"Na correct me if I'm wrong. Yall said that these here items were found in restaurants, theatres and such."

"Yeah that's right."

"Well Lt., about how many women do ya think frequent these kinds of places on a daily basis?"

"I don't know."

"Twenty, fifty, maybe a hundred?"

"I said I don't know!"

"I gotta sixteen year old grand baby that just loves her some lipstick, and I just hate it!"

A.D.A. White jumped to her feet.

"Your honor, please!"

"Mr. Cartwright no one's interested in your personal life. Please move it along!"

"Sorry yo honor! Na about this here needle, are ya sho this here is the murder weapon?"

"Yes, we're sure."

"Naw how did yall come to that conclusion?"

"It was verified by Lewis Finkle."

"Just who is this Finkle fella?"

"He's one of the state's Forensic Specialist."

"Yeah well, I think that I'm gon talk to that ole boy later. That's all yo honor. No no, wait a minute! Yo honor I'm sorry, but I done forgot something."

"Go ahead Mr. Cartwright, but let me remind you that this is your second warning!"

Mr. Cartwright walked over to his table and picked up a remote control.

"Na if the court don't mind, I'd like to show this lil ole footage from a previous news report that aired in this here fine city."

"Please make it quick Mr. Cartwright."

"Thank ya yo honor."

He pressed the button and Candee appeared on the screen. She was standing outside of the police department in front of a black sedan.

"Hi I'm Candee Harris reporting from outside the police department where decorated police Lt. Ricardo Lopez has been taken in for questioning regarding his involvement with the Lipstick Murders. It appears that a possible murder weapon was found in the back seat of his unmarked squad car. Tune in tonight for details."

Simultaneously, both the Lt. and A.D.A. White jumped up out of their seats.

"Your honor I object to Mr. Cartwright's rodeo tactics!"

Lt. Lopez then yelled out.

"What the hell is this?"

There was an uproar in the gallery, and the judge banged his gavel repeatedly.

"Order, order, if I have to, I'll clear this courtroom out!"

"Mr. Cartwright, what is this?"

"Yo honor I was merely showing that anyone can be falsely accused, my lovely client or even the Lt."

Again there was laughter in the audience and the judge slammed his gavel down. A.D.A. White shot Mr. Cartwright a look that could kill.

"That's all I have fo this here witness yo honor. Thank ya."

A.D.A. White then called her next witness to the stand. It was Mr. Charles Lancer, the guard from the theatre. "Mr. Lancer, can you tell the court in your own words what happened on the morning in question?"

"Yes Ma'am. It was a normal day and I was making my rounds when the fire alarm suddenly sounded. Moments later the sprinkler system automatically activated. The doors of the individual theatres opened and there were crowds of people trying to exit in all directions. Trash cans, movie displays, everything, was being knocked over. It was a mess! The staff members tried to maintain the crowd, but it was too much chaos. As I made my way through the crowd headed for the manager's office, I saw the defendant coming out."

"Mr. Lancer, when you say the defendant, are you referring to Miss Angie Cruz?"

"Yes Ma'am."

"Go on."

"Well I yelled at her to stop, but she kept going. That's when I saw Mr. Mallory lying on the floor. He was trying to crawl out of his office. I immediately went to his side and called the paramedics."

"That'll be all. Thank you. Mr. Cartwright, he's all yours."

"Thank ya Ma'am."

A.D.A. White just rolled her eyes at him.

"Ha yall doin Chuck? I hope ya don't mind if call ya Chuck."

"No, that's alright."

"I guess it musta been pretty crazy down there on that morning."

"Yes sir it was."

"Na, did ya actually see my client do bodily harm to Mr. Mallory?"

"Well not really, but she had to be the one that did it."

"Na hold on Chuck! Just answer my questions. On ya days off, do ya ever go watch one of them picture shows?"

"Sure, doesn't everyone?"

"No siree! Me myself, I rent mine! I love that ole boy John Wayne!"

The A.D.A. was back on her feet.

"Your honor this line of questioning has nothing to do with anything!"

The judge glared at Oliver once again.

"Mr. Cartwright move on or sit down!"

"Sorry yo honor, Ma'am."

Again she rolled her eyes at him.

"Chuck, I notice that you wear eyeglasses."

"Yes that's right, I have for years now."

"I notice a lil ole thin line runnin across them. What is that fo?"

"These are bifocals."

"Haw they help ya?"

"One area of the lens helps me to read, and the other helps me to see far away."

"Yeah I wear em too, but I think they just make me look funny!"

There was laughter in the courtroom again, and again the judge banged his gavel.

"Quiet!"

"Na yall said that the sprinkler system was rainin down water."

"Yeah that's right."

"Was ya wearing them there glasses at that time?"

"Sure I was."

"Why that's funny. When I wears mine and it starts rainin, I takes mind off. When I gets rain all over em, I can't see a damn thang! Na Chuck, did yo glasses get wet that morning?"

"Yeah, I guess they did."

"So ya tellin the court that wit all that excitement and water drops all over yo glasses, you were able ta focus on one individual?"

"Yes sir, that's right."

"Are ya sure Chuck?"

"Yes I'm sure."

"Well Chuck do ya mind if I give ya a lil ole test?"

A.D.A. White stood up.

"Your honor I object! This is ridiculous!"

"Yo honor I'm just tryin ta establish a fact. If yall don't mind, I brought along a certified Optometrist. I wanta call him up and have em give ole Chuck here a test."

A.D.A. White was back on her feet.

"Objection! Your honor this is a complete waste of time!"

"Yo honor my client's life is on the line and Mr. Lancer's ability to see under extraordinary conditions can make all of the difference in the world!"

"Ok, the two of you approach my bench! Look, I'm getting tired of this wrestling match going on between you two. Mr. Cartwright, if this is going to be another one of your circus moves, don't do it! Miss White, you've got to stop jumping up every time Cartwright makes point! Now let's get on with it so we all can go home!"

A.D.A. White took a seat and Mr. Cartwright called Dr. William Cane forward. When the doctor approached he carried a one foot square piece of Plexiglas, a spray bottle full of water, and two photos.

"Na Chuck ole buddy, can ya tell the court how far you were from the defendant on the day in question?"

"I'd say about 20 feet."

Mr. Cartwright took the Plexiglas and water bottle from the doctor and paced off 18 feet from the witness stand. The doctor stood behind him holding up one of the photos. He then returned to the stand and sprayed the glass with water and held it up in front of Mr. Lancer.

"Na Chuck I want ya to take a look at these two photos and tell the court which one is Angie Cruz."

Mr. Lancer took a nice long look at the two photos.

"She's the one in the first photo."

Without saying a word, Mr. Cartwright walked over to the jury and showed them the name on the back of the photo. He then went back to the stand.

"Na Chuck, do ya mind removing yo glasses?"

Dr. Cane held up the two photos again. This time it took Mr. Lancer an even longer time to make a decision. Again he choose the first one, and again Mr. Cartwright revealed the name on the back to the jury.

"Thank ya Chuck, that'll be all. Yo honor, I'd like to have Dr. Cane here sworn in."

"I'll allow it."

Dr. Cane took the stand and was sworn in.

"Na doctor, to please the court can you tell us what your findings of that lil ole test is."

"Well first of all I agree with Mr. Lancer's own doctor. He does have problems with seeing distance."

"What else did you find?"

"Judging from my experience, the prescription that he's currently wearing is out dated. He's long overdue for an exam and new lenses."

"Doctor what was the most disturbing thing you found?"

"Well in both cases, with and without his glasses, he chose the model, not your client."

There was mixed emotional sounds in the courtroom audience. Then suddenly silence fell across the courtroom.

"That'll be all, thank you Doctor."

The judge then asked Miss White if she had any questions for the doctor. Her reply was no your honor. He then banged his gavel.

"This court is in recess until tomorrow morning at 9:00am."

All rise, said the bailiff. As the courtroom started emptying out, A.D.A. White walked over to Mr. Cartwright.

"You Jackass!"

He just tipped his imaginary hat and smiled.

By time he and Dad's secretary packed up everything and got outside, A.D.A. White already had a crowd of reporters around her. While walking down the stairs, Mr. Cartwright also was pounced on by reporters. Dozens of questions were yelled at him all at once.

"Na na fellas, yall know I can't talk about what went on in there! I will say that I'm having a good ole time in this here fine city of yalls, and A.D.A. White is a darlin woman. Na yall have a nice day!"

Everyone climbed into the vehicle they came in and they were escorted away. Mr. Cartwright immediately called the Silver Fox.

"Howdy, well ones down and who knows how many mo. It was interesting, but all and all it went pretty well. Hey, I'm in the mood for a cocktail. Why don't you boys meet over at that ole City Block place, so we can chew the fat a spell? I'm gon have this ole boy drop me off and take yo secretary on home."

"Alright, we'll see you there Oliver.

# THE CITY BLOCK: 69

The four of us walked into the Block and took a seat at a table. Carman, Mai, and Louie pounced on us just like the reporters did to Mr. Cartwright. Unfortunately, we knew no more than they did. We ordered a round of drinks and waited.

The TV was on but the sound was being drowned out by the music. We were on our second cocktail when Mr. Cartwright finally walked in. Again the bar crew swarmed us, but I asked him the first question.

"So how did it go Mr. Cartwright?"

"Well son, it was like fishing in a bucket. I'll say one thing though. That ole boy Lt. Lopez is one nasty son of a gun! Yeah I had to cut him down to size right away. Me and that lil ole philly yall call Candee."

"Candee!"

"Yes indeed. I played that report she did on the big screen. The one where that ole Lt. was hand cuffed and being taken in for questioning. Mannn, that ole boy was pissed! In my mind I was wearing a big ole shit eating grin. I had stung his ass twice!"

Dad was next up.

"How did the jury respond to him?"

"Well it was hard to tell, but the courtroom audience sho did eat it up! "So I take it that I ain't finished wit that ole boy." I gotta find a way to get the jury ta think that he ain't worth a three leg horse at a rodeo!"

Mr. Cartwright caught a glimpse of himself on the TV.

"Man I look right handsome on a sunny day!"

We all laughed and Dad just shook his head. After a few more drinks and a few more laughs, we all paired up and began leaving.

It was now day two, and the scene outside the court building was a carbon copy of yesterday. That included Candee with another on the spot report.

"Good morning, and welcome to day number two of the Lipstick Murder Trial. So far the A.D.A. and the Defense teams have been pretty tight lipped about what went on yesterday in the courtroom. As always, we here in the media have our own opinion. Let me show you an example."

She then held up a local news paper. On the front the page in bold letters were the words, YOU JACKASS! Underneath the statement was a picture of Mr. Cartwright on one side and A.D.A. White on the other. She then folded the paper under her arm.

"Rumor is that A.D.A. White made that statement to Oliver Cartwright following the trial. I guess you can say that there's no love lost between these two. Hang in there folks, it's just heating up. I'm Candee Harris coming to you live outside the court building."

Inside the show was just getting underway.

"All rise! The honorable Phillip T. Evans presiding."

A.D.A. White started the day by calling Dr. Lewis Finkle to the stand, the state's Forensic Specialist. After he was sworn in, she went straight to evidence found at the scenes.

"Dr. Finkle, can you tell the court what your findings were from the evidence provided to you by the police?"

"Yes Ma'am. Regarding the lipstick tubes, there was no finger prints found on any of the tubes found at the scenes."

"Dr. Finkle did you find that to be strange?"

"Well in most cases there are a woman's finger prints on the tube."

"What did you think when you didn't find any?"

"It made me wonder what the purchaser's intentions were."

"What about DNA doctor?"

"In each case, the only DNA found was that of the victims."

"Did you find that strange as well?"

"No, not really."

"Why not doctor?"

"Seeing that there were no finger prints, I didn't expect to find any DNA other than the victims."

"At that point did you suspect foul play?"

Mr. Cartwright quickly rose from his seat.

"I object to this line of questioning yo honor!"

"What's the problem Mr. Cartwright?"

"Dr. Finkle is a Forensic Specialist. He's not a crime investigator, and his personal opinion on rather or not someone was intending on committing a crime is irrelevant!"

The judge hated to agree with Mr. Cartwright, but he did.

"Strike that question. Continue A.D.A. White."

"Dr. Finkle, what did you discover regarding the needles?"

"I found that they had residue from several chemicals, your garden variety for exterminating rodents."

"If these chemicals were digested by a human being, what would the result be?"

"For starters it would affect the flow of blood possibly leading to a blood clot, which could cut off oxygen to the brain."

"Is that all?"

"Well depending on the amount taken, it could do muscle damage and nerve damage."

"Are you saying that this chemical cocktail could kill a human being?"

"Yes, if left untreated long enough."

"If a person did survive, would their life be changed?"

"Yes Ma'am, it would be."

"How so Doctor?"

"It could vary from muscle damage or in some cases psychological damage. The worse would be that the individual is left in a vegetative state for the rest of their life."

"Thank you Doctor. Your witness Mr. Cartwright."

"Dr. Finkle, do you think that a farmer might use these here chemicals maybe to keep rodents outta his barn?"

"Yes, I guess that's possible."

"How about the janitorial closet in let's say a commercial building?"

"Maybe."

"Well Doctor let me ask ya another question. Ya ever been to a movie house and the lights came on when the movie ended?"

"Sure, hasn't everyone?"

"Well I have, and man there's popcorn, gummy bears, you name it, all over the place. Na it kinda make ya wonder if those good people at the movie house got a mouse in ta house. Would you agree that's possible?"

"Yeah, I guess so."

"Doctor, does one need some kinda license to purchase these here chemicals?"

"I wouldn't know sir."

"Well let me answer that fo ya. Na I did a little research before this here trial. I went right over to ta neighborhood hardware store and told the lil ole gal at the counter that I had a rodent problem. Her name was Suzy, sweet as an apple blossom."

Laughter came from the audience and the judge banged his gavel.

"You're pushing your luck Mr. Cartwright!"

"I'm sorry yo honor. Well Suzy took me right to it. There it was just as plain as day. It was sitting right there, next to the mouse traps. Man them puppies look painful!"

This time the judge just shook his head.

"I also found that just about anyone could walk in there and buy the stuff. There's one mo thang Doctor. Those needles yall was talkin bout. Are they hard to come by?"

"By law you can only get them through a prescription written by a physician."

"Ya mean fo someone that might have sugar?"

"The term is Diabetes."

"I'm sorry."

"Yes."

"That's all Doctor. Have a good day."

He then turned and faced the judge.

"Yo honor, if Miss White and ta court don't mind none, I'd like ta call up a fella that's somewhat of an expert on needles?"

Miss White and the judge had no objections.

"Thank yall. I'd like to call up to the stand Mr. John Collins."

Mr. Collins took a seat at the stand and was sworn in.

"Mornin. Ya mind telling the court just what it is you do Mr. Collins?"

"I'm the director of a non-profit rehabilitation clinic."

"What kind of people do yall specialize in rehabilitating?"

"People with chemical dependencies."

"Ya mean like heroin addicts and such?"

"Yes sir."

"Tell me sir do any of ya patients use needles?"

"Most of them do."

"Can ya tell the court where they get them from?"

"Those of them willing to tell us get them from AIDS prevention centers."

"Is that so?"

"Yes sir. Their mission is AIDS prevention among users, so they hand them out without asking questions."

"So would it be safe ta say that getting these needles these days ain't that difficult?"

"No, not if you know where to look."

"One mo question Mr. Collins. Does any of yo clients have criminal backgrounds?"

"Unfortunately, yes."

"Thank ya fo yo time. Miss White."

"The state has no questions for this witness."

The judge took advantage of the moment.

"In that case, this court will recess, and resume at 2:00pm."

Bang!

All rise!

# THE CITY BLOCK: 70

During the break Mr. Cartwright called and gave Dad an update. Dad's main concern was Mr. Cartwright's plans for the afternoon. He planned to drive the final stake into Lt. Lopez's heart. He believed that he just may be able to blow the A.D.A.'s case right out of the water. He felt that everything she had was based on the investigation of Lopez.

At 2:00pm sharp, the judge came out of his chambers.

"A.D.A. White, would you like to call up your next witness?"

"The state would like to call to the stand Dr. Michael Conrad, Chief of Staff at Goodwill Mercy Hospital."

He was sword in and she approached the stand.

"Thank you for being here."

"You're welcome."

"Dr. Conrad, were you on duty when Mr. Mallory was brought in?"

"Yes I was."

"What exactly took place on that day?"

"At the time I was in a meeting. My understanding is that the trauma team was ready and waiting for his arrival."

"Did your team know right away that he had been poisoned?"

"No Ma'am, if it's not a household accident with a witness, we never know."

"So in a case like this one, what's the procedure?"

"We start out treating each individual problem that the victim has. That's followed by a series of test. In the meantime, any organs that may be failing we sustain with aid of machines."

"Would it be safe to say that the time between getting test results and providing treatment determines the amount of damage?"

"Yes, that's a fair statement."

"What kind of life style changes do these people face?"

"It varies depending on the dosage of poison they ingested. Some return to a normal life style. Some have minor muscle or nerve damage. The worst case scenario would be a loss of physical and mental capabilities. In layman terms you could say that the person would be unable to function as a normal human being."

"From your experience Doctor, what does the future look like for Mr. Mallory?"

"In all honesty, it's too soon to say."

"Thank you Doctor, that'll be all."

Mr. Cartwright stood.

"The defense has no questions fo this witness, but we would like ta recall Lt. Ricardo Lopez to ta stand."

Lopez took the stand and the judge reminded him that he was still under oath.

"Lt., just haw many people do yall accuse my client of murdering, or attempting to murder?"

"Five people total."

"Are yall sho of that?"

"Yes I'm sure!"

"Are yall sho it's not six, or maybe yall just investigated five?"

"What are you getting at? Of course I'm sure!"

"Well Lt. I'm glad ya asked. Why don't ya look at that big ole TV screen over there?"

He then pressed the remote. It was Candee doing another live report. This time it was from a residential neighborhood.

"Hi, I'm Candee Harris coming to you live from a normally quiet blue collar neighborhood. It appears that the Lipstick murderer has struck again."

He then stopped the footage.

"Do yall remember this case Lt.?"

"Yeah, I guess it was six."

"Why don't ya bring the court up to date? Ha far that yo investigation get in this here case?"

"Not too far."

"Did yall have any of them fancy specialist fellas go over and check out the house?"

The Lt. began to get pissed off.

"No, it wasn't necessary."

"Well why not?"

The Lt. then jumped up out of his seat.

"Don't tell me how to do my job!"

That's when the judge banged his gavel several times.

"Lt. if you jump out of your seat one more time, I'm going to have you and your testimony thrown out of my courtroom! Now sit down and answer the questions!"

The judge didn't like Mr. Cartwright, but he also didn't like cops that thought that they were Gods.

"Na Lt., did yall ever interview the victim's wife?"

"No we didn't."

"Why not?"

"She couldn't be located."

"Has she been located since then?"

"Not that I know of."

"Has the police department done any follow-up on this here case?"

"No sir."

"Well ya know somthin, I been doing a little follow-up myself. Ya know it's kinda funny. I drove by the victim's house and there was a fore-closure sign on the front lawn."

There was a variety of moans and groans in the gallery.

"I just couldn't help myself, so I talked to some of the neighbors. They was some real nice folks too! They say yo victim was an ornery ole polecat and he treated his wife somethin awful! They say they ain't seen no hide or hair of her in a month of Sundays!"

The chatter in the gallery got louder. This time the judge banged his gavel.

"Quiet!"

"Yall know what else? Them folks all thought that I was the police. Ain't that funny? They say they done been waiting fo the police to come talk to them, but they never did."

The courtroom fell silent. They couldn't belief what they were hearing. Mr. Cartwright looked over at A.D.A. White and she dropped her head and wouldn't make eye contact with him. That was too bad, because Mr. Cartwright was just getting started with him. He stalled for a few moments, and pretended to be going through his paperwork.

"Tell me somthin Lt. Prior to that so-called high speed car chase involving Mr. Sherman Brothers, did ya know that ole boy?"

"No I didn't."

He looked at A.D.A. White again. She knew that he was lying.

"Fo the sake of the court, I'd like to remind Lt. Lopez that there's a law in this here state fo committing perjury while under oath. Na ya sho ya didn't know that boy?"

"Yes I'm sure."

"Alrighty then, have it yo way! Let me ask ya another question? Lt. do ya have a habit of working on unsolved cases with the aid of folks not in the police department?"

"No, of course not!"

"Are ya sho ya don't wanta think about that?"

"I said no!"

"Well ya leave me no choice but ta remind ya that there's a law against perjury."

Mr. Cartwright picked up the remote again and pressed the button. This time the scene was inside what looked like a cocktail bar. Three people, one by one entered and took a seat at a table. He then froze the frame. Both A.D.A. White and the judge couldn't belief their eyes!

"Na, fo the sake of the court, can you tell us who these three people are?"

The Lt. didn't say a word.

"What's the matter Lt.? Cat got ya tongue? I'll tell yall who they are!"

Using a laser pointer, he pointed at them one by one. This pretty lil ole thang here is Miss Candee Harris, that lil ole reporter gal. Na this ole boy over here, he's special. Ya know why? He's none other than Mr. Sherman Brothers. Na some of yall might not know, but I done did some diggin, and I found out that ole boy is licensed by the State of Illinois to be a Private Investigator."

Once again the audience blew up and the judge did his thing!

"Na this last boy right here, I think that everyone in the courtroom knows who he is!"

As he looked around he couldn't tell who was more pissed off, the Lt. or A.D.A. White.

"Na there's one mo thang that I wanta sho yall."

He started the footage again. It showed me placing a note on the table. He then froze the frame again.

"What's that lil ole piece of paper about Lt.?"

"I don't know."

"It doesn't mean nothing to ya?"

"Yeah that's right."

"Alrighty, have it ya way!"

He started the footage again and this time you could see the Lt. clearly read the note and jump up out of his seat. You could tell that he was pissed off. He began yelling at Candee and me. To make matters worse, it was obvious that he had drawn the attention of other people in the bar. Mr. Cartwright turned and looked the judge straight in the eye.

"Yo honor I'm sorry, but I don't think that I should ask this ole boy any mo questions in yo courtroom."

The judge laid his face in his hands for a few moments.

"Miss White, do you have any questions for this witness?"

"No your honor, I don't."

"This court is in recess until tomorrow morning at 9:00am."

He then banged his gavel so softly that you could barely hear it.

"All rise!"

Mr. Cartwright had done it. The Lt. had proven that he was a disgrace to the legal system. As Mr. Cartwright began gathering up his materials, A.D.A. White made a beeline past him without saying a word. It had been a good day for the firm, but he knew that tomorrow A.D.A. White would show up with the big guns drawn.

Outside the courthouse the scene was the same as previous days. The protesters were on the verge of getting out of control and the media was doing their thing. At the bottom of the stairs Mr. Cartwright was greeted by the press and saw faces that he had come to know, but today was different. He loved the legal system and what happened today had left a nasty taste in his mouth. Normally he'd have a little fun with the reporters, but this time he said no comment.

# THE CITY BLOCK: 71

On day number three Mr. Cartwright woke up knowing that today would be a short one. There was very little to bring forth, however he'd be just as vigorous as the previous days. He prepared himself and waited for his driver. On the ride over to the courtroom it was apparent that he was tired of bickering with A.D.A. White. He imagined that she felt the same. Maybe today they could put their differences aside, do business and wrap this thing up.

At 9:00am sharp the judge entered the courtroom.

"All rise!"

"Good morning. Miss White, would you like to call your next witness to the stand"

She stood up and paced for a moment.

"I'd like to draw the jury's attention to the TV monitor."

Mr. Cartwright was thinking this is good, it's just what he had been waiting for.

"Ladies and gentleman what you're about to see is still photos taken from security cameras at each of the murder scenes. What you're going to see are five women with different color hair and hair styles. What I'd like you to pay attention to is the body size, shape, and habits. The state believes that all five of these women are one in the same, our murderer."

With that she pressed the button on the remote. On the screen five women appeared just as she had said.

"Ladies and gentlemen take a close look and let your eyes decide."

Mr. Cartwright had to admit to himself that they did have similarities, but he was on the other team. For about five long silent minutes everyone in the courtroom stared at the monitor. A.D.A. White then turned it off. She took a seat and the judge motioned to Mr. Cartwright.

"Thank ya judge. Yo honor, if yall would bare wit me, I'd like ta call up a group of folks that yo honor and the jury will find quite interesting?"

The judge threw his hands up in the air.

"Well so far Mr. Cartwright I haven't been able to stop you!"

"Thank ya yo honor. Oh there's one mo thang."

"What is it Mr. Cartwright?"

"Do ya mind if I have the jury close their eyes fo a spell?"

The judge didn't put up a fight. He waved his hand at the jury and they all closed their eyes. Mr. Cartwright turned to Dad's secretary that was sitting in the rear of the courtroom. In a single file line, all five of the hired models walked up to the front of the courtroom.

The gallery was taken completely by surprise. Mr. Cartwright faced the gallery and put a finger to his lips. He then had the models stand side by side in front of the jury box. He then looked at the judge asking him to instruct the jury to open their eyes. When the jury saw the women, there were real human expressions on their faces for the first time during the trial. It appeared that they couldn't belief what they were seeing.

As they looked at the models Mr. Cartwright asked A.D.A. White if she'd put the still photos back on the monitor. When she did it the gallery couldn't hold back any longer and the chatter was out of control. The judge demanded order in the courtroom.

"Na ladies and gentlemen of ta jury, what I'm tryin ta do is show just how much we can and can't depend on technology. Na I don't know bout yall, but from where I'm standing, any one of these lovely ladies could be ta murderer. Na I'm gone have em turn around a bit so yall can see em from every angle."

On his command they turned slowly. After a few minutes he asked the jury to look at the monitor again. He thanked the models and they left the courtroom in a single file line. The judge looked at A.D.A. White.

"Does the state have any more witnesses?"

"No your honor."

He then asked Mr. Cartwright.

"Yo honor I'd like to call up one more witness."

"Please proceed."

"Thank ya. I'd like to call to the stand Nurse Linda Mason."

She took the stand and was sworn in.

"Ma'am, do ya mind telling the court what yo capacity is, and what yo relationship is to my client?"

"I'm a Registered Nurse and I'm in charge of the daily care of Angie Cruz."

That's when Mr. Cartwright brought up a picture of Angie lying in her hospital bed.

"Na is it true that you were involved in a very special activity a while back?"

"Yes sir, it's true."

"Do ya mind tellin the court the details of that activity?"

"Over a month ago I organized a small group of medical staff to help set up and operate a blood drive on Angie's behalf."

"That musta taken an awful lot of doing?"

"Yes sir, it was quite a task."

"What exactly was the reason fo the drive?"

"Angie has Sickle Cell Anemia. The only thing that would give her a fighting chance was finding a matching blood donor."

"So what was yall gon do after finding this here match?"

"The next step would be running test, and if everything went well, we'd do a bone marrow transplant."

"Tell us Nurse Linda, did that indeed happen?"

"Yes sir it did."

"That's mighty fine to hear! So I take it that she's as good as new?"

"No sir, that's not true."

"How so?"

"It can take months before we find out if the transplant was success-ful."

"If it's that serious, why was she allowed to be at home?"

"During the waiting period a patient's status can be up and down. Sometimes your life can seem as normal as anyone else, and you feel better in your own home. Getting better can be hard sometime when you spend weeks with tubes and an IV running into your body. If you're strong enough for a period of time, it's allowed. In a case like this, a good spirit goes a long way."

"Well how do yall monitor these folks when they're at home?"

"Mostly by phone, but there's also visits to the home."

"What is the risk that these folks take when left on their own?"

"Things could change for them on a daily basis. They can experience high temperatures, vomiting, fainting, and poor judgment of what's going on around them."

"What happens if they find themselves in this state and not get treatment?"

"Death would be possible."

"Let me ask ya one mo question? If Mr. Brothers hadn't come along when he did, what would've happened to her?"

"Without medical attention, she would have slipped into a coma, and eventually died."

"Thank ya Nurse Linda. That'll be all. Yo witness Miss White."

"Is Angie Cruz a personal friend of yours Nurse Linda?"

"I only know her from the hospital."

"It seems like you put forth a lot of effort for someone you hardly know."

"Well she's a dear friend of a mutual acquaintance."

"That will be all, thank you."

 With that said, the judge spoke up.

"If there's no more evidence or witnesses to be called, we'll go to recess and tomorrow we will listen to closing arguments."

"All rise!"

As usual Mr. Cartwright allowed A.D.A. White to exit the building first. He took a moment to give his models instructions on how to leave the building.

"I want you ladies to slowly walk side by side down the stairs, and we gon be right behind ya."

His plan was to get his money's worth out of the media. When they stepped outside the plan came together like a well oiled machine! Camera flashes were going off like the models were Hollywood movie stars at the premiere of a block buster release!

Once again Dad got an update from Mr. Cartwright. Following his conversation our little group broke up and the guys went home. I now had the rest of day to kill. Tomorrow would be closing statements and this thing will finally be coming to an end. The plan was for everyone to relax tonight.

I decided to order a pizza and watch a good movie. With the remote in my hand I started running through the movie listings on the TV. Just as I was about to give up, something caught my eye. It was The Hustler, starring Jackie Gleason.

"Right on, now that's what I'm talking about!"

I ordered my pizza and waited. While waiting my phone rang. I was delighted to find that it was India.

"Hi, I was just thinking about you!"

"Yeah I know!"

"How did you know?"

"Because that's how we roll!"

"Ha ha, that's real funny!"

"So what are you doing Mr. Sherman?"

"I ordered a pizza and I'm about to watch an old black and white movie."

"It sounds like you're just fine without me!"

"I'm just trying to occupy my mind. I can't keep running the streets, trying not to think of you."

"You know girls dream about being wrapped up with their man watching a good movie."

"I always thought that you guys went for fancy dinners and flowers!"

"Nope, we only do that to see if you men can hang!"

"Oh really?"

"Yeah, and I'm sorry, but I've got to go sweetie."

"Ok, be good!"

CLICK.

It was really nice to hear from India, but now I was wondering where my pizza was. Just as I was wondering my doorbell rang. I went to the door and buzzed the pizza guy up. Moments later there was a knock at my door. I took a look through the peep hole and saw a guy with his back to me holding a flat box. It wasn't the regular. This guy wore a baseball cap and had a long ponytail. I opened the door and there standing was India holding my pizza.

"Please don't be mad at me!"

"Get in here and put that pizza down!"

"I hope you like surprises."

"Not when they come in the form of a heart attack!"

"I'll only stay until tomorrow, and then I'll have a shuttle pick me up! All I want you to do is make love to me."

"Where is your bag?"

She stepped back and reached into the hallway.

"Here it is right here."

"Follow me. This is the bathroom and here's the bedroom. If you need to freshen up, there's clean linen in the hall closet and I'll be in the living room."

"Sherman."

"Yes."

"You didn't hug and kiss me yet!"

I took her in my arms and I could feel her energy penetrating my body.

"Hurry up, the movie is about to start!"

I stretched out on the sofa smiling. I haven't been this excited in a long time. Just as the movie was starting India walked in wearing some-thing that looked like it was straight out of a Victoria Secret catalog!

"Do you always dress like that to eat pizza?"

"It depends!"

"It depends on what?"

"How far I have to fly and who I'm sharing the pizza with!"

"Maybe I should order pizza more often!"

Both the pizza and the movie were great! I then looked at India.

"Are you ready for bed?"

"I thought you'd never ask!"

# THE CITY BLOCK: 72

India's surprise visit was incredible to say the least. My only worry was our relationship becoming purely physical. Let's face it, if that's what I wanted, I could've given in to Candee, which reminds me that I'm still in dept to her! For now I sit alone. India's shuttle has come and gone. The only remaining clue that she was here is the smell of her perfume on my bed linen.

Today final arguments will be given in the courtroom. All I can do is wait to hear from Dad or one of the guys. The end is almost here. I've dreamed of this day, and now that it's here, it's kind of scary. A guilty verdict will destroy Angie. There's no doubt in my mind that Mr. Cartwright has done a great job, but the fact is that it's all in God's hands.

The scene in the courtroom had been set. It was so quiet that you could hear a pin drop! While waiting, respect was being given on both sides of the courtroom. A.D.A. White wasn't giving Mr. Cartwright nasty looks, and he wasn't giving her shit eating grins. This was the moment of truth and all personal feelings had been put aside. The tension in the air was so thick that you could cut it with a knife. Suddenly the bailiff spoke.

"All rise!"

The judge kept everyone in suspense as he shuffled through his paper work. At one point he even leaned over and whispered something to the court reporter. Finally he said good morning to everyone.

"Before we get started, I'd like to have the full attention of each and every juror. This morning you'll be hearing the closing arguments from both the prosecutor and the defense. Before this trial began you were instructed to make your decision based on the evidence and the testimony given. It will be expected of you to make your decision based on facts, not emotions. In addition to this, your findings are to be beyond a reasonable doubt. I know that everyone here is on edge, so let's get this over with. A.D.A. White, you have the floor."

She stood and faced the jury.

"Ladies and gentlemen you've spent the last three days enduring grueling testimony and evidence. I'd like to personally thank you for your time."

With the remote control in her hand she pointed at the monitor. On the screen appeared a picture of the victim's family, a woman, a teenage girl, a little boy wearing a Cub Scout uniform, and a little girl with curly gold hair.

"Ladies and gentlemen, what you are looking at is a wife that no longer has a husband, half of the team needed to raise a family."

Using a laser pointer she pointed at the teenage girl.

"This teenage girl will never be able to talk her dad about her boyfriends. She'll never have him walk her down the aisle and give her hand away in marriage. This little guy in the Cub Scout uniform will never go another fishing trip with his dad. Trust me folks, this little guy doesn't want his mom tagging along on a camping trip with the other scouts! If she's a real mom, she'll go anyway, and sleep on the ground in the woods because that's what his dad would have done. This three year old little cutie barely knows what's going on. All she knows is that daddy acts different, and mommy look's sad. I can't begin to tell you the future of this little girl without her daddy."

A.D.A. White pointed the remote again and the picture changed to Mr. Mallory lying in his hospital bed.

"I'm sorry for doing this to you again, but take one more look at what's left of this father and husband. The last three days you've listened to testimony from the investigating officer, experts in the field, and the security guard that witnessed the attempt. You've seen countless photos from security cameras. There's one more thing that I'd like to bring to your attention. Throughout the trial, not once that the defendant deny being at the scene of the crime. I have faith in all of you. I know that after you've reviewed all that has been given to you, you'll reach the same conclusion that the state has. You'll see that beyond a reasonable doubt Angie Cruz is guilty of four counts of Premeditated Murder and one count of Attempted Murder. Again I thank you all."

Mr. Cartwright didn't stand right away, but when he did, he appeared different. No Texas charm, no funny remarks.

"Ladies and gentlemen, I know that A.D.A. White and I look like enemies, but the truth is that we both fight hard to reach the truth. Na I do agree with her on one thang. You folks have endured a lot this week. Ya know it's kinda funny. We go through our lives punching the clock, paying taxes and voting. We never think that one day we'll be called on to participate as a citizen in this fine country. There's no way that any of you could have prepared yourself for this trial. From my experience you all have risen to the occasion, and proven to be real Americans. It's folks like yall that makes this country a wonderful place. For that I thank ya.

Folks I'm going to start off with the testimony of the guard himself. First of all he was not physically present to see the crime committed. My Optometrist proved that his current vision capacity would not allow his eyes to see what he said he saw. He himself proved that it was physically impossible. That fact alone not only makes his testimony unaccountable, but irrelevant.

Na I did bring in models that appeared to look like the images you saw on the security footage. Some may say that it was a underhanded trick, but think about it. If your life was on the line, wouldn't ya want yo counselor to do whatever the law allows? There was reasonable doubt, and it was my job to bring it to your attention.

There's one mo thang that I wanta talk ta yall bout. That would be the testimony of Lt. Ricardo Lopez, one of Chicago's finest. Na I'm not gone go into any details simply cause it make my stomach turn! Yall are all smart people and I know what you saw and heard when the Lt. was on the stand."

He stopped talking to let the thought sit in their minds for a moment.

"Ladies and gentlemen I'm proud of who I am, and there's a reason for that. Ya see folks, yall, the judge, A.D.A. White, the bailiff, the court reporter and myself are the legal system. I'm sure that everyone of you can feel what I feel. That feeling is one of utter shame! Why, because one of our own has shamed us all. How do the kids say it, his testimony sucks!"

After pacing a little he pointed the remote toward the monitor. On the screen appeared Angie lying in her hospital bed.

"Ladies and gentlemen this is a picture that you've all seen before. This is my client. For the last few months she's been dying and didn't know. About a month ago she was lucky enough to find a matching donor. Since then she's had a bone transplant that may, or may not work. It's still up in the air. She's spent more time in the hospital than anyone I've ever known."

Mr. Cartwright took a seat and silence fell across the courtroom again. The judge shuffled around his papers and then spoke.

"Ladies and gentlemen of the jury, you've been given instructions. You've heard and seen evidence. You know the job that's ahead of you. On behalf of Cook County and the State of Illinois, I thank you. You're dismissed until you return with a verdict."

The jury stood and left the courtroom. The judge then gave his attention to courtroom audience. This court is in recess until the jury has reached a verdict. You'll be notified."

BANG WENT THE GAVEL!

"All rise!"

Both teams took a sigh of relief. It was over! No words were spoken between them as they prepared to face the media circus waiting for them outside. There was no shortage of pandemonium on the stairs of the court building. There was so many camera flashes going off that Mr. Cartwright could barely focus on the steps as he walked down. Instead of having his usual fun with the reporters, all he wanted to do was get the hell out of there! He shielded Dad's secretary until they reached the Towne Car.

Once inside the car she couldn't help but speak up.

"You know Mr. Cartwright, this is the first time that I've been scared all week."

"Don't ya worry none, we ain't gon let nothing happen to ya!"

"Thank you Mr. Cartwright."

"Why don't ya start callin me Oliver?"

"Ok Oliver."

He called Dad and told him that the worst was over.

"Why don't you and the boys meet me at that lil ole watering hole? I could use a good belt or two!"

# THE CITY BLOCK: 73

Mr. Cartwright thought that the ride over to the Block was taking forever. When he walked in he received a round of cheers from everyone.

"Hold on na! The jury's still out, and I don't think that we're gon hear from them folks tonight! That's why I'm gone have a drink! Na why don't yall just sit a spell and have some of them ole spirits that Mr. Louie got back there?"

We took a couple of tables and relaxed.

"So Mr. Cartwright, do you think that tomorrow's the big day?"

"Well I've said all along that this jury looks like a smart bunch. I don't think it's gon take em a long time. There's one thang that I gotta say. That woman sho put on a powerful closing statement! Hell I damn near starting crying myself!"

"So what's your gut feeling?" Asked Dad.

"Well I did all that I could to shut down everyone that she called to the stand. Absolutely none of em could hold water! Unless the jury is blind, we should come out looking pretty good, but I gotta tell yall, in the past I've seen the police department under this kind pressure befo and strange thangs happen. Yall boys are fogettin somethin!"

"What's that, I asked?"

"Didn't you boys tell me that ole judge is running fo governor? Come on na, this ain't no jaywalking ticket! This here is the big league! Angie might not be nothin but a pawn. I hate ta say it, but I done seen mo folks go to jail in the name of politics then yall can shake a stick at! We done put on a damn good sho, but listen to me. If that ole boy is running fo governor, you can damn bet that's there's a wagon load of bank rollers supporting him! Fo cryin out loud, this ain't no dog and pony sho! Remember that we're all a team, win or lose. Tomorrow let's get everybody over here, the models, everybody! Louie yall got some champagne back there?"

"Yes sir, we sure do."

"Well keep it chilled just in case. Yall can camp here til ya hear from me."

It wasn't his intentions, but Mr. Cartwright was taking the wind right out of my sails. He didn't feel good about it, but he had to prepare us for disappointment.

Morning came and Mr. Cartwright along with his one woman team made their way across town to the court building. After entering the court building they were escorted to a conference room where coffee and Danish was provided. After an hour and a half there was a knock at the door. It was the court bailiff.

"If noon rolls around, you may want to grab some lunch in the cafeteria."

Sure as hell they ended up having lunch. At exactly 1:00pm there was another knock at the door. It was the bailiff again.

"It's time!"

They were out of their seats and out the door in a flash! When they walked in A.D.A. White and her team was already sitting down. Just as they were about to sit down, the bailiff said all rise. The judge walked in and banged his gavel.

"This court is now in session. Bailiff, please bring in the jury."

The jury came in and took a seat in the box. The judge didn't beat around the bush!

"Will the jury foreman please rise?"

The first gentleman on the left end of the roll stood.

"On the count of Premeditated Murder of Kevin Crocket, did the jury reach a verdict?"

"Yes your honor. The jury finds Angie Cruz not guilty."

Mr. Cartwright let out a breath of air and there was a uproar from the courtroom gallery. The judge banged his gavel to restore order.

"On the count of Premeditated Murder of Dr. Marc Kenner, did the jury reach a verdict?"

"Yes your honor. The jury finds Angie Cruz not guilty."

There were groans in the gallery again. Mr. Cartwright took his teammate's hand. A.D.A. White had a horrible nervous look on her face.

"On the count of Premeditated Murder of Donald Kelly, did the jury reach a verdict?"

"Yes your honor. The jury finds Angie Cruz not guilty."

At this point A.D.A. White was visibly shaken. She knew that Lopez had blown the case and ruined her reputation.

"On the count of Premeditated Murder of Leo DeSando, did the jury reach a verdict?"

"Yes your honor. The jury finds Angie Cruz not guilty."

This time the judge gave A.D.A. White a serious look. They both were thinking the same thing. Ricardo will pay for this with his badge! Not only did he cost the state thousands of dollars, but he disgraced the legal system. There was no doubt in the judge's mind that this case would come back and haunt him when he begins to campaign for governor.

"On the count of Attempted Murder of Frank Mallory, did the jury reach a verdict?"

The jury foreman took a deep breath and let it out.

"The jury finds Angie Cruz not guilty."

This time the gallery went bananas! The judge had to stand up and bang his gavel.

"This court is still in session!"

Mr. Cartwright turned and gave his teammate a big hug. The judge then addressed the jury.

"On behalf of Cook County and the State of Illinois, I'd like to thank you for serving. You're now excused."

BANG WENT THE HIS GAVEL!

"All rise!"

The judge wasted no time going straight to his chambers. Mr. Cartwright looked over at A.D.A. White, but she couldn't look him in the eye.

Back at the City Block we were all glued to the TV screen. We could see that something big was happening at the courthouse because the big doors blew open, and a huge crowd came rushing out. There was a stampede of reporters trying to get interviews and a equal number of cops trying to keep control.

Dad tried to reach Mr. Cartwright on his cell phone, but had no luck. All we could do was watch and wait. Finally one of the cameramen got right in Mr. Cartwright's face and he took advantage of it by winking at us with a smile. That's when the City Block totally blew up! We all went crazy jumping up and down and screaming! We then saw Mr. Cartwright take out his cell phone as he made his way down the stairs with his arm around Dad's secretary.

"Tell Louie to break out that champagne!"

During his ride over, the Block was being transformed into what looked like a campaign headquarters. Pizzas were being ordered and buckets of champagne on ice were being placed on the tables. When the two of them finally arrived, there was cheers, yelling and hugging all over the place. Music was playing and the atmosphere was incredible.

Carman went into the back office to call Angie with the good news. It was the only place that she could hear herself think. After a few minutes she motioned for me to join her. She gave me the phone and left the office.

"Hi Sherman, it's me Angie. I just wanted to thank you so much! You mean the world to me! As soon as I can I'm going to give you and that Mr. Cartwright a big hug."

"Angie you're family, and if I had to do it all again, I'd do it in a heart-beat! I love you and can't wait to see you. This place isn't the same without you!"

"Thanks Sherman, I'd better go now, bye."

CLICK.

When I went back into the bar area I was surprised to see Mai holding Barney in her arms. A big smiled stretched across my face because I was finally going to see Rebecca. I scanned the entire place but she was nowhere to be seen. That's when Carman came to me and handed me a small envelope. I opened it immediately.

"My dearest Sherman, if you are reading this you know what has happened."

I stopped reading and looked Carman in her eyes. I went back to the office with her trailing me. She closed the door behind us and I began reading the letter again.

"Meeting you at the lake was a breath of fresh air for both Barney and me. You made me smile and reminded me of my own silly youth. When my health started failing I didn't want you to see me this way. I had a dream that you met the right girl. I told Barney about her he was sure that he could learn to love her. He also agreed that no one in the world would love and take care of him the way that you will."

It was then that Carman saw me do something that she's never seen me do before. Tears rolled down my cheeks. She sat on my lap and wrapped her arms around me as I laid my head on her shoulder.

# LIFE AFTER THE TRIAL

It's been over two months since the last Lipstick Murder, and even though Angie has been cleared of all charges, the state's prosecutor as well as the police still believes that she's the killer. With their case destroyed by Lt. Lopez, and nothing but circumstantial evidence, they've decided to drop the investigation. The media has called off their hounds, and there's no ink in the headlines of the daily papers. Local law enforcement has returned to focusing on regular robberies, dope peddlers, and internet crimes. Things have returned to normal at the City Block and Sherman has moved on to other investigations.

Sherman now has a new member in his household. Due to Rebecca's unfortunate passing, he's inherited Barney, the Jack Russell Terrier. Due to the fact that Louie has chosen to keep his life style in the closet, Sherman's the only one that doesn't see it. Will he ever put two and two together, who knows, but the ladies in his life finds it funny that he refuses to believe it.

Angie does recover from her illness and continues to live a healthy life. For now she's content with the revenge that she's gotten, and thanks to Oliver Cartwright, her skeletons will remain locked in the closet forever.

As for Carlton Jr. and Rex, they'll have to carry the burden of their dirty deed for the rest of their lives, and forever look over their shoulders.

Rebecca's dream of Sherman finding the right girl does come true. He and India will form a life together and manage to sustain a long distance relationship by sharing their homes off and on in Atlanta and Chicago. There's still times when Sherman finds that reporter Candee Harris is a useful tool in his investigations, which sometimes drives a wedge between him and India, but they manage to work through it.

The Silver Fox still finds himself sitting alone in darkness from time to time dwelling on his past now that he's convinced that he's Angie's father. The news that Sherman possibly has a sister only adds to his worries. He wants so much to open up to both of them and be a real dad, but he knows that they'd be devastated. There's a lot of love among this group of people, but there will continue to be a lot of secrets.

As for Lt. Lopez, due to the fact that he insisted on sticking to his story during the trial, he shamed the legal system as well as his brothers and sisters in law enforcement. Obviously he's fallen from grace, but the degree of discipline he'll be facing is yet to be determined. Judge Evans sees a future of becoming the state's new governor, and A.D.A. White looks forward to being the next District Attorney. Neither of them is willing to let the actions of Lt. Lopez get in the way of that. Their plan is to squash his career. In the meantime Sherman has been able to move around the city without receiving the occasional kidney punch from the Lt.

# About the Publisher

## LIFE TO LEGACY, LLC

Let us bring your story to life! Life to Legacy offers the following publishing services: manuscript development, editing, transcription services, ghost writing, cover design, copyright services, ISBN assignment, worldwide distribution, and eBooks.

Throughout the entire production process, you maintain control over your project. Even if you have no manuscript, we can ghostwrite your story for you from audio recordings or legible handwritten documents. Whether print-on-demand or trade publishing, we have publishing packages to meet your needs. We make the production and publishing processes easy.

We also specialize in family history books, so you can leave a written legacy for your children, grandchildren, and others. You put your story in our hands, and we'll bring it to literary life!

Please visit our website:
www.Life2Legacy.com

Or call us at:
877-267-7477

You can also email us at:
Life2Legacybooks@att.net

www.ingramcontent.com/pod-product-compliance
Lightning Source LLC
Chambersburg PA
CBHW031100030726
47496CB00002BA/311